ALPHA BRUTE

SARA FIELDS

Published by Stormy Night Publications and Design, LLC.
www.StormyNightPublications.com

Fields, Sara
Alpha Brute

Cover Design by Korey Mae Johnson
Images by iStock/MRBIG_PHOTOGRAPHY, iStock/bazilfoto, and iStock/MarsYu

This book is intended for *adults only*. Spanking and other sexual activities represented in this book are fantasies only, intended for adults.

PROLOGUE

lijah Baumann

The Crimson Shadow pack had a problem and right now I was staring at it straight in its face. The man grimaced and for the briefest of moments, his eyes flashed bright red. This was the third attempt to break into the pack's territory in a week and this particular vampire had come the closest to actually being successful.

Honestly, it was becoming something of a nuisance.

His upper lip rolled slightly, his nose crinkling along with it. A harsh scarlet glow burned around the edges of his irises, the veins surrounding his eyes darkening as his teeth lengthened to sharpened points capable of piercing through human flesh. This was a newly born vampire; all the signs were there, including the desperate lack of control when it came to hiding his true nature.

They were the only ones with the audacity to challenge someone like me. Overconfident pricks that deserved nothing more than a thick stake right through their still-beating hearts.

I swung my arm around and caught him in the side of the temple hard enough to make him growl anew. My ring cut his cheek, but it healed right before my eyes in no more than a fraction of a second. Annoying little perk, really. I'd just have to hit him harder.

"Why are you here?" I roared. The vampire should have shuddered in fear, but he did something far more stupid. He challenged me instead.

"I don't have to tell you anything," he snarled. His lips rolled again and he hissed. I didn't hold myself back.

I punched him again, the crunching sound loud enough to make even Theo grimace beside me. The vampire hardly even flinched. God damn supernatural healing. Sometimes it was so incredibly inconvenient and this one seemed even more resistant to pain than usual.

What was he on? Was it some new drug? Ecstasy? Meth? Something else? What the fuck was going on here?

There was an oddly deranged gleam to his gaze, something more than just the fact that he was a newly sired vamp. It was sharper. His pupils were dilated, his eyes bouncing back and forth so rapidly that a normal person wouldn't even have picked up on it. Something was off. I could feel it.

Tomorrow, my alpha Amir was supposed to meet with the leaders of the Malkovian clan to sign a peace treaty, which was all pomp and circumstance. This guy had probably been sent to throw a monkey wrench into all of that. Maybe it was another jealous clan wanting to move in on our territory. I didn't know.

Whatever it was, it was my job to handle it.

Slowly, I took a step back, taking stock of the situation before I decided on a course of action. I was nothing more than a soldier within the Crimson Shadow pack, but I hadn't gained the respect of my men by making reckless decisions in the past.

I looked at the well-groomed Venetian-style gardens all around me. It was well into the night, but the moon was bright, illuminating the flowers below in an ethereal glow. The rest of the grounds were silent, but that didn't stop my hackles from rising all the same. This didn't make any sense. Why would any of the nearby vampire clans send several lone men into our compound knowing that they'd be easily overpowered and killed as a result? What could their reasoning possibly be?

This one hadn't exactly been quiet in his approach. He'd triggered pretty much every motion capture camera and had seemingly set a direct course for a run-in with me and my men.

Something was going on and this newbie vamp was only a piece of it.

"I'm not afraid of you," the vamp goaded, but I didn't respond. Instead, I studied him more closely. My existence in the pack was well known. I was unbeaten in a fight, so much so that people were intimated by nothing more than my simple presence when we were together in a room. It had worked well for Amir in the past, especially when he wanted to procure a deal that wasn't necessarily fair for the potential recipient, which he took advantage of. Again. And again…

I was the one who did the dirty work for him. I always did.

The vamp struggled in his bonds, but he wouldn't be able to break them. The ropes I'd used were too strong, threaded with blackthorn to keep him weak. He rocked back and forth, trying to tip the heavy stone bench Theo and I had secured him to. He was strong enough to move it just a little bit, probably a perk of the extreme strength of a newly sired vampire. He continued to goad me, but I no longer took heed of him. There was something more to his presence than what appeared to meet the eye. I could feel it in my gut.

He was dressed in all black, which was usually a token of the Lasombre clan, but it could also be just a cover to use in the shadows of the night. He had the look of a vampire that might have been compelled, which might explain the insanity I could see within his eyes. He didn't carry himself in the haughty way a vamp from the Malkovian clan would, plus they'd been allies with the Crimson Shadow pack for centuries. Maybe he was a member of the Asamire clan, but that would mean he wasn't a very good assassin if he'd gotten caught this easily.

It was possible he could be Venuti, but they'd gone quiet ever since their run-in with the Council last year in New Orleans.

"Whom do you serve?" I snarled. His maniacal laughter followed, slowly rising in pitch until it burrowed into my eardrums and made every single hair on my arms stand on end. His pupils dilated even further, the red of his irises only a thin border now encompassing pitch black spheres.

A woman screamed in the distance.

Impossibly, his laughing surged to a deafening decibel as his psychotic derangement took over completely.

"You're too late," he sneered gleefully. On instinct, I surged forward and gripped his skull. With a hard wrench, I tore his head from his shoulders and tossed it aside, ending him so quickly he hadn't even gotten the chance to panic that his life was over. The rotten scent of vampire blood pierced my nostrils and I scowled with disgust.

The woman screamed a second time, and I burst forward. The sound had come from the northern reaches of my alpha's compound, where his daughter's quarters were located. Knowing speed was of the essence, I shifted into my wolf form and sprinted across the gardens. I rounded the corner and leapt up onto the second-floor balcony to catch sight of nearly a dozen vampires crawling up onto the third. I grasped one by the ankle and jerked him down hard, throwing him to the ground below. He landed on his back with a grunt and was just about to leap at me when Theo made a grab for him and dislocated his angry head from his shoulders with a ruthlessness that had more than earned the position of my second in command.

I howled and the vampires looked back at me with surprise, almost as if I'd caught them off guard. They hadn't expected to be discovered at all.

The other vampires had been a diversion. They'd sent loners in enough times to lull me into a false sense of security when their real goal had been something else entirely.

They wanted Ashleigh. They wanted to kidnap the alpha's daughter.

I wasn't going to let them.

Behind me, my soldiers answered with excited yips as they jumped up onto the balcony along with me.

"Get out!" Ashleigh screeched and I pushed onward. My men would follow me. They had walked through fire for me, and this time would be no different. My claws dug in between the mortar of the rock, pulling me up onto her terrace with frightening speed. Once I reached the top, I shifted back into my human form. A blond-haired vampire was climbing through her window, not caring that he was slicing himself open on the broken glass in the process. I rushed toward him and reached for him, grabbing the hair at the back of his scalp in my fist so hard that it stopped him dead in his tracks. I reached down to my belt and un-holstered a thick wooden stake, quickly spearing him straight through the heart with the violent force I was known for.

His body twitched for several seconds in my arms before I threw him aside. I didn't bother pulling the stake back out.

Ashleigh screamed bloody murder and I looked back to see her fighting off a vampire that had made it all the way inside. Her small size put her at a distinct disadvantage to his much larger one, no matter how hard she fought. His hand closed around the back of her neck, whipping her around so that her back was pressed against him. With his other hand, he boldly pressed a silver blade firmly against her throat. She stilled, trembling in both fury and abject fear.

She was completely naked, water still dripping down her damp glistening skin.

She must have just gotten out of the shower. There was a towel on the floor. Her chest rose and fell, her nipples tightening in the chilliness of the night air, and I watched a single bead of water roll down between her swollen breasts, down the flat expanse of her lean stomach and the toned surface of her right thigh. Her wet hair framed her face, more water dripping from the soaked ends. Several strands were plastered to her left cheek and her throat, dark mahogany that was almost black against the paleness of her skin.

A breeze whipped through the room from behind me, catching me by surprise.

I wasn't prepared for what came with it.

Her scent was something like a gift from heaven. Men had described the sensation to me in the past, but a gift like this was too incredible to be put into words. I knew the signs, what it was supposed to be like, but this was something I had never really understood until this singular moment.

When I felt the call of my mate.

It was so much more powerful than I'd imagined it would be.

She trembled in the vampire's arms, her full breasts bouncing just the slightest bit as she tried to break his hold. Her pale flesh was still slightly pink from the hot water of her shower and her gaze met mine, bright green emeralds glimmering with fear. The vampire only needed to wrench the silver knife across her throat to end her. Nothing more than a single flick of the wrist and her life would be over.

I wouldn't allow that.

My hand dropped back down to my belt, gripping my gun next. I whirled my arm outward and aimed directly at his head. Without hesitation, I fired that gun, catching the man right in between the eyes with a bullet.

A normal bullet wouldn't pierce a vampire's skull, but this wasn't any normal bullet. It was a new development in the weapons world, a sun fire bullet. At its core was a magnesium ribbon. Once it was exposed to oxygen, it would explode with enough light and power to simulate the sun.

A particular weakness of the bloodsucking monsters with pointy teeth.

The bullet penetrated the vampire straight between the eyes and a burst of violent light shattered his skull from within. The explosion was too bright to look at directly, so I chose to look into Ashleigh's burning gaze instead.

In an instant, I saw fury, humiliation, and most intensely, her wounded pride that I was standing there in front of her, a lowly soldier staring at the alpha's daughter completely naked. I could see everything, from the pink peaks of her nipples to the trembling in her thighs. She breathed in deeply and started, narrowing her eyes in my direction.

Had she caught my scent too?

The arms holding her captive loosened and the body teetered sideways. She took a step forward, shivering with disgust as the vampire's headless corpse collapsed to the floor with a sickening crunch. His blood was spattered all over her face. She used her palm to try to swipe it away, but it only ended up smearing across her blushing cheek.

Behind me, the rest of my soldiers made quick work of the remaining vampires. None of them had been particularly well equipped with weapons. Not even one of them had a gun or silver bullets. Just silver knives from the look of it.

I shifted back into my human form now that the threat had passed, taking a step toward Ashleigh with wild intent. The wind whipped around me, surrounding me in the deliciousness of her scent and a primal instinct deep inside me awakened.

I wanted to take her there and now.

"Stay back, soldier," she spat. She knew my name; I was sure of it. She raised her chin haughtily, looking down at me with revulsion as if she was too good for me.

Her defiance only made me want to claim her even more. It also made me want to throw her down on her own bed and teach her a lesson at the end of my cock about who was in charge, only after I marked her pretty little ass with my belt.

I went to take another step toward her, and the door burst open, two dozen members of my pack filing in ahead of Amir. His aristocratic gaze flicked from me to her, taking in my wild state and her very naked one.

Ashleigh looked away from me, breaking the moment as she rushed to grab the towel at her feet. Hurriedly, she wrapped the massive towel around her beautiful body, and I was deeply aggravated at the sudden loss of it, that she hadn't asked me for permission to cover herself first.

My palm twitched. How would she look when I put her over my knee?

It was as if there was a wild beast that had suddenly emerged from deep inside me. It wanted to dominate her so completely that she had no choice but to admit that she was mine, that I was the only one who could leave her trembling and satisfied after I was through with her, that I was her destiny and her mate.

"Elijah," Amir purred, and the powerful judgment of the alpha was upon me. His stare searched mine, like he was daring me to take another step toward his daughter and for a long moment I considered defying him. Her scent was still running strong through my veins, an intoxicating sensation that was too intensely potent to ignore. With every single breath I took, it spiraled, lodging its place so deeply in my soul that I knew I'd never be the same again.

The entire room was tense for several long moments and when I eventually managed to pull my gaze away from Ashleigh, the savage beast inside me quieted only a little.

"Alpha," I finally managed, but my voice rumbled with need so powerful that even Amir flinched.

Ashleigh gripped the towel tighter, hiding from me as she moved back behind her father. She still held her head impossibly high, looking down at me from her place of royalty at Amir's side.

"You should be wary of the treaty tomorrow, Amir," I said gruffly, but I didn't look at him. Not even once. My gaze was firmly locked upon the haughty glare that painted my mate's face. It was clear that she thought herself too high-born for a man like me, that her father would never approve of me, and that our pairing would be impossible.

Amir was in the process of arranging a highborn marriage for her. I didn't know the details, but I knew that whatever man he chose for her wouldn't be the one meant to have her because that man was me.

I took a step toward her, letting myself reach my full height. She was maybe five foot two or five foot three. I towered over her at six foot eight. She might be one hundred thirty-five pounds soaking wet, but she didn't stand a chance at my three hundred fifty pounds of solid muscle.

As if she sensed the imposing inevitability of her claiming, she maneuvered herself completely behind the wall of her father and his closest guards.

She wouldn't be able to hide from me. I'd take her eventually.

I took a deep breath, attempting to control my wolf. I drew up to my full height and Ashleigh took another step back until she was fully hidden by the much bigger form of Amir.

He pulled his shoulders back protectively. His gaze was judgmental and threatening. I should submit to him. He was my alpha, but I wanted to do nothing more than shove him aside and take what was mine.

"I'll take note of your warning, soldier," Amir replied idly. He looked around at the mess of dead vampires that littered his daughter's room. "See to it that this is all disposed of by morning," he continued pointedly.

I nodded once as if I understood my duty, but my gaze never left Ashleigh's as she rushed out of the room in a nervous hurry. Her fingers had gone white, she was clutching the towel so tightly. Her hair was still dripping down her back. She'd looked back once, wide-eyed and furious, but I couldn't be certain if it was directed at me or at herself because of her body's own betrayal.

She shouldn't respond to me. I was beneath her. She'd looked down on me her whole life from the pretty pedestal that was the position of the alpha's daughter.

I could read it all over her face.

None of that changed the fact that I could literally smell the sharpness of her arousal dripping between her thighs as she fled. She could deny it all she wanted to, but her body knew her place.

In time, I would teach her what that meant.

CHAPTER 1

 lijah

The arrogance and sheer pompousness of the whole event was staggering. Not only was there enough food and wine to feed an entire army for more than six months, but there were naked human women wandering the whole castle so that the vampires we were meeting with wouldn't go thirsty for even a moment.

Some of the vampires were even whispering about the fact that a few of them might be virgins, but I'd seen none of the telltale intoxication in their eyes to suggest it. Likely, that was a treat reserved for only the highest born royals in the Malkovian clan, not for the vampires that weren't even remotely ranked.

Every year, the Crimson Shadow pack and the Malkovian clan met to make a show of their alliance, like they were screaming to the world about their combined power and how afraid of it everyone should be.

The whole thing was just a big formality. The Crimson Shadows and the Malkovians had been in alliance for hundreds of years. This meeting would change nothing. It never did.

I stood guard at Amir's side for most of the gathering, but I didn't partake in much of the ceremony. This was a celebration of those high in the aristocracy reveling in their power and money, namely Amir, his beta Isaac, Ashleigh, and anyone else that was highborn enough in pack hierarchy to play a role in the festivities.

I took orders. That was it.

Ashleigh avoided my gaze as much as she could, but that didn't change the fact that she was reacting to my presence in the same way she did last night. Her dark brown hair hung in waves down her back, occasionally falling in front of her pretty face. Her dress was a deep forest green, luxuriously elegant in the way it wrapped around her body.

None of that hid the scent of her arousal from me.

I was there to guard Amir from a nonexistent threat, but I didn't pay attention to him all that time. I was watching her.

I knew she could sense me staring at her. From the stiffness in her shoulders to the way she kept turning her back to me, she gave every sign that she would flee from my presence at the first chance she could.

For one moment, she let down her guard though and we locked eyes. She started for the briefest of seconds, but then she remembered herself and tried to hold her ground.

Amused, I decided to let her try.

I cocked my head to the side, sliding my gaze up and down her body, imagining her just like I saw her the night before. My cock hardened painfully, my balls squeezing so tight I thought I would burst. I breathed in deeply, surrounding myself in the utter perfection of her. Her face tightened as she remembered herself, glancing away quickly and grabbing a goblet full of wine in an attempt to distract herself. She brought the glass up to her mouth, sipping daintily. All I could imagine were those pretty lips wrapped around my cock. As if she could read the direction of the thoughts in my head, she took an even bigger gulp as if she could hide her own need from me. I smiled knowingly in her direction, and she choked, coughing into the back of her hand as she struggled to get a hold of herself.

It was difficult, but I fought the urge to give chase and teach her a lesson about who was really in charge.

My alpha would never approve of such a match. I knew that, but that didn't stop my instinct from flaring intensely inside me anyway.

Amir's hard stare caught mine and I leveled him boldly with my own. Arrogantly, he held it for a short moment before turning away to continue talking with the Malkovian clan kingpin. He just expected my obedience and that annoyed me.

I flicked my gaze back to Ashleigh, listening closely in on the conversation between Amir and Augustus at the same time. She turned away and started whispering with another member of the royal court beside her. I didn't know her name.

"With the downfall of the Asamire in the western hemisphere, there is an opportunity for us to take their place," Augustus whispered, and my ears perked up. Las Vegas had been a vampire-run town ever since its establishment; that was until recently. From what I'd gathered, they'd clashed against a wolf pack and lost in a major way.

"What do you mean?" Amir asked, a sense of boredom clear in his tone. He was watching one of the naked women walk by with a tray full of wineglasses. By the heavy metallic scent on the air, not all of them were wine either. He probably didn't know what Augustus was talking about. He often thought more grisly matters were beneath him, so he depended on men like me to keep him informed.

"Their absence opens a new trade for us," Augustus explained patiently. He nodded his head suggestively toward the woman Amir was staring at and smirked gleefully. "These women could make us an awful lot of money, both on the auction block and on their backs."

Taken aback, I stopped observing Ashleigh so closely and turned my eyes to the two kingpins about to procure a new deal right in front of me. I gritted my teeth, disgusted to take in the excited expression on Amir's face. He was seriously considering what Augustus had to say. He absolutely worshipped the highborn vampire. Augustus could probably spit in his face and Amir would simply thank him for it while asking for more.

It was unnatural.

They lowered their voices, but I was listening. They talked in detail about the taking of women from foreign countries, the selection of those who wouldn't be missed and the kidnapping of virgin women with the express purpose of selling them to vampires who were addicted to the feeling of getting blood drunk.

The more I heard, the sicker I felt.

I'd done my fair share of dirty work in the past. As Amir's head soldier, I'd killed for him. I'd defended him. I'd fought the battles he refused to fight as he grew old and fat as alpha. I'd fought fiercely to hold our turf against any pack or clan that dared to cross us. If Amir had a problem that could be solved with fists, he called on me to take care of it.

Every. Single. Time.

There were lines I refused to cross though.

I didn't hurt women and kids. I most definitely wouldn't take part in a trade as dirty of the trafficking of them either.

Amir looked far too interested. I shouldn't be surprised. He'd been so closely aligned with the vampires for so long it was almost as if he was one himself. Vampires were supposed to be the enemy, but Amir was so taken with Augustus that the fabric of our very nature no longer mattered to him.

It did to me though.

I couldn't hide my scowl anymore. Beside me, Theo noticed the direction of my gaze and it didn't take long for the topic of their conversation to become clear to him too.

"He can't be serious," Theo whispered furiously, and I grunted with revulsion.

"Elijah!" Amir called out and a sickening feeling rumbled in the pit of my belly. With a sigh, I walked over to the table and nodded my acquiescence. Amir's excited glance was almost too much, and I had to bite my tongue to keep quiet.

He was the alpha. I was nothing more than his subordinate. I kept reminding myself of that simple fact, but it was getting harder and harder to submit to.

"I have a job for you, Elijah. You're going to head a brand-new division for me and Augustus," he declared.

"And what is that?" I pressed. I knew the answer, but I needed him to say it anyway. Every hair on my body bristled with unmatched fury. I took a deep breath. I told myself to hold back, but it just felt like a matter of time until my fists met his face.

"Women," he answered gleefully, and my fury sizzled past the breaking point.

"No," I replied. My voice was soft at first. Amir looked at me in disbelief, like he had imagined the word that had come out of my mouth. His eyes narrowed as he stared, almost as if it had never occurred to him that anyone would ever defy him, especially in the presence of the Malkovians.

Until me.

"What did you just say?" he said quietly. I lifted my chin slightly, leveling him with a glare as ferocious as his own.

"I said no," I repeated.

His mouth closed into a firm line, his brow furrowing with annoyance. He stood up and I took in the state of my alpha for the first time in a long time.

He didn't stand a chance against me.

When he tried to make himself appear bigger than he was, I almost laughed. He was well past his prime, approaching his late fifties. He had stopped keeping himself fit years ago, relying too heavily on men like me to solve his problems for him. His belly was round, his arms skinny, his legs weak. His hands were soft like a child's, the product of not having to put in a hard day's work in decades. If I faced anyone that amounted to someone like him in a fight, I could win without even really trying.

Defeating him would be easy. Taking his place would be child's play.

His hair had long started to turn gray. He had to look up at me from below since he was almost a foot shorter than me. I smirked as he tried to capture his role as alpha once more, but I detected the slight quiver on his lips. He was afraid of me. To be honest, he should be.

"You can't say no to me. I am your alpha. I will not stand for this kind of defiance," he spat.

My grin widened as I felt the pull of his alpha fade the longer I stood in front of him like this. I rolled my lip and crossed my arms in front of my chest.

"I'm done taking orders from you," I answered him boldly. I wasn't backing down from something like this.

"I can have you killed where you stand," Amir growled.

"Who would win in a fight against me? You?" I dared. He visibly grimaced at the prospect of facing me in a fight. He and I both knew who would win if we clashed. His hands twitched and his eyes flickered around the room. The room had gone silent. There was no doubt in my mind that everyone was watching.

Ashleigh included.

I allowed my gaze to slide over to her. She'd taken her seat at the head table. Her green eyes were stormy, fully focused on the exchange between me and her father. She looked furious that I would challenge his authority like this.

I was about to take it one step further.

"How dare you!" Amir exclaimed furiously.

"How about it, Amir? Could you defeat me?" I taunted him.

My inner wolf roared with excitement. The alpha I'd always resisted burned through me with wild abandon and at long last, I finally let him out.

For as long as I can remember, Amir had sat as the head of our pack unchallenged, like he had forgotten that his seat of power was an earned one rather than an inherited one. He'd kept it by way of money, blackmail, and unending nepotism. An alpha challenging another alpha was a basic law of nature that would never disappear and now that I'd done it so publicly, he would be unable to sweep it under the rug like he usually did.

Amir picked up his wine goblet, covering up his distress with a big gulp. Augustus sat beside him with obvious arrogant interest. No matter how much he allied himself with Amir, it was clear that the vampire still thought himself better than all of us.

"Of course I can," Amir blurted, and I grinned knowingly. I took a step toward him, and he visibly flinched, which only made the beast inside me preen with glee.

"Seize him!" Amir exclaimed and I stood a bit taller. I turned my head, catching Theo's gaze and then the rest of the soldiers that typically followed my orders. None of them made a move toward me. Instead, they looked to me for direction first. I grinned. They would choose me over him in a second.

I'd earned their respect. Amir, on the other hand, had not.

"Amir, I challenge you as alpha. I will save you the embarrassment of a drunk fight since you've partaken in much of the free-flowing wine here tonight. Tomorrow, we will determine who is worthy of the title of pack leader of the Crimson Shadow pack," I declared boldly. My voice reverberated off the walls all around me and the ensuing silence that followed was like music to my ears.

Amir's face paled and beside him, Augustus looked like he was witnessing the most exciting entertainment in the world.

"I'm not afraid of the likes of you, Elijah. I accept your challenge." Amir's gaze was furious. By the way his fingers were clenching, he was having extreme difficulty keeping his anger at bay.

"Good. Then I will see you tomorrow here at noon," I spat, and I turned away with every intention of leaving.

"I did not give you permission to go," Amir snarled.

"Are you going to stop me yourself?" I asked pointedly, glancing around to the men who surrounded us. None of them made a single move toward me. Amir's hands tightened into fists and his nose scrunched in anger. He lifted his chin to say something more, but the loud scrape of a chair against the tile echoed throughout the room instead.

Ashleigh had stood up and slammed her hands on the table.

My gaze slid to hers.

Her eyes burned into mine, showcasing in a single instant more spirit than her alpha father. Her fierceness drew me in, and I turned my full attention to her. I wanted to reach out, wrap my hand around that pretty, dainty throat, and kiss her like she'd never been kissed before.

Ashleigh had been expected to marry a high-standing gentleman of a rival clan a while back, but she'd refused the match and now her father was scrambling to marry her off to another in his vie for more power. It didn't matter though. She was my mate.

I wouldn't allow her to refuse a man like me, not ever.

"Get out," she snarled.

"Or what, Ashleigh?" I answered gently.

Her upper lip curled adorably, but I could see her nipples pebbling through the draped fabric of her dress. I cocked my head to the side and made a show of scenting the air.

The aroma of her arousal was just as sharp as I'd expected it to be. I cleared my throat and decided to reveal my intentions for her, at least a little bit.

"When I defeat your father in combat tomorrow, I'm going to take not only your pack, but you as my prize," I vowed, and her face twisted with anger.

"I'll never be yours. You're nothing more than a brute," she spat, almost in disgust. Her pretty lips pouted as she turned away, both scared and aroused at the prospect of belonging to me. There was a very slight hint of curiosity in the way her eyes flicked back to meet mine, but I turned away first.

"It's only a matter of time, mate," I promised, and I walked out of the room with my head held high, thoroughly enjoying the way the scent of her arousal only grew stronger after that.

* * *

That night, I waited up in my room. I was not foolish enough to sleep the night I challenged my alpha for his position. I peeked out of my window, watching how a number of wolves had been positioned strategically on the grounds in a way to cut off any escape routes. Boldly, I walked out onto my balcony, looking over the compound and watching as the Malkovians took their leave. The treaties had been signed, the deals made. The show was over now.

By morning, it would just be wolf shifters here. Amir

probably didn't want the vampires to witness how gloriously badly he would do in combat tomorrow.

In the distance, I could see the main house. Much of it had gone dark. Amir and Ashleigh had probably gone to bed by now.

I started at the sharp squeak of my bedroom door. I could have oiled the hinges long ago, but I'd left it that way on purpose so that no one would ever be able to sneak up on me in here. I lived a dangerous life, and I had my fair share of enemies. Tonight, I'd added one more to the list.

I dropped down and armed myself with a knife, sneaking into the room. It was pitch black, but I could see the form of a large man inside it. Just when I was about to spring, a familiar voice rang out.

"Elijah, it's me," Theo whispered gruffly.

"Theo, you should know better than to sneak up on me like that," I chided him quietly. "What are you doing here?" I grabbed the curtains and whisked them shut before I turned on a light so I could see him.

"It's Amir. I came to warn you of his plans," he replied immediately. My expression sobered quickly at the seriousness in his tone. "Augustus offered him assistance. He agreed to loan out his best men in order to kill you tonight. I placed the rest of us on the perimeter just in case they try to sneak in from out there. I came as quickly as I could so you could be prepared along with us."

"Theo, you shouldn't risk yourself for me. Nor should the others," I said softly, shaking my head.

"It isn't a risk. I'd rather follow you than a man like him, even if it means exile or death. He treats the vamps like they're better than his own kind. The rest of the men feel the same," Theo spat.

I stared at him. He was a loyal soul who had done nothing more than fight by my side for much of his life. He was always kind, a bit sarcastic at times, but a true soldier. I reached out my hand and he took it. With a firm handshake, I nodded.

"Thank you for coming to warn me, Theo," I replied. "When is the attack?"

"They could come at any time," he whispered.

"Then we'd better be ready, shouldn't we?" I answered and his face lit up with an excited grin. I cleared my throat and walked over to my bed, grasping the mattress and flipping it up.

I'd built a storage compartment that functioned as my own personal armory. It was full of guns, knives, stakes, crossbows, and herbs that both wolf shifters and vampires were weak to. I grabbed two 9 mms, loading each magazine with sun fire bullets. I shoved multiple stakes into the slots in my belt. Just as I slammed two more full magazines into my pockets, the door burst apart in a shower of thin splinters. I quickly whipped up my arm to cover my face, wincing as the tiny pieces of wood scratched at my flesh. The sting faded quickly.

Vampires weren't the only ones with supernatural healing abilities.

I leapt into the fray with Theo at my side. One vampire after the next flooded into my room, but Theo and I tore through them as if it was nothing more than a game. The visceral feel of slamming a stake into as many of them as I could was invigorating, and I howled as I whirled through the room with the full intentions of ripping through every single one until there wasn't a pointy toothed fucker left.

One of them came at me with a silver knife and I caught his wrist in my hand. I wrenched it to the side, the sounds of bone splintering sharp before I pulled him in hard and viciously pierced his heart with my last stake.

Quickly, I threw his limp body to the side as I unholstered both guns from my belt. More vampires were pouring in the door, and I started squeezing the trigger. Each gun was equipped with a long silencer that quieted the gunshot substantially, but soon the sound of the constant pop was the only thing echoing throughout the room.

The entryway exploded into a fiery display of bright light as one bullet after the next ended each vamp before they could enter. The doorway soon became thick with bloody headless corpses, one dead vamp piling onto the next until the ones coming began to trip on them.

I was a good shot. I didn't miss, not even once. When my magazines ran empty, I replaced them with the skill of someone who'd done it a thousand times. By the time I was finished with those, there wasn't a vampire left standing.

The ripe scent of their deaths was harsh on the air. I lifted my chin and had to force myself not to gag.

"Damn, Elijah. You could have left some for me," Theo joked. "I only got, what, five to your two dozen?"

"Sometimes I'm greedy," I joked back. As the smoke from my gunfire began to clear, I took state of the fallen carnage. My walls were splattered with blood. My carpet wouldn't be able to be salvaged, not by a longshot. From behind, I heard the sound of boots landing on my balcony and I looked back to see my pack members.

"Let's clear this out. I have an appointment tomorrow at noon," I added and Theo's answering grin was contagious.

"You wish is my command, alpha," he replied, and I chuckled.

"In time, my friend," I answered.

CHAPTER 2

*A*shleigh Wyss

The next morning, I sat down to breakfast with my father. I watched as one of the servants brought several platters of food and placed them on the table. With boredom, I sighed as they were each uncovered, revealing mountains of eggs, sausage, bacon, toast, and pancakes. There were bowls of fruit, but none of that looked even remotely appetizing.

I reached forward and held up my mug. When the servant beside me didn't fill it fast enough, I growled with warning before he rushed forward and grabbed the carafe of coffee. I watched the delicious black liquid pour into my cup.

"Leave some room for cream," I added.

"Yes, mistress," he answered quickly. When he was finished, I grasped the handle of the bowl of creamer and poured enough into my coffee to lighten it to my preferred taste.

I hadn't been sleeping well. Not for the past few nights.

Not since Elijah had rescued me from the vampires that tried to kidnap me.

My body was hot. Even the soft fabric of my clothing felt scratchy and tight. I wanted to rip it all off. A bead of sweat gathered at my brow, and I rushed to wipe it away before it dripped down my forehead. I took a deep breath and took a sip of the delicious brew, sighing with feigned contentment.

I hoped it would make it better, but deep down I knew it wouldn't. There was only one thing on my mind, and it wasn't coffee. It was the massive six-foot-eight man who had dared to gaze at me naked with an expression that said he would devour me from the inside out.

That single look had set my body on fire.

I couldn't let that happen. I was too valuable of an asset to the Crimson Shadow pack to lower myself and mate with someone below my station. My father expected better of me.

But already, the first marriage he'd arranged had fallen through. My potential husband had been caught sleeping around with a chambermaid and it had garnered enough publicity that I'd been forced to decline the match at my father's insistence. He'd had me do it so he could save face, but the second I'd given my word that I was no longer interested, he'd gotten to work on another more advantageous match. He hadn't told me the man's name yet, but chances were the marriage would make him a shit ton of money in the process.

I was his only daughter. It was my duty to marry high enough to bring my family even more power.

I looked out the window as I sipped my coffee, taking in the mountains in the distance. Just beyond those peaks was the city of Vienna, a beautiful place I'd spent much of my life shopping and exploring with my friends.

I glanced at my father, and he looked over me like I wasn't even there. I swallowed a mouthful of coffee, carelessly burning the roof of my mouth in the process. It always felt like he hated me because I'd had the audacity to be born a daughter and not a son.

Not only that, but I'd killed my mother. My father had insisted she give birth in the privacy of our own home and there had been complications. Something terrible had gone wrong and she'd started to bleed. It escalated too quickly and by the time help finally arrived, she was already dead. They'd said I'd been a miracle.

To my father, I was anything but.

He hadn't taken another by his side since her death. In some ways, I think he mourned her but in others I think he just didn't want to share the power he'd acquired since she'd died. He never told me much about her. Everything I had learned had been from other people, mostly the ones who had taken care of me since the day I was born.

My father hadn't brought himself down low enough to take care of the likes of me. He simply ruled over me from afar, directing his demands through other people and just expecting me to follow without complaint.

I sighed, taking another sip of coffee more slowly this time so that the tender roof of my mouth didn't burn any more than it already was.

My stomach growled, but I didn't want to reach out and touch even a single bite of food. My core protested, spiraling tight enough to hurt and I hardly quieted my groan before it escaped my lips. The servant beside me leaned down and cleared his throat.

"May I serve you anything, miss?" he asked.

I fanned my face with my napkin, hurriedly shaking my head.

"No. Thanks though," I spat out and he sat back. My father must have noticed the exchange because he deemed me fit to actually look at this morning. His expression was thoughtful, but I knew he only thought of me as a mode of currency and not as his daughter.

"I have news for you, Ashleigh," he said expectantly. It was so rare that he spoke to me that I hated the way I hung onto every word. Even after all this time, I still wanted to please him. I still wanted to make him proud.

"What is that, Father?" I asked with a smile.

"Last night, Augustus and I came to an agreement regarding the problem that is your hand in marriage," he began.

My brow furrowed with confusion. My last match had been procured from another wolf shifter pack that was rising in power alongside us in Europe. What could the Malkovian vampire possibly have to do with my future husband?

"The Venuti have been vying for power since they were clipped in New Orleans some time ago. Since then, though, they've been laying low and growing here in Europe. They have offered both Augustus and me an incredible amount of money and potential trade deals in exchange for you," he explained, and I stiffened visibly.

"I'm not sure I catch your meaning," I answered quietly.

He wouldn't agree to wed me to a vampire, would he? Such a match was forbidden by the Council. Not only was it against the law, but it went against the very fabric of our nature.

"Vincenzo Venuti will take your hand in marriage," he said firmly, his voice carrying an air of finality to it. I swallowed hard.

"You can't be serious," I said, unable to stop myself.

He slammed his hand on the table.

"You will wed Vincenzo Venuti and that's final. You will sit in your chair like a dutiful daughter should and do what your alpha tells you, do you understand me?" he spat.

"But he's a vampire. Father, please. It's forbidden," I whispered, trying to hide my horror and utterly failing.

"Do not dare to question me, daughter," he roared, and the table rattled as his fist slammed down on it again. Every servant in the room had frozen, afraid of him lashing out at them next.

"Yes, Father. I'm sorry. It took me by surprise is all," I whispered, staring down at the milky swirls of coffee that trembled in my cup, and I slowly realized that my hands were shaking.

"This afternoon, you will meet with the best dress designers in the country. You will pick out the dress of your dreams. Augustus has graciously offered to pay for it, and you will thank him properly when you see him next. Next week, you will fly to Rome, where the ceremony will take place," he continued.

"I understand, Father," I answered.

"Good," he replied curtly.

I kept staring into my coffee, feeling both cowed and angry. My emotions surged inside me, but the sense of pure disgust had free rein. I tried to take another sip of coffee, but it tasted like ash in my mouth.

My father had sentenced me to life as a vampire's wife. My stomach roiled, threatening to upheave the contents onto the floor if I didn't get a hold of myself quickly. I braved a glance up only to see that he'd gone back to stuffing his face full of pork sausage and I had to turn away before I threw up.

I closed my eyes and the door slammed open so hard it crashed into the wall behind it. The floors rattled. I tore my gaze up only to see the man who had haunted my dreams for the past few nights.

Elijah.

He sauntered into the room like he owned the place with a sizeable group of men at his back. I recognized Theo and several others, all of them lowly soldiers who did my father's dirty work. They were the ones he sent when words wouldn't solve something. They were his fists and Elijah was at the head of them.

"It's almost noon, Amir. Were you planning on standing me up?" Elijah began dangerously and the look of raw shock that passed over my father's face was comical. He covered it up as fast as he could, but I'd still seen it anyway.

"You should be dead," my father spat.

I opened my eyes in surprise. I should have known. As pack leader, he had to take Elijah's challenge no matter what. My father would never lower himself to a fight and had probably done something to avoid it last night.

"You should know it would take an army of vampires to kill me," Elijah answered with a cocky grin. His shadowy gray eyes found mine and it was just as jarring as the first time.

With a single look, he possessed me. I felt as if he'd reached out and torn my clothes right off of me, like he'd bared my soul with nothing more than his gaze. The powerful intensity behind those gray fortresses was enough to suck the air right out of the room. My heart pounded in my chest, the temperature of my skin rising with every prolonged second that his stare held mine.

I'd thought that Elijah would back down and remember his place in the pack. I had hoped that it was just maybe the booze talking, that the pressures of the night sharing the compound with the Malkovians had just gone to his head.

With a heavy swallow, I realized that I couldn't remember him drinking a single drop last night.

He drew his shoulders back, dragging his sordid gaze up and down my body. I turned away, trying my best not to breathe.

But I did. I caught his scent.

My blood boiled. I had long resigned myself to never experiencing the full power of a mate bond. I was the alpha's daughter. Our pack reigned over Austria along with the Malkovian clan. My life was one of duty. I was never meant to find love.

His scent though. Fuck *me* sideways…

Sometimes some of my friends would whisper about the possibility of finding their fated mate one day, but I'd never paid them any mind because it would never be something I could ever even hope to have.

I told myself I couldn't, not even now.

But the pull of his scent was like gravity and my resistance faltered. It vibrated at the very edges of my nerves, pulsing as it surrounded me in the security of its thorough embrace. With every breath, it sank deeper into my soul, and I whined softly at the terrible temptation.

I tried to breathe through my mouth, shunning the delicious mixture of citrus, smoke, bourbon, and the sheer masculinity of Elijah. As I opened my lips, the taste of his scent burrowed into me like the sharpened tip of a blade. I whimpered, the sound nearly silent. It was as if his very existence had consumed everything and there was nothing else other than me and him.

Elijah cocked his head to the side as if he knew what I was thinking. Feeling. Experiencing.

As if he understood me.

My father cleared his throat, breaking the long stare between us with its harshness. I shook my head and desperately grasped at my coffee. I gulped it down, trying to wash away the taste of him. It didn't work.

"Vacate the room," my father blurted out to the wait staff.

The servants disappeared within seconds, leaving my father, Elijah, me, and the rest of the pack members that had dared follow him.

"What if we made a deal?" my father suggested. I hazarded a glance in his direction. His face had paled underneath his graying beard. His eyes were frantic, like he was scraping the bottom of the barrel for any possibility of avoiding Elijah's challenge and a sickening feeling descended into the pit of my belly.

"What would you offer?" Elijah answered, looking pointedly at me and then back to my father. I slammed my lips shut, too flustered to allow myself to say anything at all.

"I've changed my mind. You've been such a loyal servant all these years that I want to reward you, not fight with you. With that in mind, I want to give you the gift of peace. You may start your own pack with any of the men that wish to follow you if you leave the Crimson Shadows' territory. You may go anywhere you wish in the world. I will not raise a finger to stop you," my father growled.

Elijah's grin was enough to send my stomach into flutters. I suddenly wished for a black hole to open up beneath my feet and swallow me whole.

The heavens would never smile on me like that.

"I will agree to your suggestion on one condition, Amir," Elijah answered, and the rumbling sound of his voice was enough to send my core into a spiraling overdrive. My chest rattled as the air rushed from my lungs. What the hell was wrong with me? Why was I reacting to him this strongly?

"Whatever you want, soldier," my father answered, and time seemed to come to a screeching halt.

"I will be taking Ashleigh with me as my mate. I claim her as my prize," he declared, and his pronouncement was enough to force me to my feet.

"I am no man's prize," I spat.

Neither man answered me. They didn't even hazard a glance in my direction. It was as if I wasn't even in the room, like I had no power in deciding my fate.

"Take her. She's yours," my father answered, and I stared at him in shock. No matter how angry he made me, I'd been groomed to be his obedient daughter. But this... this was too much. I wouldn't be bartered like a prized horse.

I turned my fury straight to the source. Elijah.

"How dare you? You're worth nothing more than the dirt beneath my shoe. I am our alpha's daughter. I would never go with the likes of you," I vowed. I lifted my chin proudly.

Elijah was a brute. He was good at one thing, fighting. He carried no status with him and even though my father had offered him a deal in exchange, it was nothing more than a veiled offer of exile.

The most important thing to my father was loyalty and Elijah had shown that he would no longer give him that.

He was probably already planning his revenge in his head. Elijah was as good as dead. I could see it in my father's eyes.

Elijah leveled his intense glare at me. His gray gaze glimmered with power, and it was all I could do to remain standing there in front of him. I took a shallow breath and lifted my chin even higher, playing the part that was expected of me all my life. He smirked as if I didn't stand a chance against him and maybe I didn't, but I wasn't going to be taken by a man like him quietly.

His eyes darkened dangerously, and it took everything in me not to start trembling right then and there.

"Ashleigh, I will give you a choice. The decision is up to you, but if the next words out of your mouth aren't an apology and a humble request to be punished like you deserve in the privacy of our bedroom, then I will take that to mean that you need your bare bottom marked with my belt before I mount and claim you right here in front of everyone watching," he warned.

I stilled, words failing me in that moment. My mouth opened and closed several times as a heated shiver raced across my skin. I turned my head away, desperately needing to break eye contact with him for only a second.

"Do you want your spanking and fucking right now, Ashleigh?" he pushed, and I had enough sense to shake my head quickly. When I didn't answer right away, he took several steps in my direction and something inside me cowed before him.

He was so massive. I was so much smaller than him. He could snap me in half with nothing more than his hands. There was a scar across his left eyebrow, a jagged mark left behind from a blade that had gotten too close. His furrowed brow made him seem even more fierce than he already was. A thick beard covered his chin, a bit wild and untamed. It was dark, like woodsy mahogany. The hair that covered his scalp was trimmed and well kept, but it was the shadows in those gray eyes that scared me the most.

My fingers trembled with fear, but it was the rest of me that reacted with visceral intensity. His sheer overpowering dominance surrounded me. With every breath, it grew more overwhelming until it was the only thing that consumed my thoughts. His fingers reached for me, grasping my chin lightly.

I expected him to strike me, but he didn't. Instead, he was gentle.

The fiery tendrils of his touch set my skin ablaze. My heartbeat quickened, but it was my pussy that reacted the strongest.

My panties had dampened the moment he walked into the room, but now that he was close enough to touch me, they were absolutely drenched. His heavy-handed threat has caused my pulse to surge, and I glanced down at the thick leather belt around his waist.

A part of me wanted to stand up and fight against him, to show that I was strong enough to stand toe to toe against him and come out the victor, but I was smarter than that. Challenging him like this in front of everyone watching would be foolish.

He could pin me over the table and lift my dress. No one in the room would stop him. Intervening during an alpha claiming was forbidden. To do so would be a direct challenge and going against someone like Elijah would mean most certain death.

I didn't want anyone to see me taken like that.

I stood no chance against a man like him. He was so much bigger, so much more experienced, and so impossibly strong that it would be sheer stupidity to push him further.

"Do you really mean that?" I breathed. There was no challenge in my voice.

"I do," he whispered firmly. His thumb grazed across my cheekbone and the sheer size of his hand against my face settled me. I didn't want to find out what it felt like as punishment in front of my father and all of his men.

This was a battle I wasn't going to win. Not like this.

I swallowed my pride. I would get out of this in some way; I just had to wait for the right time. My destiny wasn't with him. I just knew it.

"I'm sorry, Elijah. Please punish me in private. Not here," I whispered and the glower of victory that crossed his face made my anger flare at the same time my clit throbbed with anxious arousal. I wanted to reach out and slap him, but I didn't want to tempt him any further here in front of all of these people. As if he could sense my disquiet, his grip tightened only slightly. It didn't hurt, but somehow it felt comforting in a way.

"Good girl," he murmured, and my pussy tightened with irrevocable excitement. His praise did something to the frigid expanse of my heart, but I refused to face it. I pushed it away with as much force as I could muster. This was just a temporary situation. That was it.

I would figure out some way out of it.

Elijah released my chin and my flesh burned long after as if he was still touching me. I licked my lips and I looked up into the sinister depths of his gaze.

"I'm going to take you away from here now, Ashleigh. I will make you a promise. As my mate, I will give you the world," he declared quietly, and my heart squeezed. I did my best to ignore it.

I said nothing as he leaned down and wrapped his arms around my waist. With an air of daunting effortlessness, he tossed me over his shoulder. My backside felt impossibly high in the air, and I squealed with distaste, but he smoothed his hand over the backs of my legs, just glancing against the bottom curve of my cheeks.

I stilled.

No one had ever touched me like this before.

45

"Put me down," I shrieked. The sheer ferocity in my voice echoed throughout the room. No one said anything in return.

His hand slapped my ass, hard. The sting that followed was sharp and terrifying. My left cheek pulsed for several moments before the sensation descended deeper into my core. My hand rushed to cover my mouth and hide my resulting cry, but the sound had pierced through the air anyway. He pulled at my sundress suggestively, as if he was warning me that he could flip it up and bare me right then and there. I didn't dare lift my head for fear of seeing anyone else's reaction to him smacking my ass like that. I couldn't bear it.

"I'm sorry," I said quickly.

His enormous hand settled over my ass, and I stilled. My pussy was practically convulsing at the proximity of his massive fingers, and I quaked beneath him. I didn't want to think about how I wanted those thick fingers pressing in between my thighs.

"Please, not here," I begged.

His hand squeezed in warning.

"Then you will do well to remember yourself, little wolf," he snarled.

CHAPTER 3

A shleigh

Elijah carried me through the house. My ass still smarted from that single smack, but my wounded pride stung that much more. I chewed my bottom lip, watching the thick carpets and expensive tile floors fly by beneath me until I turned my head and pressed my forehead against his back. I tried to calm myself, but my mind kept reeling with his threats of punishment. My arms hung down behind him, just grazing against the soft leather of his belt.

It was dark brown, embroidered on top and on the bottom with black thread. It was worn in and thick. To the cursory touch, the full grain leather felt like butter, but I knew it wouldn't feel that way if he used it the way he'd said he would.

Maybe he wouldn't really do it. Maybe that had all been a show in front of his pack and my father so that he could take me and make me compliant in front of all of them.

I knew his reputation was pretty grisly, but I didn't know much else about him. I'd never heard word of him hurting anyone that didn't deserve it, namely my father's enemies and anyone that dared make a move against his pack and his alliance with the Malkovians.

"Please let me go," I began again, and he slapped my right ass cheek this time, harder than the first. I yelped quietly and grasped at him, wrapping my fingers around the very belt he'd threatened me with in the first place. The feel of it made my soul shudder at the possibility of him using it on me.

"The sooner you accept you're mine, the easier this will be for you, Ashleigh," he murmured, and my stomach spiraled so hard that it hurt more than my stinging ass.

"I don't want this. I'm not meant for you," I continued, and he stopped. Very quickly, he lifted his foot and hoisted me in the air to deposit me over his leg. My hands and feet couldn't reach the floor. I was suspended and helpless and before I could do a thing to fix it, he started to spank me.

I shrieked.

"You don't have a choice in this, wolf. It doesn't matter whether or not you want to come with me. The more you fight me, the harder your punishment is going to be," he growled.

I yelped as he gripped my dress in his fingers and lifted it straight up. I panicked. What panties was I wearing? Were they pretty?

Why did that even matter?

He pulled them down, baring me so quickly that I could scarcely breathe. I tried to kick, but it threw me off balance. I cried out, afraid of landing on my face on the floor below. I tried to bring my thighs together and hide my most private of places.

I couldn't think of anything to say in return because his massive hand was smacking my ass once again. My bottom bounced, the sting piercing deep into my flesh. There was nothing I could do except yelp and suffer over his thigh.

I tried to ignore how incredibly wet I was. I tried to disregard the intense throbbing in my clit and how my pussy seemingly had a heartbeat in his presence. I didn't want to think about how it grew stronger the longer he spanked me like a naughty little girl over his knee.

"Please! I'm sorry!" I wailed. Apologizing had worked before, maybe it would now. Instinct surged and I waited, hoping that would be enough to stop my spanking. I didn't lift my head, not wanting to see if there were any witnesses to my humiliating punishment. It was bad enough anyone nearby would have heard the deafening sound of his palm smacking my flesh. I couldn't bear seeing it too. His palm smoothed over my burning cheeks, soothingly even.

He didn't pull my panties up or my dress down right away.

"If you continue fighting me, I will tear your dress off and put you over my knee in the front yard completely naked. Your bare little bottom will be bright red before it's marked from my belt. Do you think everyone will enjoy watching you get the punishment you've needed for a very long time?"

"I understand," I managed to whisper. My heart was pounding in my chest, but my clit was pulsing even more frantically. I closed my eyes, trying not to think about the fact that he was staring at my naked bottom. My thigh muscles tensed.

"This is your last chance, Ashleigh. You need to under-stand that you are going to be punished. The only thing that is up to you now is whether it will happen in a very, very public way, or with me in the privacy of our bedroom," he warned and the blood in my veins practi-cally sizzled.

"The bedroom, please," I wailed.

His palm had settled on my backside, a constant burning reminder of what I had coming.

"Now, you will very quietly think about how much my belt is going to sting when we get there. Be a good girl for me or else I will decide where your claiming will take place," he continued. His hand lightly massaged my backside and he hummed with desire.

I swallowed my protests.

"This little ass is so very pretty when it's been spanked bright pink. I can't wait to see what it looks like after it's been very thoroughly marked from my belt," he declared, and his words made me rattle with shame. I could feel his eyes gazing over my nakedness and when his fingers just lightly grazed my wetness, my embarrassment only grew stronger.

"Please," I begged. He didn't say anything more, which made the following silence that much more unnerving. That single finger slid back and forth against my damp skin for several more moments until he reached down and pulled my panties back up. Carefully, he pulled my dress back down and I breathed a sigh of relief as he wrapped his hands around my waist, lifting me back over his shoulder with incredible ease.

My stinging pride kept me quiet. I dared a glance up, looking around me. There was no one there and I gasped in relief that no one had seen him handle me like that. My bottom burned beneath my dress as he strode off. His arm was wound tight around my waist, holding me steady as he continued on down the hall. I recognized the hardwood floor of the foyer before he burst out of the house into the warmth of the sun.

I had to bite my lower lip to keep from saying anything at all. I swallowed hard as we passed the waterfall feature in the center, hoping that he wouldn't change his mind and decide to sit down and punish me right there after all.

Punish.

That single word played in my head, over and over again with every beat of my heart. My panties were soaked through now, the surrounding warmth only resulting in making me even hotter than before.

He carried me across the front lawn, through the gardens to one of the smaller houses. The front door slammed open when he burst through it, rattling against the wall before he closed it behind him. The sound of the lock clicking shut was damning and my heart leapt into my throat as he climbed up the stairs. I hazarded a glance out of the window, seeing his men circle around the house in a defensive ring.

I had been nervous before but seeing them make a formidable wall to stop anyone from rescuing me from this man was the most terrifying thing at all. I started to struggle over his shoulder, ignoring the burning across my bottom in the idea of self-preservation. I'd thought I'd be able to find a way out of this. I didn't realize that he'd intended to deal with my punishment this soon.

He strode into the master bedroom with purpose. I suddenly found my feet back on the floor as he closed the door and slid the second lock home. I trembled and held my hands up in front of my chest as if I could push him away if I just tried. I knew better than that.

When he turned around, his fiery gaze practically set me ablaze.

"Strip," he demanded. His command was simple, but it was singularly polarizing in a way that left me entirely frozen. I couldn't push away my skepticism. This couldn't be real. Was I dreaming? Was this just a nightmare?

He didn't say anything for the longest time, his gaze simply devouring me. I took a step back, glancing around the room. A massive canopy bed built of sturdy wood took up much of it, but there was still enough room for me to put some distance between him and myself. His brow furrowed with warning, but I didn't stop.

Although we were still in the same room, the gap between us was enough for me to catch my breath. My wildly racing heart began to calm, and my body cooled, at least a little. I lifted my chin and the storm of my fury finally flared back to life. I took a hold of it, and I let it bloom into something magnificent.

"How dare you? I will not lower myself to the likes of you. I will not strip simply because you command it," I spat. I expected him to be angry with me, yet he didn't lash out and he didn't insult me. He did something else.

He smiled, which was more terrifying than any of those things. I swallowed hard as he cleared his throat and I watched anxiously as he casually dropped his hands to his belt.

"I was hoping you would refuse, little wolf," he said softly. The tone was so dangerous that my legs quivered at the sound, even as my pussy clenched tight with need.

No. This couldn't be happening.

His grin grew wider, more ominous and my heart practically leapt into my throat. I went to take another step back, but my calf grazed against the bed, and I looked back frantically. There was nowhere left to run. We'd gone up several flights of stairs to get here and even if I shifted into my wolf form, he would still be bigger and stronger than me. I could jump out of the window, but I doubted I'd be able to get that far even if I tried. He would catch me if I ran. I knew that.

"Release me at once," I demanded, and he chuckled with such sinister intent that I couldn't help but gasp at the sound. His eyebrows perked up and I held my ground even though I knew that a reckoning was soon coming.

Like cornered prey, I would fight until my last dying breath.

His hands shifted on his belt. My clit hammered with sensation as he slipped the end through the buckle, the sliding sound of leather especially damning. I couldn't look away as he took the thick silver clasp into his hand. He jerked it out of the loops of his pants quickly enough to make my pulse speed up and I stopped breathing.

He folded it over in his hands, looking pointedly in my direction as he did so. The soft, flexible leather hung from his fist as he took a step toward me, drawing my attention with the power of the gravitational pull of the sun and the stars. I stood taller, trying to be brave in the face of such danger, but when his other hand flew forward and grasped my right wrist I cried out in alarm. He pulled it high over my head and grasped the other one with a swiftness that left me reeling. With a cruel jerk, he gathered both wrists in one hand and wound the belt around them roughly. I tried to pull away. He was too strong for that.

I'm not sure how he did it, but he bound me so swiftly with that belt to the canopy overhead that it left me reeling. He'd stretched me taut so that my heels were arched clean off the floor, forcing me up to my tiptoes with a rough jerk. The belt cut into my flesh just enough to ache, but it didn't really hurt. I was far more concerned with the way that he was looking at me right now, like he could devour me whole with nothing more than his savage gaze.

His hands drifted down the expanse of my arms. I shook as the fire of his touch burned across my skin. When his fingertips brushed against my throat, I gasped. He continued down the sweetheart neckline of my dress. Just when I'd relaxed the slightest bit, he grasped the neckline and roughly ripped it apart.

The sound of tearing cloth reverberated through my body like a drum. I tried to pull my wrists free, but the belt held my wrists fast. I twisted my body away, but that only resulted in assisting him to shred my dress even further. He wrenched his hands apart and ripped through the expensive fabric like it was nothing more than a sheet of paper.

As a wolf shifter, he was strong, but this was something else.

"Are you afraid, little wolf?" he asked, his lips brushing against my ear and setting my soul on fire. I shivered and turned, shaking my head defiantly.

"No," I dared.

I could feel him smile against my cheek. My rapid pants filled the air, my chest rising and falling in a desperate feat to cool myself down.

It didn't work.

With cruel, ruthless abandon, he rendered the rest of my dress nothing more than a shredded pile of cloth. He tore every piece of it from my body.

"You should be," he growled, and I stood my ground, clenching my teeth together.

"You're nothing more than a brute," I spat.

"You're playing with fire, little wolf. You should be careful before you get burned," he purred, and my insides practically turned molten at the suggestive insinuation. His hand wound around my throat as he tossed the last remnants of my pretty dress to the floor. His thumb slid along the bottom curve of my chin, and I couldn't catch my breath no matter how much air I pulled in.

Tell him to fuck off. Tell him. Be strong. Do it.

The words died on the tip of my tongue, so I did the next best thing. I threw my body to the side and drew my knee up hard, attempting to strike him right in the balls. He moved too quickly, as if he'd sensed my rebellion before I could go through with it. He swung his arm down and caught my leg from behind my knee. He lifted it straight up, forcing me to abandon my mission and focus solely on keeping my balance so that I didn't fall.

I seethed beneath him.

Slowly, he removed my ballet flat and tossed it aside. Then he knelt down and wrapped my one leg over his shoulder before he took my other foot off the floor. Left completely off balance now, I had no choice but to lean on him as he took off my last shoe. Weightless, I tried to be brave, but the more this continued the more nervous I was getting.

Carefully, he placed my foot back down and uncurled the other from his body. I struggled to keep standing as he slid a finger beneath the front connector of my bra. He took his time before he flicked it open, the cups springing apart as my breasts bounced free. With a hard tug, he tore through the thin lace and tossed it aside with the rest of my dress.

My nipples peaked right in front of his eyes in a show of my body's traitorous arousal. I turned my head aside, humiliated, as he brushed the tips of them with his palms, dragging them across each peak, which only made them harder.

His hands dropped down to the last piece of clothing that covered my body. He ran his fingers just beneath the lacey hem of my light blue panties, teasing me slowly, which made my body burn with devastating heat.

"Please don't," I managed.

His wicked grin made my hopes sizzle away into a pile of ash. He gripped my panties in his fist, pulling them so the fabric was yanked taut against my clit. I quaked, unable to bat his hands away or do anything to fight him off. My clit tingled and he pulled the cloth even tighter, making the ache that was so very centered in my core spiral that much more into twisting pain.

I was trapped and he held the most sensitive part of me in his fingertips right now.

He dragged that soaked fabric up and down and despite everything in me that tried to fight him, it started to feel good. It soon became useless trying to keep my hips still. They arched into his movements, rocking back and forth until I moaned.

I *fucking* moaned for him.

Mortified, I stiffened and looked away. I hoped he hadn't heard it, but when he chuckled deliberately, I knew that he had.

"Hmmmm. I like the sounds you make. I can't wait to hear them when I have you bouncing on my cock," he whispered, and my legs grew weak.

It was that moment when he decided to tear my panties clean off. The fabric that had been roughly rubbing my clit pinched it brutally hard and I screamed. It felt like a stinging firebrand, stealing my entire focus for what felt like eternity. I cried out several times, each one with rising pitch until at long last the terrible hurt began to fade to a more throbbing ache.

His hands surrounded my waist, smoothing over me as if he was worshipping me with them. His fingers were gentle as they dipped down just low enough to glide against the top of my mound. When he reached even further and brushed against my pulsing clit, I gasped openly, unable to hide or to stop myself from reacting to him. My lack of control was humiliating.

"I know you feel it, Ashleigh. You're fighting it, but my alpha calls to you. You can deny it all you like, but this needy little body is telling me an entirely different story," he observed, and I shook hard.

"You don't know me," I countered boldly, but my voice was trembling, and he took advantage of that by sliding his finger directly over my clit. I gasped even louder this time.

"No? Are you telling me you wouldn't come for me if I didn't press this needy clit a little harder? Would you scream for me if I slid these fingers inside of you?" he teased, and I couldn't stop the way my body shuddered with pleasure beneath his touch.

"I... please..." I whispered but he shook his head and I quieted down. He removed his hands from my body and took a few steps back. I dared to meet his sordid gaze, but he glanced downward at the cusp of my thighs and made it exceedingly clear that he was no longer looking at my face.

He took his time, studying the way my nipples were hardening under his scrutiny, the way my thighs were rubbing against one another in an effort to quell the wicked need he'd stoked between them, the way my chest was rising and falling under the instinctual power of his presence. He looked at everything. I could hide nothing, not like this.

I felt so hot, and I couldn't put a stop to it.

His gripped the hem of his shirt and lifted it over his head. My mouth went dry, falling open as I took in the rigid perfection of his chiseled chest. His pecs were hard, his stomach a toned eight-pack that only became more apparent as he tensed. His chest was covered in thick hair. I wanted to reach out and touch it, run my fingers through it and I sucked in a heated breath.

No. Get ahold of yourself, Ashleigh. Jesus Christ.

I shouldn't be losing the control I'd worked all my life to maintain around a man who wasn't even ranked high enough to be granted any sort of title or land or even money. He was nothing.

"You think you are above me, little wolf, but you will never be above fate," he chided me, and his fingers grasped his waistband, slowly popping open the button and sliding down the zipper of his jeans. He slipped his thumbs beneath his dark gray underwear and pushed them down, freeing himself in one quick motion.

I looked down. I couldn't stop myself from staring straight at his cock.

Elijah was an enormous man. His muscles were big. His body was massive. His strength was something akin to colossal, and his cock was no different.

Thick veins bulged down its length, throbbing with blood right before my eyes. The head of his cock was terrifyingly girthy and the slit at the tip was already beading with pre-cum. I licked my lips, the salacious urge to take it my mouth catching me by surprise. I clenched my teeth together, pushing against the primal need that was taking my body and holding it captive.

He'd said he was going to fuck me with that monstrosity. I swallowed hard, knowing that no matter if he was gentle or not, it was going to hurt.

He leaned against the wall behind him, lifting his foot and pressing the bottom of his boot against it. Arrogantly, he cocked his head to the side and wrapped his fingers around his thick cock. I squirmed a little even though I tried to keep myself still.

He started to stroke himself right there in front of me.

His eyes never stopped devouring me. He looked at my breasts down to the tips of my toes. He feasted on the sight of me swaying on my feet bound to his bed by his belt. He narrowed in on the wetness between my thighs, likely seeing the swollen state of my soaked pussy and throbbing clit. My nipples peaked painfully tight, and I desperately wanted to soothe them with my own fingers.

"The sight of you bound, bare, and entirely on display for me makes my cock very hard, Ashleigh," he said pointedly, using my name like a weapon. I pursed my lips and turned away, but I couldn't keep from looking back at his cock when the pressing silence grew to be too much.

His fingers tightened, stroking up and down his length as he observed at me, and I hated the fact that I liked that I made him this hard. I liked that he enjoyed the sight of me, and I loathed myself for it. This wasn't me. I didn't lose myself over something as simple as a hard cock.

Maybe he was right. Maybe I was his mate, and this was nothing more than a viciously cruel twist of destiny meant to ruin my place in the world.

"Don't," I begged, and his grin widened. He stroked himself a little faster and my lips parted. It was becoming difficult to draw in air.

"Do you want to know what is going to happen next?" he said gruffly, and my pussy practically convulsed at the sound. Every inch of my body felt like it was crackling with electricity, and I did everything in my power to hold it at bay.

"Fuck. Off," I managed.

His loud laughter twisted deep into the marrow of my soul.

"First, I'm going to begin with that defiant little pussy. I'm going to show you what happens to rebellious little girls with sassy mouths and then I'm going to teach you a lesson you won't forget anytime soon. Then I'm going to bend you over that bed and whip your perfect little ass with my belt until you are very, very contrite. You may scream. You may cry, but you will submit to your alpha in the end. You will beg for me to claim you. You will beg for me to make it hurt, and you will beg me for the privilege of coming all over my cock. Do you understand me, *little wolf*?" he roared, and I could feel my anger and defiance bowing before him.

My arousal surged forward instead.

"You don't have to…" I began before he cut me off.

"That pretty pussy was already getting spanked bright pink tonight. Now it has three licks from the belt coming too," he growled, and my lips snapped shut just as my clit throbbed ominously.

I pressed my thighs together protectively. I swallowed hard. I was far more out of my element than I realized. The more I tried to fight him, the deeper hole I was digging for myself.

"Do you understand your alpha?" he repeated. I knew I was testing his patience.

"Yes, alpha," I whispered. His cock had only gotten harder. He was aroused by the prospect of punishing me. There was a dark glint to his gaze that screamed his full intent to dominate me so completely that I never questioned I was his ever again.

He stroked his cock more slowly now, taking his time and feasting his bold stare up and down my body before he pulled his shoulders back and tucked his cock back inside his jeans. I didn't know why, but I was disappointed that it was gone. He pulled up the zipper and buttoned it closed before he pushed off the wall and took a few steps toward me.

My heart pounded wildly in my chest at his approach. He reached up and released the tension on the belt just enough for me to flatten my feet on the floor.

"Spread your legs for me now," he commanded. His voice was gentle, but there was a very serious edge to it that gave me pause. I stood frozen in front of him, still trying to figure out if he was serious or if I was just losing my mind. His expression hardened visibly, and both of his hands grasped my nipples firmly enough to make me gasp.

Cruelly, he pressed the tips between two of his fingers. As the seconds ticked by, he ruthlessly pinched them increasingly harder. I cried out, and he twisted them so viciously that a frisson of pain blossomed across my breasts. When he didn't let go, I began to panic, trying to think of anything to make it stop. I begged and pleaded for him to let go, but he ignored all of it.

"Spread. Your. Legs," he demanded.

I spread my legs. When he saw that I'd finally begun to show compliance, he released my nipples and the violent surging sting that followed took my breath away. My nipples throbbed and I choked back a cry.

He used his boots to kick my feet even wider. He didn't stop until I was obscenely spread, and I wailed when a single drop of arousal spiraled down the expanse of my inner thigh.

"That's more like it," he whispered, and I clamped my lips shut in an effort to keep my cries quiet. His fingers glided down my stomach, and I tensed, looking up at him and trying to understand what was happening. I jerked my wrists, but still my bonds didn't give. His fingers descended to my pussy. He cupped it gently and I tensed, humiliated that he could undoubtedly feel just how soaking wet his cruelty was making me. I turned away, unable to face the darkness in those shadowed gray eyes.

His other hand cupped my cheek, forcing me to look back at him when all I wanted to do was hide. His thumb played over my clit, using just enough pressure to make me quiver with sudden overwhelming need.

"You've needed me to punish you for a very long time, little wolf. We both know that, and I can assure you, I am going to enjoy every single second of it," he declared, and a piercing volley of pleasure jolted from my clit straight into the surging depths of my core.

CHAPTER 4

*A*shleigh

When his palm slapped my pussy for the first time, I couldn't stop my body from pitching forward. It caught me by surprise, the vicious sting so overwhelming that the air rushed out of my lungs in an instant. The wet splat of his palm against me was humiliatingly loud and terrible and my thighs instinctually pressed together in a haphazard attempt at protection.

It didn't work.

He slapped my pussy hard several more times. I twisted side to side, just trying to survive his brutal punishing hand and when he finally paused, I did everything I could to catch my breath.

He cupped my stinging pussy. Then he patted it lightly and I flinched, which only made him grin with triumph.

"This wouldn't hurt as much if you weren't so wet for me," he observed.

I cringed, braving a glance into his eyes and regretting it almost instantly.

"I'm not," I denied, but he shook his head and lifted his fingers so that they were right in front of my face.

"You're so wet for me that my fingers are glistening with it," he continued. I shook hard and as much as I didn't want to, I looked to see that he was right. I swallowed anxiously, refusing to answer.

"You may deny it all you want, my pretty little wolf, but you're wet. For *me*," he declared hoarsely. I shook my head, and he grabbed my chin with one hand while forcing his fingers inside my mouth. I fought him, the sweet musky taste of my own arousal on my tongue especially jarring. It was like candy, except with a salty after-taste that would remain long after he cleaned his fingers off with my mouth.

I didn't like the way his forceful dominance was making my pussy convulse. I didn't like that he'd made me taste my own arousal.

I bit his fingers hard, and he didn't flinch. Not even for a second. I knew I wouldn't hurt him. My strength was no match for him. Teeth would not be enough to pierce his flesh.

His only weakness was silver.

Carefully, he pulled his fingers out of my mouth and quickly slapped my pussy again before he knelt down and kissed the interior of my thigh. I stiffened as his lips drew closer to my pussy and I tried to close my legs. His wide shoulders stopped me cold.

"You should know better than to use your teeth, Ashleigh. Now I'm going to have to use mine," he warned, and I jerked away. It wasn't soon enough. His teeth bit down on my clit, nipping hard enough to sting. I cried out in alarm as the aching pressure twisted through me like a knife.

"Please! It hurts!" I wailed and when he finally pulled away, I sighed in abject relief.

"Open your mouth. Stick out your tongue," he demanded. With my clit still throbbing, I obeyed. He stood up slowly and roughly pushed his fingers along my soaked folds. He coated his fingers with my wetness before he smeared it all over my tongue. Startled, I went to pull away and he shook his head. The taste of myself was more overwhelming than before, sweeter yet somehow bitter at the same time.

"This is what your sassy mouth will earn from now on. Do you understand me?" he said softly, but the underlying threat was there.

"Yes," I answered meekly, unable to stop myself from trembling.

"Yes, *alpha*," he corrected.

"Yes, alpha," I repeated, feeling my face flush as he wiped off his fingers on my tongue once more.

"Now, you're going to come for me whether you want to or not. Then, I'm going to bend you over this bed and give you the belting you deserve, little wolf," he said, and I shivered hard. His fingers descended back in between my legs, roughly capturing my punished clit between them. I whined, closing my eyes as the raw pleasurable sensation jolted through me. He started to cruelly circle my clit, varying the pressure constantly and forcing me toward the edge of orgasm even as I continued to try to fight it.

I didn't want to come.

I did.

I shouldn't.

I needed to.

Everything in the world was cruelly focused on the tiny little bundle of nerves between my legs. I found it hard to remain still. Every muscle in my body wanted to spasm and I held it off as long as I could.

He slapped my pussy hard and the radiating sting was so intense that I moaned out loud. His rough fingertips returned to teasing me, forcing my desire to come to a head once again. Once I approached the edge once more, he spanked my pussy even harder. I jolted, but he started roughly circling my clit again before I could grapple with the burning sting blooming across my most sensitive flesh.

It became too much too fast. Pain and pleasure intermingled together and soon I couldn't tell one from the other. It was all just sensation and my tortured clit succumbed to him before my mind did.

My core burst open with pleasure, and I cried out. His fingers became more forceful, more demanding and my pitiful cry transformed into a needy desperate moan. I couldn't stop my hips from bucking forward, riding his incredible fingers for everything they were worth. He didn't slow when I started coming for him. He grew rougher and my orgasm deepened, blinding me with its powerful intensity and drowning me in its seemingly endless bliss.

"That's my good girl. Come for me," he encouraged, and I whimpered loudly, rocking back and forth until that brutally vicious pleasure finally began to ebb away. My clit pounded with sensation and when I drew in a breath, he used one hand to part my folds so that he could spank my clit directly.

I saw red.

My thighs slapped together, and I moaned, shaking with both the aftereffects of such an intense orgasm and the hard spanking between my thighs. I slumped down, held up by the belt and he bodily lifted me from the floor. He reached up and undid the strap, catching me in his arms. I hated how my hands wrapped around his shoulders, holding onto him as he turned me over and laid me face down over the bed.

I sighed into the firm softness of that mattress. My quivering muscles slowly relaxed and my body temperature followed. I felt more sated than I ever had before, at least until he laid the belt down on my back. I stiffened and pushed my palms against the bed in a panic, but his own on my upper back pressed me back down before I could get any momentum. I squeaked in surprise, and he cleared his throat. He ran his fingers across the bareness of my backside, and I shivered, both in pleasure and anxiety because I couldn't forget the thick strap of leather laid across my lower back.

"I've watched you from afar for a long time," he murmured, and my pussy pulsed hard. He forcibly spread my legs wide and I knew better now than to try to close them. Maybe I could convince him to fuck me now. Maybe I could make him forget that he ever wanted to belt me in the first place.

I lifted my hips, arched my back, and displayed myself for him as obscenely as I could. His fingers brushed the side of my hip as he moved behind me.

"Elijah," I whispered, and he slapped my ass hard.

"Alpha," I quickly corrected, and he made a sound of approval as he stepped to the side. "Wait! I'm sorry. Please fuck me. I'll be a good girl for you," I pleaded.

"Raise your hips. Show me that wet little pussy," he demanded.

I did. I arched so much that my back felt sore the longer I held it, but I knew it wouldn't hurt as much as his belt would. His fingertips trailed across my skin, and I shivered, but my pussy clenched in anticipation of his large cock pressing inside me.

He trailed his fingers across my lower back and picked up the belt.

"Wait! Please! I won't fight you! Take what you want," I said hurriedly, and he didn't take the bait.

"It's time I used this belt in a different way," he replied.

"Please! Not the belt!" I exclaimed desperately.

"You've had this coming for a long time, little wolf. I'm going to take great pleasure in striping this pretty little ass red," he growled and the harsh swish of the belt cutting through the air caught me off guard.

I wasn't ready for that first terrible lash.

A blazing line of fire cut across my ass, vicious and brutally cruel enough to take my breath away. I keened and another one followed, this one just a little bit lower than the first. Fearfully, I tried to close my legs and the belt descended even lower, striping every inch of my backside with a stinging ruthlessness that left me spinning.

"Keep your thighs open. I want to watch how much wetter your punishment makes you," he demanded, and I shook hard. The belt stung enough to dampen my defiance and I opened them, moaning into the sheets beneath me as the ache radiated across my bottom and deep into my core.

My sore pussy throbbed almost as if it was asking him for more.

When he paused, I bit my lip as he ran his fingers over my marks. I hoped my ordeal was over, but little did I know it was only just beginning.

"Put your hands behind your back," he instructed, and I held my breath as I did as he asked. I whimpered when he pinned them. Whatever he had planned, I told myself that I would remain strong. He wouldn't make me scream and he mostly definitely wouldn't make me cry.

"I think it's finally time for the real punishment to begin," he growled, and the belt whipped across my bottom hard enough to steal my breath away. I rasped as I tried to draw in air, but the next wicked lash of the belt was upon me before I had a chance.

The belting before had been nothing more than a warmup. This was the real thing.

One after the other, the belt licked into my flesh. The end of the belt snapped against both sides of my ass, cruel and viciously intense. He whipped my poor defenseless ass from the very tops of my cheeks to the bottom curve where my thighs began.

It was overwhelming and cruel, and I bit my lip to try to keep any cries I made quiet. I didn't want to give him the satisfaction.

I wanted to take his belt gracefully, but there was no hope of that. From the first moment that punishing belt lashed across my cheeks, I twisted from side to side in hopes of him missing. The hand that held my wrists captive pressed down more firmly on my back, holding me in place despite all of my struggling.

My teeth bit down harder on my lip as I struggled to take it. I was successful in keeping quiet for a period of time, but when the belt descended onto my thighs I cried out before I could stop myself.

The sound rang out around the room with an embarrassing echo. I slammed my lips shut, but when he strapped the backs of my thighs, I screamed out loud. His aim was perfect no matter what I did, and the overwhelming lines of fire truly began to blaze. I could feel each mark rising on my skin, thick welts that simmered long after the painful kiss of the belt.

Over and over again, that dreaded leather punished me.

My fingers curled around his wrists, holding on as he took complete control of me. I'd tried to fight him. I'd stood against him every chance I got, but here I was lying face down on his bed getting the first belting of my life.

It hurt so much more than I imagined it would.

I no longer cared that I was naked, that he'd torn my clothes off my body and pinned me beneath him. My vow to keep quiet and take his belt had long since fizzled into nothingness and I was doing everything that I could to simply survive it. The vicious whip of the belt had taken me captive, and it was all I could do to surrender to it.

My breath hitched in the back of my throat as my fingers tightened around his wrist. My eyes watered and I tried to blink several times in order to stop myself from crying.

"Please. I'm sorry, alpha," I whispered in a rush.

"I know, sweet girl, but we're not finished yet. Spread your legs. It's time that perfect little pussy got a taste of the belt too," he replied. My heart stopped and I forgot how to breathe for several seconds.

"Please forgive me. Please don't belt me there," I wailed.

"You're already earned three, little wolf. Should I add more?" he asked.

"No, alpha," I whimpered.

"Then spread your legs. That little pussy is going to be bright pink before I punish it with my cock," he declared, and shiver of fear took hold of me. I don't know where it came from, but I found the will within me to obey him. I trembled as I waited, but I was not prepared for the stinging kiss of the belt when it came.

It was more vicious than his hand or his belt across my ass. This was something much crueler. He let the sting from the first lash really sink in. I struggled to keep my thighs open, and his foot forcibly kicked them wider before the second slap punished my pussy especially hard.

It smacked against my soaked folds, the sound of leather hitting wet flesh especially mortifying but I couldn't bring myself to care. I could only think about how I had one more strike of the belt on my pussy to make it through.

"Wider, sweet girl. Show me what a good little wolf you can be for your alpha," he purred, and I whimpered as I tried to follow his instructions. My pussy was on fire and when the final lash fell on my sensitive flesh, it was meaner than all the rest.

I wailed as the pain escalated between my thighs. Every bit of my pussy felt scalded and all the work I'd done to keep myself from not crying failed. The first tear escaped me and rolled down my cheek, quickly followed by another.

"I'm sorry, alpha," I murmured, trying to sniffle back my tears. Soon enough, I was able to get ahold of myself, but the stinging of my pussy burned long after with ruthless intensity. In the wake of such a painful taking of control, though, my desire returned with incredibly powerful force. My thighs trembled with it and my aching clit pulsed heavy with need.

His fingers dipped down between my thighs and even just a gentle touch stung. I blinked several times, and he growled quietly with satisfaction.

"It's alright, sweet mate. You just needed to be taught a lesson, didn't you?" he asked. He released my hands and I pulled them forward. My fingers were shaking and clutched the bed sheets in order to make them stop.

"Yes, alpha," I whimpered.

"You're mine now, Ashleigh, and now, you're going to beg me to claim you," he demanded tenderly. He petted my pussy lightly and I was mortified to realize that even though both my pussy and my ass were incredibly sore, I was wetter than I'd ever been before. My clit throbbed even though he'd already made me come once and the only thing I could think about was his cock sliding inside me. My pussy clenched hard at the thought.

"Please claim me as yours, alpha," I whispered shakily, stepping from one foot to the other in an effort to relieve the growing sting he'd painted between my legs.

"Beg me to make it hurt," he continued, and I wailed in mortified embarrassment. I hid my face in the blankets beneath me and he cleared his throat in warning. When I didn't answer right away, he grasped my bottom cheeks firmly enough to hurt and spread me apart.

"I had planned on only fucking your pretty little pussy tonight, but I could certainly teach this tight hole a lesson instead," he threatened, and I cried out with open shame.

I couldn't believe he was looking at me there. His thumb glided down the cleft of my ass, just glancing across my tight rim and I opened my mouth so fast that my head spun.

"Please fuck my pussy! Please make it hurt!" I pleaded desperately. I shook beneath him, and he didn't let go of my ass right away.

"That's a good girl," he praised and when he finally released me, I sighed in relief. "I will leave that reluctant little hole for another day when you've been a very bad girl who needs a very hard lesson indeed," he warned, and I couldn't help but tighten my muscles protectively against his open threat.

Would he really do something like that? Would I like it if he did?

I was so caught off guard by his promise to fuck me there that I hardly heard the sound of his zipper descending before the blazing hot head of his cock pressed against my pussy.

I froze and he slowed, likely feeling my trepidation. His fingers slipped in between my thighs, lightly touching over my entrance.

"You've never been with another, little wolf," he said softly. It wasn't a question, but more of a gentle observation.

"No, alpha," I whispered hoarsely. I wasn't lying. I'd never been with a man. My father had kept me sheltered as best as he could for all my life. I'd never gone on dates or courted anyone. There had been no reason to. I'd always known my fate would lie with whatever husband my father arranged for me.

I'd never imagined my first time looking anything like this.

"I won't lie to you, sweet mate. What comes next is going to hurt, but I promise you that you are safe with me. You're mine and I will always protect what's mine no matter what," he vowed, and his possessiveness did something odd to my heart and my pussy at the same time. Both tremored with feeling and I did my best to push it away.

I heard the belt jangle behind me, and I flinched, but as he leaned forward and looped it around my neck, my pussy flared with heat. He slid the end through the clasp and pulled it tight around my throat like a leash. He didn't pull it tight enough to choke me at first, but the threat was there all the same.

I squirmed, knowing that soon he would be the man to steal my virginity.

I expected him to take me right away, but as he slid his cock up and down my wet slit, I found myself enjoying its wicked heat. I was so wet that his length simply slid against me and when it pushed up against my sensitive clit, I gasped with pleasure. I jerked away slightly, and he pulled the belt just a little bit tighter.

The belt was a message that he was very much in total control of me. I opened my legs a bit to show him that I understood.

He teased me with his cock, rubbing his heat against my clit as I squirmed beneath him. My core spiraled with need, squeezing tighter and tighter until the only thing on my mind was the next time I was going to come.

I'd only ever brought myself to orgasm in the privacy of my own room in the dead of night. I'd used my fingers long enough to have one. I'd never tried for two in the same day, let alone so close together. I trembled, bucking and rubbing my clit even more firmly against him.

He growled in appreciation.

"That's it, little wolf. I like it when you lose yourself on my cock," he purred and that only made me squirm even more wildly.

Slowly, he angled his hips back and the tip of his cock just pressed against my entrance. He tightened the belt around my throat slightly, forcing me to lift my head. I whimpered fearfully, but my pussy practically wept at the proximity of his cock. I was so wet that my inner thighs were dripping with it.

"This part is going to hurt, sweet girl, but I promise you that I will make you come for me several times before your claiming is through," he said darkly, and he gripped the belt tight as his hips surged forward.

His cock slammed through my virgin barrier with primal savagery, and I wailed as he sank himself inside me. He was so impossibly big, and my body fought against him. With every inch, he stretched me wider, and it burned hot for far longer than I had anticipated. He didn't release the belt, only pulling it tighter to show me that I was going to get fucked, that he would decide exactly when and how hard.

He thrust roughly enough for the tip to push against my cervix and my pussy spasmed around his cock. I suffered from the burning sting for several long seconds until it finally crested and started to calm. He didn't move yet, and my core tightened greedily. The edge of the belt cut into the skin of my throat, aching a little but the feel of it made me quiver with shameful desire.

It had caught me off guard at first, but I realized now that I liked it.

"You're just as tight as I thought you'd be, little wolf. This pussy is absolute perfection. I'm never going to tire of it no matter how many times you need to be put in your place," he said, and his words carried with them a wicked seduction that I couldn't ignore. My clit throbbed. He was still frozen, his cock sunk all the way inside me, and I fidgeted.

I wanted more.

I needed more.

"Please," I begged. I couldn't see his face and I didn't know what his intentions were, but I did know I needed him to do something because the passionate desire in my core was demanding it.

"What is it, Ashleigh?" he pressed. There was an amused air to his voice, like a man that knew he'd irrevocably won.

"Please fuck me," I begged, and he slowly pulled out of me only to slam back inside. Hard. I cried out, but the delicious friction was too magnificent to ignore. The burning ache that soared across my bottom and my pussy from his belt only made it that much more intense.

Pleasure. Pain.

It was everything.

"I'm not going to be gentle with you, Ashleigh. If you are going to come again for me, I'm going to make sure it hurts," he warned, slowly sliding his cock in and out of me at a leisurely pace. It was enough to drive me mad with fervid arousal.

"I don't care," I wailed.

His grip on the belt tightened and he slammed his cock into me several times very quickly. I cried out in shock, my body continuing to fight the monstrosity that was inside me. It hurt, but I wanted more of it at the same time.

This was madness.

Raw instinct took ahold of me as my body clutched around him. There was nowhere to run and nowhere to hide.

"You need this, don't you? You need an alpha that isn't afraid to put you in your place at the end of his cock," he murmured and my pussy spasmed around his length. I gasped, the choking sensation from the belt around my neck making me feel lightheaded with delicious insatiable desire.

"Yes, alpha!" I howled, and my fucking truly started. The shame from being so thoroughly punished rattled through me as his cock surged in and out of me, rutting me from behind so hard and so thoroughly that I feared I would burst into flames.

The more his thick length speared into me, the more I lost control of myself. The belt around my throat and the hammering ball of need pounding in my core was more than I was prepared to handle and soon enough, I was teetering on the edge of orgasm. It felt like a balloon filling to the brim deep inside me and I moaned, too over-whelmed by pain and pleasure to do anything but feel.

"Come for me. I want to feel how much tighter this sweet pussy gets when you're coming all over me," he demanded, and his words were too much for me. I lost it and my world exploded into a fiery display of white-hot bliss. Helpless under its terrifying thrall, I could do nothing but survive its wonderfully vicious onslaught.

Unlike that first orgasm, this one came with a deeper intensity. It was intermixed with stinging pain and burning pleasure. I moaned and the sound was so lewdly sordid that it raised the hair on my flesh. My hips rolled, taking his cock deeper with every hard stroke. My body wanted more, and my head was already reeling.

"Fuck, such a good girl. You're going to come for me again," he roared, and my pussy convulsed around his cock salaciously. He groaned and a shiver of arousal coursed down my spine.

I liked that sound. I liked hearing him enjoy my body.

I shouldn't have, but I did.

He jerked the belt a bit harder, tightening the loop around my throat in the process. I choked just the slightest bit at the sudden change in intensity, but my pussy absolutely flooded with sensation.

Despite my initial reluctance, my clit throbbed to life, and I wailed at the fire that whipped through my body like a freak storm. Lost in its clutches, I bucked beneath him, and he mounted me even more viciously.

He wasn't making love. This was a claiming with his cock. This was what it meant to be rutted by a beast.

I moaned. I screamed. I lost myself to another orgasm before I was ready for it.

It slammed into me like a tidal wave, cruel and brutal and so deliciously intense that it overwhelmed me with savage force. His thick length was ruthless, thrusting in and out of my pussy so hard that I saw stars. I closed my eyes, reeling under the delicious absolution of pleasurable bliss.

My back arched and his cock slammed into me even deeper. He demanded my surrender, and I gave it to him, losing myself completely to his brutal beast. I bowed before him. I raised my hips for him. I gave him everything.

I lost control as I shattered for him for a third time. I could feel my inner walls clutching at his girth, both greedily wanting to pull him in at the same time I wanted to push him out. My fingers clutched the blankets so hard that my knuckles turned white. Every stroke of his cock was painful, but so was the way my clit ached after that third orgasm.

"Put your hands between your thighs, pretty girl. Play with that little clit for me," he commanded, and my pussy squeezed so tight that he groaned. He fucked me more slowly for several seconds before picking up the pace once again.

Tentatively, I followed his instructions.

The blossom of fiery pleasure at the initial touch of my fingertips was enough to make me moan. My clit was so swollen, so firm beneath my fingertips.

It felt the way it did right before I had made myself come in the safety of my own bed.

"Ride your fingers for me, little wolf. It's about to get rough and I want another hard orgasm out of you," he demanded.

"I can't," I wailed. He jerked the belt harder, and my pussy convulsed. I sucked in a loud breath as the blood rushed to my head.

Fuck.

I really shouldn't like that so much. But I did. A lot.

My body writhed beneath him as my fingers danced over my clit. My legs tensed and his cock surged in and out of me with a savagery that would leave me sore long after he was done. My own pleasure flared wildly inside my core, billowing outward like a bonfire that had escaped its confines. It consumed me and I began to scream.

He slammed the entire length of his cock into me with a hard thrust and the base began to expand. I screamed louder once I realized what was happening, knowing that I could do nothing to stop it.

He was knotting me.

When he'd talked about claiming me, it hadn't been that he just wanted to fuck me. He'd had the full intention of forcing the mate bond on me from the beginning and I hadn't realized it.

My desire to come for him overwhelmed anything in me that would have fought that realization. What should have been anger escaped from me as a wretched moan. What should have been resistance transformed into an utter willingness to take everything he gave me and more.

I arched back, taking him as deeply as I possibly could.

This was complete insanity.

He leaned over me, kissing the cusp of my shoulder sweetly. I twisted my head just enough to see his face. His canines were extended to sharp points indicative of a wolf, and he snarled. I looked back down as his teeth tore into my shoulder, marking me as his once and for all.

His knot kept expanding, stretching my body wider with an incredible burn that made me cry out. My eyes watered and his bite stung, but then my entire world collapsed.

A sensational white light enveloped my body, surrounding me completely with warmth as powerful as the sun. Every nerve trembled with tumultuous electricity, set on edge so completely that my body didn't stop shaking.

The bond exploded in my chest. My heart pounded hard several times and the blood surged through my veins. My eyes rolled back in my head and my orgasm crashed into me, taking my breath away from the start.

My fingertips crackled with energy as the bond spiraled through me. It was as though I was falling into a black void and all I could do was wait for the inevitable breaking that came with it.

My screams bounced off the walls. Magnificent bliss blinded me, and the world fell away from beneath me.

Pleasure and pain were two sides of the same coin. I couldn't tell one from the other, and in the end, it didn't matter.

It was evolutionary.

I moaned desperately. I writhed wildly. I shattered completely.

His seed spurted deep inside me the moment his knot hooked behind my pelvis. We were locked together now, and the only thing left to do was to ride out the storm.

Each spurt was like a firebrand inside me, painful and wonderful and incredibly fulfilling all at the same time. It drove my release to greater heights.

My orgasm was seemingly endless as one incredible wave after another soared through me. Eventually, my pleasure peaked, and each surge lessened. My body quaked, my muscles tightening with powerful aftershocks that stole my breath away.

When it was finally over, my cheeks were stained with tears. They dripped down my face and puddled beneath me on the bed. I blinked several times, staring down at the wet spot almost in a daze.

His hands reached forward and loosened the belt around my neck. He unwound it from me carefully and I pressed my forehead into the mattress, just doing my best to draw in one lungful of air after the next.

Strong arms surrounded my waist and lifted me up. His knot finally began to deflate, and his cum leaked out of me. Its warmth dripped down my thighs, but I didn't have to energy to try to wipe it away. To be honest, I sort of liked how it felt.

He curled me into his chest, and I burrowed my face into the crook of his neck. His arms squeezed tightly around me, and I sniffled, enjoying their warmth and safety more than I should have. I closed my eyes and breathed in his overwhelmingly perfect scent.

The scent of my mate.

I swallowed hard as my panting began to slow down, trying to understand the fundamental changes happening in my body. I could feel the connection to him inside my heart and it threw me off balance in a way I wasn't prepared for.

This wasn't supposed to be my fate. I wasn't supposed to be his, but here I was in his arms anyway, naked and claimed. My shoulder throbbed, not with pain but with that same connection that was slowly threading into the depths of my soul.

He kissed my forehead sweetly and I melted even further into his embrace. His fingers petted up and down my back in a soothing motion, but when his touch ventured up to the back of my scalp, I shivered with aching bliss.

"You see, my little wolf, I can be a brute when I need to be, but I can be gentle too. Will you let me show you?' he whispered, and I hummed into his chest.

"Yes, alpha," I answered hoarsely.

"There's my good girl," he crooned, and my heart expanded at least three times its size in my chest.

CHAPTER 5

lijah

The two of us were meant to be. Fate had decided that. She was made for me.

She was sheer and utter perfection. There was absolutely nothing more I could have asked from her. With every moan, every soft sigh, every wistful smile that she didn't know she made, it was as if she had been created from every dream and fantasy I could have ever asked for.

Her body was flush against mine. She fit me like a glove. I dragged my fingertips up and down her spine and her lips opened with a soft sigh of contentment against my throat.

The mating bond pulsed inside my heart. I'd read about it. Sometimes, my men would talk wistfully about the possibility of ever experiencing one when we were killing time at a stakeout or late at night at a poker table. I'd never thought I'd be lucky enough to find mine and to know that she was right under my nose this whole time was almost a little saddening, so I squeezed her to me tighter.

Her breathing had leveled out and soon enough, I could tell she had fallen asleep in my arms. I pressed my lips gently against her temple, wanting to savor every moment with her. I knew that I would never let another man touch her. If anyone ever hurt her, I would rip their heart out right through their throat. I couldn't imagine a day without her.

When the mate bond was in play, there was no dating or falling in love slowly. It was fast, savage, and brutally hard.

I'd been a man solely focused on loyalty. I followed orders and I got the job done no matter what it took. I'd taken out my fair share of men along the way, human or vampire. On rare occasions, I'd even taken care of a few shifter packs that dared to tread on our territory.

Now, though, none of that seemed important.

Ashleigh trembled faintly in my arms. I reached to the side while disturbing her as little as possible, grabbing a blanket off the foot of the bed. I quickly wrapped her whole body with it and her quivering slowed down until it disappeared entirely. I would have stayed there like that with her forever until a knock sounded on my door. I adjusted the blanket around Ashleigh, making sure that she was covered. She didn't stir in my lap.

"Come in," I called out softly.

The door swung open slowly, the hinges squeaking just a little in the process. Theo ducked his head in, and I nodded in greeting.

"Amir sent a message. He will prepare a convoy for us to leave first thing in the morning. Be prepared to leave at ten a.m.," he explained quietly. He kept his voice down and the sleeping bundle in my lap never stirred.

"A convoy?" I questioned.

"Yes," he answered simply.

"For how many?" I pushed.

"There's about one hundred of us that want to follow you, boss," he replied.

I was taken aback for a second before I nodded.

"You will be a better alpha than Amir could ever dream of being. We all have faith in you."

I stared back at his hard brown eyes. Theo was often sarcastic, even in the face of danger. Once, he'd walked straight up to a vampire holding a gun loaded with silver bullets and put his finger directly over the end of the barrel. He'd dared the man to take the shot, but to be careful where he aimed because he might enjoy it. The vampire had frozen just long enough for Theo to get close enough to separate his head from his torso.

It had been a sight to see.

"I want guards posted. Take shifts and make sure everyone gets their rest tonight. I want them on their toes tomorrow. I don't trust Amir as far as I could throw him. He has never granted anyone exile before and we need to be prepared if he decides to throw anything at us," I warned.

"Consider it done, boss," Theo replied with a grin. He glanced down at the top of Ashleigh's head and then back to me.

"Taking her might mean repercussions, Elijah," he said gently. His eyes searched mine, full of concern, but he posed no challenge whatsoever.

"She is more than worth it, Theo. If the men are to follow me, they will have to accept their alpha's mate," I answered. "It's just that simple."

"I understand, alpha," he replied seriously.

"One last thing, Theo. See to it that Ashleigh's things are packed. Bring a bag of clothes for her to me so that she may dress in the morning," I said quietly. He nodded once and lowered his eyes.

He bowed his head and left the room. Ashleigh finally stirred in my arms and lifted her head. Her cheeks pinkened when she realized that she'd fallen asleep in the comfort of my lap. Her embarrassment caught her by surprise, and she worked hard to quickly replace it with indignation. She tried to pull away and I didn't let her.

I allowed my hand to slide down her back, over the blanket to her backside. I could still feel the heat my belt left behind and she stiffened just a hair. I simply used my fingers to lightly circle the small of her back several times and after a few moments, she relaxed once again.

I wrapped my arms around her and stood up. With much care, I tucked her under the covers and brushed the hair out of her face.

"I should wash up," she muttered, trying to sit back up. I pressed her back down firmly as I crawled into bed beside her.

"No. Tonight, I want my seed marking your skin. I want you to go to sleep knowing you're mine," I whispered, and she shivered against me. The scent of her arousal on the air was fresh again and I pulled her in flush against my frame.

I reveled in the fact that she didn't fight me. There were small signs that she was comforted by my presence. Her back arched, not a lot, only slightly. Her body curled against mine as I wrapped myself around her, using my body heat to keep her warm and her small fingers found my own. She clutched at them like she never wanted to let them go.

My heart throbbed with hope.

Yesterday, I'd been nothing more than a foot soldier in the Crimson Shadows mafia family. Today, I'd claimed my mate. Tomorrow, I would become an alpha of my own pack with her at my side.

I closed my eyes, happy and content.

* * *

The next morning, I opened my eyes to see the early morning rays of the sun cutting through the dark gray fabric of the curtains. I blinked away my sleepiness, but there was a part of me that didn't want to let the sleeping woman in my arms go. It still felt too soon.

I muffled a groan as I glanced at the clock on the wall. We would have to get moving and soon.

She was still fast asleep, so I reached up and brushed the hair from her face. I kissed the side of her neck, softly at first as she slowly began to respond. She sighed quietly and nestled in closer to me as if she didn't really want to get up either. With a reluctant groan, she rolled against me, and I grasped her chin firmly. I made her kiss me.

To my surprise, she kissed me back without a moment's hesitation.

That made me want to devour her even more. I ravaged her with my kiss, and a deep-seated hunger within me flared to life. I'd never see another woman again. I would never want for another because the only one in my life was her now.

I growled as I kissed her, and she moaned right into my mouth. I swallowed her sounds and when I finally pulled back far enough to allow her to breathe, her face was flushed.

"It's time to wake up, little wolf," I purred, and that beautiful blush deepened.

I would be the only one to ever see it. I knew that now. She was mine and I planned to keep every beautiful piece of her surrender to myself.

I kissed her again, only this time I was rougher, more insistent and she responded so very beautifully. Her chest arched toward me, and I wound my arm around her back and pulled her against me hard. She gasped and I deepened the kiss, possessing her completely in that single moment. She quaked with pleasure beneath me.

"Now that you're awake, we can take a shower," I offered, and her bottom lip protruded just slightly in an adorable pout. Her thighs tensed beneath me. She didn't breathe a word of confirmation, but I didn't need it. I could smell it.

She was soaked. She'd come several times for me yesterday, but that was the power of the mate bond. It would never be enough, and I felt exactly the same way.

"You can be a good girl for me and get up and shower, or we can start the morning with a trip over my knee," I warned her, and her cute pout grew a bit bigger. Even though I wanted to stay in bed as much as she did, the longer we stayed the more time Amir had to plan something that would put us all in danger. We had to leave and soon.

When she didn't make any effort to move, I grasped her wrist and jerked her hard enough to put her exactly where I'd threatened. My big palm settled on top of her right bottom cheek, and she stilled. Oddly though, she made no effort to escape me.

It was as if she wanted a spanking. My cock was hard as a spike.

When I'd made the threat before, I hadn't exactly intended on following through, but I was only a man. I couldn't resist something like this. I couldn't fight the temptation of her.

I decided to test her. If she needed a spanking, she would get one.

"You're my mate now, Ashleigh, and when I give you a directive, I expect your obedience," I scolded lightly. I rubbed over her bare bottom, admiring the pale pink marks that my belt had left behind last night.

"Yes, alpha. I'll do better next time," she replied.

"Will you get up and take a shower with me like a good girl or do I need to redden your bottom, little wolf?" I pressed. Her hips wiggled slightly, legs falling open just enough so that I could see the glistening arousal on her thighs.

"I don't want to get up," she whined. I had to hide my smirk. My belt had done nothing to quiet her feistiness, not that I thought it would.

It simply released something within her that she'd never known about herself. She liked when a man took control. Deep inside, she craved it.

"I didn't give you the option to stay in bed. Either the two of us take a shower together, or you get a spanking and then you will take a shower with your bottom burning. Whatever you choose, you will not be allowed to stay in bed," I warned her.

For several moments, she was quiet, likely deciding what her next course of action would be. I guessed that she was probably thinking about how I'd bent her over the bed and whipped her perfect ass with my belt. Maybe she was thinking that I'd give in and take care of that needy little pussy with a good hard fucking. I knew she could feel the rigid hardness of my cock under her belly. We had both slept naked and when she wriggled her body over my thighs teasingly, I knew what needed to happen. I'd given her multiple outs, but she very clearly wanted a red bottom.

I would be the man to give it to her, but at the same time she needed to know I was in control. She'd get spanked, alright, but it was going to be just a little harder than she expected.

I squeezed her bottom hard and she yelped. I wrapped my other arm around her waist and pinned her over my thighs. Her body shivered with anticipation.

I slapped her left bottom cheek hard. She gasped, almost as if she had forgotten a punishment like this was supposed to hurt and I smacked the other side. Her pale, slightly pinkened skin went white for a moment, before my handprint blossomed up in its place. She whined, but I knew what she needed.

I started spanking her gorgeous little ass in earnest. I started at the tops of her cheeks and worked my way down, ensuring that I didn't miss a single inch. When I reached the bottom curve of her cheeks, I lifted her hips and spanked that spot harder than the rest. I wanted her to remember this moment every time she sat down today, that she was the one who earned a spanking and she'd gotten everything she deserved and more.

She struggled over my thighs as I took control. She might have thought she was ready for it, but she would eventually learn that she would always be out of her element with me because that was exactly what was making her little pussy wet right now.

She had challenged me this morning and I would make sure that I surpassed her expectations.

When my palm descended onto her thighs, she yelped out loud. I punished them hard with my hand and she began to give in.

"Please! Elijah! I'll go shower!" she exclaimed, but I wasn't done with her yet.

"Open your thighs, little wolf," I demanded.

"Please don't spank me there," she whined.

"Is it up to you?" I asked. I'd given into her playfulness thus far, but I would only go so far.

"No, alpha," she whispered.

"When you need to be punished, I will decide when and how, so if you don't want me to take my belt to you next, you will be a good girl and open your thighs for the spanking you deserve," I chided her.

"Yes, alpha," she whimpered. She struggled to obey me. Now that she knew her pussy was about to get spanked, it was hard for her, but I was proud to see her thighs open very slowly.

"This needy little pussy is the reason you're over my knee in the first place, my little wolf, isn't it?" I began and she shuddered hard. Her entire body was flushed with arousal, and I could see that the sensitive skin of her inner thighs was practically dripping.

"Did you think you could tempt me with this beautiful body into getting the hard fucking you deserve?" I quizzed her next. I brushed her hair out of her face just in time to see her mouth open and close with disbelief. I'd hit the nail right on the head.

She wanted to come for me. I would allow it, but it would be on my terms.

I slid my hand between her thighs, and she flinched.

"Answer me, little wolf," I pushed.

"Yes, alpha," she whined. Her hands flew to cover her face as if she could hide her shame, but I could feel her arousal against my hand. I already knew.

"That was very, very naughty," I scolded her, and she shivered. I slid a single finger very lightly over her clit. Then I slapped her pussy firmly enough to sting. She cried out and her thighs instinctually tightened around my wrist for several moments.

"Open. I'm not done," I commanded, and she wailed into the sheets even as she obeyed me.

In quick succession, I spanked her little pussy hard three more times. She squirmed over my knee, trying to avoid my firm hand, but I didn't let her. When she caught her breath, she opened her thighs without needing to be told.

I repeated the three, bringing the number of slaps in between her thighs to seven. She had three more to go.

Her entire body undulated over my thigh, trying to fight me and attempting to take it for me at the same time. The wet sound of my palm against her very soaked pussy was loud and I took several moments between each set of spanks to rub her heated flesh until she was writhing with need.

These last three were going to be the slowest and hardest of all.

"Is your little pussy sore?" I asked her. One of my fingers was teasing her clit. I wasn't pressing hard enough to make her come.

"Yes, alpha," she whined, just as she tried to ride my fingers more firmly.

"Naughty girl. Trying to make yourself come without permission," I scolded her, and I firmly spanked down directly over her clit. She cried out at once, but I slapped her quickly after it before she could tense up. She writhed, struggling in the throes of insatiable need and sharp stinging pain. Even though it hurt, her desperate little clit found my fingers once again.

The combination of both sensations was turning her on. Last night wasn't a fluke. She was made to respond to me this way.

"I want your thighs as wide as you can get them for this final one. I want to make sure I leave this little pussy very, very sore," I instructed. Like I expected, she obeyed, but to remind her I was in charge, I cleared my throat. I wanted more and she gasped, spreading her thighs wider for me in the process.

Good girl.

I cupped my hand around her pussy, and she flinched, but she held her thighs open for me anyway. My cock throbbed beneath her. I wanted nothing more than to fuck her, but I resisted. It was not yet time.

She lifted her hips, opening for me even wider.

God damn. She was perfect.

I slapped her little pussy as hard as I dared, wanting the last one to sting more than all the rest. She cried out at once, and the whimpers that followed were the most delicious things I'd ever heard. Gently, I cupped her pussy and she whined. It was likely that even the light touch of my fingers stung too, but I wanted to feel her need in the most primal way.

Her clit was very hard and swollen. It would not take much for her to come for me at all.

I admired her bright red bottom and the evidence of her neediness in every movement she made. Her breathing was heavy and when I leaned forward, I could see her pussy was not only soaked but bright pink too.

She couldn't keep still. She wanted to come, badly.

"Now, little wolf, you will climb off my lap and come with me into the shower," I said. If she followed my instructions, she'd soon find herself full of my cock.

I couldn't see her face. She was probably pouting as she pushed herself up, but I didn't care. She'd listened without complaint.

I slammed her back down on the bed, flat on her back. She gasped in surprise, but my mouth was between her legs before she could say anything at all.

I kissed her inner thigh.

"That's my good little wolf. Now you're going to come for me. I want to taste you before I take you in the shower and fill you with my cock," I growled.

CHAPTER 6

 *shleigh*

When his mouth closed over my clit, I wasn't ready for the warm envelope of wetness. It felt like heaven itself, and I arched clean off the bed. I grasped at the sheets beneath me, trying to keep my thighs open and not pull away from him even though every soft touch made my pussy sting at the same time that my desire for more soared.

I'd woken up impossibly needy, but I wanted to be taken. I didn't understand it, but I wanted it to hurt too in some way. The idea of being taken over his knee this morning had been too much for me to resist and I'd deliberately pushed him into it. Now my bottom and my pussy had both been soundly spanked, far harder than I'd wanted to begin with, and now I was more aroused than I should have ever been.

I liked it when he took charge of me. I liked it when he made it hurt, but I liked when he pushed me even more.

His tongue flicked my clit and I gasped out loud. I couldn't keep still, and his hands grasped my waist and pressed me down onto the bed. He maneuvered his shoulders between my legs, ensuring that I couldn't close my thighs either. I gripped the sheets more firmly as my entire core pulsed with spiraling need. My swollen, stinging clit throbbed and I couldn't help but arch toward his mouth.

"I won't allow you to get off this bed until you come hard for me, little wolf," he purred, and my body vibrated with need. I chewed my bottom lip, but when he kissed my clit directly my eyes practically rolled back in my head.

His teeth nipped at me, but I was so aroused that I moaned. Sensation roared through me as he focused so thoroughly on my pleasure that I knew it was only a matter of time before I came in my mate's mouth for the first time.

My *mate*…

Yesterday, I'd wanted to hate him. I'd wished terrible things on him when he'd taken me against my will, but now I wanted nothing more than to succumb to his every desire because those desires were also mine.

My hips rolled, surrendering to the pleasure he was forcing on me. My clit pulsed against his tongue and soon my little moans became desperate pleas for mercy as he teased me with that perfectly extraordinary mouth.

I let go of the sheets and started to tweak my nipples just like he had done before. I pinched them harder and twisted them side to side, enjoying the way the delicious tremors of pain sank down and were lost in depths of pleasure begging to be set free in my core.

Elijah teased me with his mouth. I was already at the edge of orgasm, but he taunted me with it. He brought me to the edge again and again, but just as I was about to fall, he'd lighten the pressure and I couldn't quite get there. I cried out, the stab of denial exceedingly cruel but brutally arousing at the same time.

He'd controlled me with pain. Now he was bringing that same lesson home with pleasure.

"Please let me come," I begged.

"Are you going to come hard for me?" he asked, and I wailed in response.

"Yes! I'll come so hard for you, alpha," I quickly answered, and he licked all the way from my entrance to my clit. I shivered hard as the pressure was almost too much.

"Good. I wouldn't want to have to get my belt," he said darkly, and I shuddered, remembering the sordid ways he'd used it on me last night.

I was so hot, I almost couldn't stand it.

"Please, alpha. Let me come for you. Let me be your good girl," I pleaded, and I was rewarded once again with the sweet bliss that was his mouth. I teetered on the edge of that knife, and I started to beg again. Soon enough, my words didn't even really make any sense.

He flicked my clit several times and just when I was ready to come, he sucked my needy bud in at the same time that he caressed it with his tongue.

There was no holding out when he did that.

I arched, pressing myself into him as I lost control and came hard, just like he wanted and I needed. My body started to shake, overwhelmed by sensation and completely consumed by it. With his focus entirely on me, I could do nothing but succumb to his expert touch. My core contracted over and over again as my inner walls grasped around empty air.

He'd promised to fill me with his cock.

My clit pulsed under the firm pressure of his tongue as I writhed beneath him. My hips bucked, but he held me firmly in place. He'd made it clear I was going to come for him and nothing, not even I, was going to stop that from happening.

My fingers dug into the mattress as my world exploded. I closed my eyes, the light from the morning sun far too bright. With a low moan, I simply let my pleasure take hold of me until at long last, it peaked and began to ebb into the beautiful aftermath of sated pulsing bliss.

I sighed happily, content as waves of warmth washed over me.

He hadn't cared that I'd woken up with bedhead or morning breath or his seed still sticky on my thighs. He'd wanted me all the same. When he'd kissed me, he'd looked at me like I was the most beautiful woman in the world and that made me feel special.

Could I find happiness with him? Was that even possible?

I lay languidly on the bed as Elijah stood up front of me, watching me with a deep satisfaction that made me squirm a little bit in embarrassment. I glanced down for a second, wanting to see the magnificent sight of his cock and it was even bigger than I remembered. My pussy flinched with both reluctance and anticipation, knowing that soon I was going to have to take every inch of it inside me.

I wanted it, but it made me nervous at the same time.

He offered me his hand and I took it. I didn't realize my legs felt like jelly until I stood on them, and I faltered, but he was quick to catch me. He hoisted me into his arms, and I wrapped my legs around his waist as he carried me into the attached bathroom. He turned the shower on and waited until the steam billowed up around us until he carried me inside.

I gasped at the hot water as he slowly dipped me under it. He didn't rush to put me down though. Instead, he slammed my back against the wall. I stared back at the ravenous expression on his face and licked my lips. My nipples hardened into tight little points.

"This needy little pussy still needs to be taught a lesson, doesn't it, little wolf?" he growled, and my stomach practically leapt into my throat. With the steam of the shower surrounding us, it felt like we were up in the clouds. The head of his cock brushed against my entrance, and I gasped with anxious arousal.

"Yes, alpha," I breathed. He hadn't forgotten. I was going to get fucked after all.

The hot water dripped down my body, scalding against my freshly spanked flesh. I bit my lip, and he captured my lower lip with his teeth.

"Keep doing that, my sweet mate, and you're going to get fucked hard. I had intended on being gentle with you," he growled, and I stared into the gray depths of his gaze. They were turbulent like a storm, and I felt myself drawn into their wicked darkness. I gave into temptation.

I bit my lip again.

He thrust forward hard, forcing himself inside me before I was ready. I cried out and he swallowed my screams with a rough kiss that would leave my lips sore long after he was done with them. My pussy felt like it was stretched to the limit, and it hurt, but as he began to piston himself into me, I started to crave it. I wanted more.

I rolled my hips with a gasp. The head of his cock brushed against a place deep inside me and my entire body began to shudder.

I knew I was going to come again, just as hard as the first time. The mate bond flared deep in my heart, and I lost myself in its beautifully delicious purity.

Weightless, I bucked on top of his cock as he fucked me. He wasn't gentle and to be honest, I didn't want him to be. I wanted his roughness. It felt dangerous and perfect, and I couldn't get enough of it.

I wrapped my arms around him and dug my nails into his back, holding on while I lost control. My orgasm seemed just out of reach, and he growled into my ear. My body shook, vibrating with visceral intensity and I keened against him.

I dug my nails in deeper.

He growled louder, demanding that I give him everything and I did. Stars studded right before my eyes and I closed them, crying out into his chest as my orgasm took hold.

My pussy clamped down around his cock and he roared with a savage pleasure of his own. He slammed his cock all the way inside me, and the first spurt of his seed hit me like a brand. His cum filled me to the brim, but it didn't stop. He roared and slapped his hand against the tiled wall, thrusting into me roughly and repeatedly.

"One day, you're going to carry my baby in your belly," he growled, and the thought of our child together twisted my heart with hope.

My core pumped with one convulsion after the next. My inner walls milked him of every spurt of seed. When it seemed like he was finally empty, he didn't pull out right away. He kept his cock fully inside me, keeping his warm seed locked there.

When he did pull out of me, I had to bite back a sigh of disappointment. He took a step away from the wall, holding me steady in his arms as I slowly unwrapped my legs from him. I pressed my feet down to the floor as he circled me in his embrace. For several long moments, I just caught my breath as the hot water steamed down all around me.

He reached over to the left side and grabbed a bottle of shampoo. He squeezed it into his palm.

"Lean back for me," he directed, and I obeyed without question. He massaged the soap into my scalp, causing me to moan out loud at the delicious feel of it. I honestly hoped it would last forever, but when he eventually rinsed it out, I had to keep my disappointment at bay. He soaped up a loofah next and very gently washed my body, taking extra care to cleanse off the seed dripping down my legs. When he was done, he directed me under the spray. I enjoyed the feel of the water pounding against my sensitive skin and when I'd rinsed all the soap off, I sighed and pumped several spurts of conditioner into my hand.

I massaged it into my hair, running my fingers through its length in an attempt to ease out all the knots. Beside me, Elijah started to soap up himself. When he shampooed his thick brown hair, the suds dripped down his body. I licked my lips, savoring the sight until he caught me watching him. I rushed to take my eyes off him.

"Like what you see, little wolf?" he chuckled knowingly.

I was too proud to tell him that I did, but my clit pulsed as if it was answering for me. I ignored it. There wasn't a chance in hell that I'd reveal that to him either.

I finished rinsing myself off under one of the shower-heads while catching glimpses of him. His cock was impossibly hard again and I made the mistake of biting my lip once more. His brow furrowed and his eyes narrowed. I swallowed hard and blushed.

"I'm going to count how many times you bite that pretty lip today and when we get to our destination, you're going to have to come for me that many times in a row," he warned. He reached for me and pinched my nipples, pulling me toward him by the tips. I whimpered and he captured me in a kiss that left me reeling before he shut the water off. He kept a steadying hand on my lower back as he stepped out and wrapped himself in a towel.

He handed me one and I wrapped it around myself. I made my way over to the counter where there were fresh toothbrushes and toiletries laid out. I brushed my teeth first and then I worked a brush through my wet tangled mop until I was certain I got all the knots out.

When I finished and walked into the bedroom, there was a duffle bag on the bed. I looked from it to Elijah with a raised brow.

"Your father has arranged a convoy for us in preparation for our departure. I have taken the liberty of having your things collected so that you may keep them," he replied.

His thoughtfulness caught me off guard. I appreciated the fact that I would have my favorite pieces of clothing, but it was heavy handed all the same. I opened my mouth to tell him that, but he cleared his throat, which gave me pause.

"I suggest that you say thank you gracefully, unless the only thing you want to wear on the journey are the marks from my belt," he warned, and I blushed hard.

"Thank you, Elijah," I said in a rush, and he smiled knowingly. My bottom clenched, the memory of the strap around his waist still very fresh in my mind.

"Good girl," he replied, and my pussy pulsed as if it was answering for me once again. My face heated and I turned my head, focusing instead on unzipping the duffel and seeing what was inside. There were a few different outfits, but it appeared that most of them were dresses. I started to pull them out one at a time. By the time the bag was empty, I'd come to realize that there wasn't a single pair of pants inside it. Also missing was even a single pair of panties.

I turned toward him, raising my eyebrow.

"I want a pair of jeans and whoever packed this forgot that underwear is a basic necessity," I declared.

"No. Wearing panties is a privilege, little wolf," he answered calmly.

I looked back at him like he had two heads. I crossed my arms over my chest, and he very casually picked his belt off the bed. He slid his finger up and down the edge and I bit the inside of my cheek. I was treading on dangerous ground.

"You will not cover that pretty little pussy without my permission and right now, you do not have it. I want it bare as a reminder that every beautiful piece of you belongs to me," he continued.

My traitorous little clit pulsed in response.

"If you choose to disobey me in this, you will learn what a spanking with a wooden spoon feels like on that perfect little pussy," he warned, and I nodded quickly.

That was something I would desperately try to avoid. Getting a spanking with his belt between my legs was bad enough. I had no doubt that a wooden implement would sting that much more.

"I'll be a good girl," I blushed.

His answering smile was so full of pride that I couldn't tear my eyes away. My heart was suddenly surrounded in his warmth, the bond making me feel safe and secure with him far more quickly than I ever imagined I'd be with a man.

A man who was now mine.

I fingered one of the dresses on the bed, having trouble choosing which one because my mind was so consumed with what was looking to be my new life. He must have seen that indecision cross my face, because he put the belt down and walked over to me. Possessively, he wrapped an arm around my waist and perused the options I'd laid out on the bed.

"This purple dress will look especially beautiful on you. Not only that, but it will make your green eyes pop perfectly. You will wear it, for me," he decided. His hand squeezed my torso a bit tighter, and I couldn't help but lean into his embrace.

"Yes, alpha," I breathed. I smiled softly as he released me. There were a few bras inside the bag thankfully and I pulled one over my shoulders before clasping it behind my back. He watched me as he dressed himself, and I turned my back. He growled with desire once he saw my ass. It was still pretty sore and from my glimpses in the bathroom mirror, it was likely still red from my spanking. There had been several light pink marks from his belt too.

I thought seeing marks like that would have made me angry, but it was the exact opposite. I carried them with pride. I didn't understand it, but then again, I didn't really need to.

I slid the dress over my head and tied it around the waist. My pussy felt extremely bare and the knowledge that he knew it was that way made me feel even more naked beneath my sundress. I shrugged on a thin sweater to cover my arms, knowing that sometimes air conditioning made me chilly.

I slipped my feet into a pair of sandals and packed the rest of the dresses back in the bag.

He'd dressed in a pair of black slacks and a dark gray button-up shirt, which only made his eyes seem even more intense than usual. When he was done, he grasped my bag with one hand and took my hand in the other. His grasp was soft, gentle even, and I found myself wanting to follow.

He led me out of the bedroom and down the hall. I didn't really pay attention to the path as we went. Eventually, the two of us ended up outside where there was a long line of black SUVs waiting. Elijah's second in command walked up and I studied his face. I vaguely remembered his name to be Theo and I nodded in greeting. His smile of acknowledgement was warm and receptive, which put me a little more at ease about leaving.

"There was no further action during the night, boss. Amir has been true to his word," Theo explained, and Elijah slid his thumb along his chin thoughtfully.

"Have the vehicles he provided been inspected?" he asked.

"Yes. All of them have been scented and there is no evidence of foul play," Theo answered.

I studied both of them intently. "Scented?" I repeated.

"For bombs. The last thing your father will want is for the world to find out he's lost a segment of his soldiers. To the other packs, and especially to the surrounding vampire clans, it will be seen as a sign of weakness," he explained.

"He wouldn't put me in danger," I scoffed, but Elijah's gaze never lost its serious edge.

"I think you may underestimate how much value your father puts on his place of power," he continued, and I swallowed hard. I could deny it all I wanted, but I knew that my father would not be above sacrificing me, especially if it meant that it would grant him an even higher seat in the world in some way. He'd already shown that by arranging my hand in marriage to a vampire.

"No. I understand," I answered plainly. I didn't expand on the issue, and he didn't ask any further questions. His eyes searched mine for a second, likely sensing my disquiet. I turned away and he let me. I expected him to demand that I look back and explain myself, but he didn't. Instead, his hand squeezed mine and he continued talking about other small details of our departure with Theo.

I gazed over the place that had long been my home. I'd grown up here under the guidance of others here. There had been many happy memories here, but there also had been many lonely ones. As an alpha's daughter, I didn't

SARA FIELDS

have very many friends that weren't simply there because they were told to be.

I'd grown up all my life believing it was what I wanted and needed, that it was my future that I was bound to inherit someday. Was that really my own dream or had that just been my father's expectations all along?

The mate bond in my heart made all of that feel empty.

Elijah tugged my hand, breaking me out of my inner reverie and bringing me back to the present. I smiled quickly, trying to cover up what I was thinking.

"It's time to go now, Ashleigh," he said softly, and I nodded. I pulled my hand from his and held my head high. I would not go like a wolf with her tail in between her legs. I still had my pride.

I walked by his side all the way to the car. Like a gentle-man, he opened the car door for me, and I climbed in. He closed it and walked to the other side, while Theo got in the driver's seat in the front. A good many familiar faces strode by and climbed into the other vehicles all around us. I lost count quickly, but it was clear that my father was losing an extraordinary number of men today.

Elijah was right. There wasn't a chance in hell that he would let that stand.

Warily, I sat back. I took note that we'd climbed into one of the SUVs in the center of the group, so we'd be guarded on both sides by Elijah's allies. We sat still for several minutes before Theo started to pull away.

120

I don't know why, but I breathed a sigh of relief at that.

Elijah pulled me toward him, surrounding me with one arm. The protectiveness of the gesture warmed my heart and my fingers instinctually found his. I felt him smile against my scalp and I snuggled into him even more closely. I lost myself in the security of his scent.

I was quite certain that it was one of the first times in my life that I'd ever welcomed such attention, not that I'd ever had an opportunity to experience it before. I wanted to close my eyes and rest, but I also didn't want to miss out on even a moment of this, so I chose to look out the window at the mountains surrounding us.

"Where are we going to go?" I asked with interest.

"Before I came to confront your father, I made several calls. In my position as your father's head soldier, some of his allies are infinitely more loyal to me than him simply because I was the one that handled problems for them personally. One of those men is the owner of a chalet in the mountains just outside Zurich. As a token of appreciation, he offered it to me as tribute, but he did warn me that the place is currently infested with a vampire clan," Elijah explained.

I stiffened, but his arm simply tightened around me.

"What vampire clan?" I asked.

"I think they were once members of the Ravnos clan, but they were exiled for ignoring the rules some time ago. It was either that or death. Since then, they haven't really amassed any power or prestige to my knowledge. I've been informed that they are a pretty vicious lot, so we need to be well prepared, but it's nothing that we can't handle," he continued.

"Are you sure?" I asked. I remembered the night they'd broken into my bedroom. I could still feel that vampire's cold touch on my naked flesh as if it were only minutes ago.

"Yes," he answered. When I was silent in return, his fingers sought out mine.

"Are you worried, little wolf?"

"Yes," I replied. I hated how my voice wavered, revealing just how fearful I actually was of walking straight into some kind of attack or ambush.

"When we get to where we're going and I've made sure it's a safe place for both my mate and my pups, you and I will spend time training together. I will teach you how you can use your smaller size to defend yourself," he offered.

"I'd like that," I whispered, curling in closer to him.

"Do you know what else, little wolf?" he asked and there was a darker under layer to his words that hadn't been there the first time.

"What?" I asked carefully, pressing my thighs together as if I could stem the pulsing in my clit. With him, I was insatiable. I told myself it was just the mate bond, but a part of me knew that wasn't all it was.

"As your teacher, I'm looking forward to implementing a very special system of punishments and rewards," he murmured, and I blushed heavily into his chest.

The thought excited me, and I was sure it did him too. His hand reached down and massaged the side of my hip. The whole idea of learning how to fight and defend myself was remarkably sweet.

I knew I didn't yet know him completely, but it seemed that although he expected my obedience, he didn't seek to control me or keep me in a cage like some kind of trophy. I needed to be sure though, so I decided to be blunt.

"What do you expect from me as your mate?" I asked.

"I expect you to hold your head high and stand by my side as the queen of my pack. You will defer to me and only me. No one will touch you except for me and I expect that in times of my absence, you will handle yourself as I expect an alpha's mate should," he replied.

"I see," I answered. I took some time to process his words and he slid a finger under my chin and forced me to look up at him.

"I will be a fair mate to you. I will love you fiercely, but I will expect your obedience. I think you know what will happen if you defy me, isn't that right?" he pushed.

"Yes, alpha," I answered truthfully. I did understand.

"Tell me..." he pressed.

"You'll punish me," I whispered, wanting to be quiet so that Theo wouldn't hear.

"I will. It'll hurt, won't it, little wolf?" he continued. His other hand fell casually to cup my bottom cheek and I swallowed anxiously, trying to willfully ignore how wet my bare pussy felt beneath my dress.

"Yes, alpha," I blushed.

"Good girl. Keep that in mind, my little wolf," he murmured as he kissed my forehead sweetly.

For some reason, the whole conversation settled me. A blanket of security folded over me, and I closed my eyes. His arm wound around me, and I pulled it close. Soon enough, my breathing evened out, and my body started to feel heavy as the comfort of him surrounded me.

I'm not sure when, but I fell asleep in his arms.

lijah

The sleeping bundle in my arms hardly stirred and when we arrived at the airstrip, I didn't have the heart to wake her. With as little jostling as possible, I carried her onto the plane myself and tucked her into one of the oversized seats in first class. I wrapped her in a warm blanket, and she snuggled into a tight little ball. I brushed the stray hairs off her forehead, sitting close by and just letting her sleep.

The drive to the airport had been far smoother than I thought possible. Theo had sent a number of wolves on ahead in the morning just to look for signs of ambush or potential places of attack, and there had been nothing.

I wasn't dumb enough to believe that we were out of the window of danger yet though. It was true that putting more distance between Amir and my pack would be safer, but I had made a powerful enemy. I couldn't forget that. Not ever.

I sat down in the seat next to my mate and pulled my laptop out of my bag. I made several more inquiries with both humans and monsters alike in my quest to fully secure our new position in the world. I heard back from a few of them very quickly. I had several allies swear their fealty to me rather than Amir. I was in a strong position already.

The only thing to do now in preparation for our arrival was to give my pack a name. It would be my legacy.

I closed my eyes and pressed the back of my head against the seat behind me. My mind raced with possibilities, but none of them seemed right until the Rising Sun wolf pack occurred to me. In time, I aimed to eclipse the power of the Crimson Shadows.

My email pinged with the satellite images that Antonio had provided for me. In the center was the chalet itself. The surrounding territory had small areas that were circled and labeled as vampire dens. I had information from multiple sources that there weren't that many vampires defending the place, but it seemed off that they'd spread their forces out over such a large plot of land. Maybe they were just that inexperienced and hadn't had to defend their territory before, but I wasn't willing to take any chances by underestimating their power.

He'd provided heat map data along with the satellite images, but it was essentially useless to me because the vampires wouldn't show up on the scanners anyway. I had no intentions of hurting any of the humans living there, just ousting the vampires that held them captive.

I studied the topography, trying to get a handle on the layout of the roads and paths to each potential strong-hold. The more I became familiar with the territory, the more I began to realize the surrounding dens were just outposts spread out to maximize their ability to guard their territory.

I understood the idea of it. The placement of each one was strategically situated to oversee much of the moun-tains and the main points in and out of the area. It was a respectable strategy, but the terrain would also limit their ability to effectively defend each outpost and their central place of power. They'd need at least double the number of vampires in practice, and all my sources indicated that they didn't have anywhere close to that.

I knew what we had to do once we arrived.

I could feel the plane beginning its descent and I closed my laptop. I slid it back inside my briefcase and grasped Ashleigh's hand in mine. I squeezed it a little. Still asleep, she unconsciously reached for me, turning her body toward mine as if she was seeking me out. I jostled her arm slightly and with a groan, her bright green eyes blinked open slowly. With an adorable stretch, she yawned and tried to rub the sleep out of her eyes.

"We're on a plane?" she asked drowsily.

"I figured it would go much faster than driving all the way there," I answered with a grin.

"You're right, I guess," she murmured. Another yawn pulled at her, and I enjoyed the innocent view of her delicious-looking little throat. "Are we almost there?"

"We've begun our descent now and will be landing very shortly. I wanted to wake you myself, instead of during the landing," I explained. Sometimes landings were a bit rough. Waking her myself would be far gentler.

"I appreciate that. I've never been particularly fond of flying," she confessed.

"It's a necessary evil sometimes," I told her, and she nodded sleepily.

"To be honest, I think this is only the third time I've been on one. Father didn't usually let me travel much," she continued. I could hear a nervous quiver on the edge of her tone. Immediately, I reached out and took her hand in mine.

The moment my fingers took a hold of hers, she breathed a visible sigh of relief and the tenseness I'd seen almost seemed to bleed right out of her.

When the plane drew closer to the ground, her hand tightened around mine. The landing went smoothly, and the plane came to a stop quickly. I still didn't let go. When the time came to deplane, I was a bit more assertive with her. I kept a hold of her arm and held her close and she seemed to welcome it.

Once we were off the plane, she didn't seem bothered anymore. The airport we'd arrived at was a smaller one, and I'd arranged for all other flights to reroute other than my own. We moved quickly to the facility, where there were several vehicles waiting for us. There were two buses, a number of SUVs, and an extended Escalade waiting for me and my mate. I led her forward as the rest of my pack segmented and climbed into the rest of the waiting vehicles.

I couldn't help but admire her body beside me. Her hand squeezed mine and I smiled down at her. A chilly breeze whipped her skirt around her legs, and I smirked as she rushed to cover herself knowing full well that she was completely bare under that dress.

I didn't say a word, but her blush when her eyes met mine was utterly delicious.

I opened the car door for her. The back was closed off from the driver, which I preferred especially when it would come to dealing with my rebellious mate in the future.

I glanced down at her backside, the cloth of her dress hugging it salaciously in the wind. I would be the only one who ever saw her naked. I would be the only one who would ever punish her pretty ass when she needed it.

I would be the only one who would ever know what she sounded like when I fucked it. I stifled a groan.

With a deep steadying breath, I helped her climb inside while ignoring the iron spike in my slacks. My cock throbbed painfully. I'd taken her this morning, but I was more than ready to do it again. I got inside with her and closed the door.

Of her own accord this time, she scooted closer to me. I kissed her temple and she moved even closer, pressing herself against me. I could smell the scent of her arousal on the air. It was getting harder to ignore.

The car pulled away from the airport entrance. It would take some time to make our way to the chalet, so there was more than enough time to take care of my needy little mate sitting right next to me.

I wanted to test her obedience.

"Spread your legs, little wolf," I commanded. She looked around, likely noticing that the windows were tinted and that the divider between us and the driver was thick enough to hide whatever happened back here. She looked quizzically at me as if she was trying to decide whether to obey me. Eventually, she sat back and tentatively opened her thighs.

"Pull up your dress. Show me what's mine," I demanded.

Her chin lifted in defiance for a moment before her fingers began to dip to the bottom hem of her dress. Slowly, she lifted it for me. She paused once it hit the very tops of her thighs and I cleared my throat expectantly. It was the only chance I would give her to be obedient for me. If she wasn't a good girl for me, she would find out that I had other ways to punish her that were infinitely more shameful than a spanking.

She was a good girl though, and she pulled up her dress. Her inner thighs were glistening, her little pussy positively soaked. I grasped her thigh and squeezed it tight enough to make her whimper.

"You're very wet, little wolf," I observed out loud, and she blushed furiously.

"Yes, alpha," she breathed. Her response made my cock jump.

"Kneel in front of me with your thighs spread. I want that little pussy on display," I ordered. Her cheeks deepened in color from bright pink to red. She opened her mouth a few times, before she thought better of it and lowered herself to the soft carpeted floor before me. She rearranged her dress so that I could see all of her just like I wanted. I took a long moment to savor the sight of her weeping pussy before I flicked my gaze back to hers.

"I'm going to fuck your mouth, my pretty wolf. If you do a very good job, I will make sure you come very hard for me as a reward," I explained and just when I thought it wasn't possible, her flush deepened even more. She squirmed, visibly curious as she glanced down at my cock.

"You'll let me come for you?" she asked. There was a part of her that seemed averse to the idea of getting her pretty little mouth fucked, but it appeared that an even bigger part of her seemed to be aroused by the idea, especially when it was combined with an orgasm for her.

"I will. You'll do it over my knee. You should know something else, little wolf. You can scream as loud as you want in here. No one will hear you except me," I continued.

I watched a drop of arousal roll down her thigh.

"I've never—" she began, and I shook my head.

"I know. As my mate, you will learn. I plan to enjoy those pretty lips often," I said.

The corner of her lip lifted wistfully. I unbuckled my belt and slowly freed my cock. When it was finally free from the confines of my slacks, I groaned as I slid my fingers over its velvety surface. She fidgeted as I opened my knees, licking her pretty lips with that little pink tongue.

"Come closer. Put your hands on my thighs. You will keep them there until you have swallowed everything I give you," I directed. I could see her swallow nervously at the prospect, but she did as I asked. She took in the full sight of my cock up close. I liked that she couldn't take her eyes off of it. There were moments of hesitation, fear, and anticipation in her eyes. With my hand, I angled my cock toward her.

"Open your mouth. Start by sucking the tip and gradually work to take in more. You don't have to take it all the way inside your throat, but you will show me enthusiasm. If I think you're not putting forward your best effort, I will spank you until you're begging for another chance to try again," I explained.

"I understand," she whispered nervously.

"Good girl," I answered, and I caught her gleeful smile before she dipped her head in an attempt at hiding her eager expression. She looked away for only a second though. With excited anxiety painted all over her face, she crawled forward and placed her hands on my thighs. Tentatively, she licked her lips before leaning forward. She kissed the tip hesitantly before she licked all the way down my length.

She gazed back at my cock with a sense of worship, and I only grew harder. When she opened her lips and granted me the gift of her mouth for the very first time, I had trouble holding back at the truly decadent sight. I groaned openly when she sucked at my length and pushed just a little past the head.

Wow.

"Swirl your tongue and suck harder, little wolf," I demanded, but I was already extremely pleased with her efforts. The fear of punishment made her wetter and the potent scent of her arousal only confirmed it. She tried to bob her head up and down, slurping around me so beautifully that I knew that this moment would be painted in my memory forever.

Fuck.

Her mouth was absolute heaven.

She pushed a little further and choked, but she got a hold of herself quickly. I sat back, enjoying the way her tongue swirled up and down my cock. Her cheeks were drawn in with her efforts to suck me and before long, the craving to remind her who was in control was almost too much to bear. Occasionally, she would glance up at me in triumph, like she was the one controlling my pleasure and I knew I would have to do something about that soon.

She suckled me and I drew my hand up her arm, allowing my fingers to just glance along her neck before I fisted the hair at the back of her scalp. She started in surprise, and I moved forward just enough to gain leverage over her so I could thrust into her mouth.

"This pretty mouth just needs a hard fucking, doesn't it, my little wolf?" I growled and she whimpered against my cock. The vibration traveled deep down into my balls, and they squeezed tight, which only made me roar with pleasure. She tried to use her hands on my thighs to push away from me, but I didn't allow her that.

"You will answer me. I don't care that your mouth is full," I demanded, and she squirmed, but I sensed her arousal had only gotten that much stronger.

It took her several tries as I slowly fucked her mouth, but eventually she was able to mutter the words "yes, alpha," and the way her tongue bounced off my cock was just as delicious as I had imagined it would be.

I took over after that.

"Remove one hand and tease yourself. I want that little clit ready for me for when you go over my knee," I snarled, and she shakily dropped her right hand between her thighs. I fucked her throat faster, enjoying the warm wetness as much as I dared before I allowed myself to let go.

I could have warned her that I was coming, but I didn't. Her surprise was just as incredible as I'd imagined it would be.

She choked at first as my cum hit the back of her throat. She tried to pull her head away, but I forced her down so that she had no choice other than to swallow around my cock. I could feel the back of her throat squeezing tightly around me and I roared, pouring the rest of me into her with wild abandon. My hips savagely thrust into her pretty mouth and when I was finally finished, I groaned and released the back of her head.

"Clean off every drop with your tongue, little wolf. When you're done, you will get over my knee and come for me," I demanded. I couldn't wait to touch her and by the way she was squirming with her hand between her thighs, she couldn't wait for me to touch her either.

CHAPTER 8

 shleigh

I'd just given the first blowjob of my life.

When he'd come, I'd been taken aback by the sudden mouthful of his seed, but my core spiraled hard with arousal even as I struggled to take everything that he gave me. I'd swallowed it all while toying with my clit. It was incredibly hard beneath my fingers. I was looking forward to coming for him. I needed it. I craved it.

The taste of his cum was still so fresh on my tongue. I found that I liked it. There was a part of me that almost wanted to take him in my mouth again.

The need was too great between my own thighs, however.

I dutifully leaned forward and stuck out my tongue. Slowly, I cleaned up and down his turgid length. It was still hard, although not as much as before. I took my time ensuring that I thoroughly washed all of him with my tongue. He petted my head gently for several moments. The look of sheer joy on his face was worth every moment of panic I'd had when he'd taken control and fucked my face himself.

Eventually, he tucked his cock away. I pouted at little at the loss it, but not for long. He reached down and grasped my arm roughly. He tossed me over his knee and quickly flipped up the back of my skirt.

The sudden nakedness of my ass caught me by surprise. He knocked my legs open with his hand, forcing his hand between them. Then, very gently, he slid his fingers along my pussy, and I quaked over his lap.

"Oh!" I moaned out loud, unable to stop the way my hips lewdly rose to grant him even more access than he already had. His hands slipped over my flesh with embarrassing ease. It didn't take long for him to thoroughly coat his fingers with my arousal and he took a few moments to tease my clit before he took his fingers away.

I whined openly and he clicked his tongue in disapproval.

"You're going to come, my pretty wolf, but you will remember that it will always be on my terms, won't you?" he chided me, and I was ashamed of the way my pussy clenched in response.

"Yes, alpha," I answered.

His other hand was massaging my bottom and I couldn't help but writhe over his lap just a little. I was not expecting what he did next, though.

With his fingers, he separated my cheeks and spread me apart, revealing my asshole in one quick motion. When I tried to crawl off his lap, he used his other hand to swiftly slap my pussy very firmly. I keened as the brilliant sting burst across my sensitive folds. I closed my eyes, trying to take it gracefully, but it hurt.

I didn't pull away after that. He went back to my bottom hole. He traced his wet fingers around the rim. I couldn't help myself as I trembled, nervous and embarrassed and scared of what he planned to do.

"This tight little hole is so very pretty, my sweet wolf," he mused, and I hid my face in the seat of the car in shame. I wanted to hate him looking at me like this, but I couldn't bring myself to. A part of me wanted him to see me like this, wanted him to notice the arousal dripping from me like a goddamn faucet.

A single finger pushed against my asshole.

"You're going to come for me, little wolf, but it will be with my finger in this tight virgin asshole. Do you understand me?" he declared.

My pussy spasmed like it had lost its mind.

"Please," I whimpered. I wanted to ask him not to touch me there. I wanted to beg him to fuck me there. Swirls of confusion rattled through me, and I struggled to make sense of them. I couldn't grasp onto anything and then his finger brushed against my most reluctant hole again. A sordid twisted part of me leapt in excitement, leaving my mind reeling.

I couldn't stop the way my hips were lifting almost in anticipation. My nipples brushed against the leather of the car seat, making me quiver and arch back against his finger.

"I'm going to slide my finger inside you, little wolf," he announced, and his finger pressed a bit more firmly against my asshole.

"I can't," I protested, and he growled softly.

"You will, my pretty wolf," he answered. Pinned over his knee with my bottom spread open, I felt so very vulnerable. His finger was persistent, and it became very clear that no matter how much I tried to squirm away, it was going inside me.

"Please," I begged.

"My finger is going inside this very reluctant hole, little wolf. The only thing left for you to decide is whether you want a hard spanking too," he growled.

His hand spread me open wider.

"Yes, alpha."

"Do you need a spanking, little wolf?"

"No, alpha," I whimpered.

"What do you need then?" he pressed. His finger tapped on top of my asshole several times, making my pussy quiver and my clit throb hard.

"I need to come," I whispered hoarsely.

"How, little wolf?"

"With your finger inside my bottom, alpha," I wailed. As the words poured out of my mouth, I could feel my core practically vibrating. My thighs trembled and he circled my asshole for a moment before he forced it roughly inside.

My asshole burned from the very start. His finger was thick, and he hadn't been gentle, causing a deep sting to radiate around my asshole. It sank deep into my core, traveling up and down my spine with a vigorous thunder that left me gasping for air.

"Oh, it hurts," I cried out.

"It does, doesn't it," he purred, and he pushed his finger inside me. His knuckle was wider than the rest and a fresh wave of sensation poured over me. I whimpered, but even as the deep ache rattled my insides, an even fiercer desire soon overpassed it.

My pussy throbbed along with my heartbeat, growing stronger with every passing second. My thighs were absolutely dripping with arousal and when another of his fingers slid along the top of my clit, I gasped loudly.

A low moan escaped me. He growled low in approval.

"Such a wet little pussy, mate. I think you're enjoying yourself," he chided, and I couldn't help but quiver with shame.

The thing was, he was right.

I *was* enjoying myself and when he started to pump his finger in and out of me, I gasped. The stretching ache deepened, but an insatiable pleasure soon followed. My hips rolled back and forth, aiding him in fucking my bottom with his finger and rubbing my clit at the same time.

I dug my nails into the seat beneath me, but there was no stopping what was coming. I was going to orgasm, and I instinctually knew that it was going to be ridiculously hard.

I moaned, trying to fight it.

He added a second finger without warning. I cried out as the sudden blazing sting tore through my insides just as he increased the pressure on my clit. I was no longer capable of words. There wasn't any rhyme or reason to the sounds coming out of my mouth either. They were simply desperation, needy and frantic for release.

"Do you want to come for me?" he asked pointedly.

"Please!" I wailed. It was the only thing I was capable of at that moment.

"Come for me, little wolf. I want to hear your pretty screams," he demanded, and my body responded as if his voice had a direct conduit to my center.

My legs started to shake, and the rest of me followed.

A magnificent ball of pleasure spiraled deep inside me, circling and intensifying until it blazed hot and burst apart in a massive explosion that rendered me senseless. I wailed as my eyes rolled back in my head. I shut them, quickly blinded by the white-hot bliss rattling through me. Thunderous pleasure surged through my veins, holding me prisoner to my mate's every whim.

I writhed over his lap, arching my back so that his fingers thrusted even deeper inside of me. It felt wrong and wicked and so incredibly taboo, but I didn't care. All that mattered was how hard it was making me come.

It was incredible.

By the time my orgasm finally crested, I was shaking with aftershocks that seemed to go on endlessly. My throat felt hoarse, and I vaguely recognized that I had screamed for him, loudly. My face flushed with shame, and I chewed my bottom lip.

He hadn't pulled his fingers free from me, not yet. My asshole throbbed around him, a little sore and achy from his rough treatment. A part of me liked how it felt and as if he could read my mind, he pumped them in and out of me, like he was proving a point.

I sighed, insatiably pushing back against him. He chuckled knowingly and my face heated even further. I swallowed hard, trying to ignore the scorching fire at the same time my body throbbed with deep satisfaction.

When he finally took his fingers out, I panted at the sudden emptiness. My muscles tensed, slightly sore even though he was no longer touching me. I liked that.

"That's my good girl," he murmured as he pulled my dress back down. Tenderly, he wrapped his arms around me and lifted me to sit in his lap.

My heart pounded in my chest, slowly coming back to normal. I curled into him and closed my eyes, just letting the satisfied bliss of the aftermath of orgasm and the safety of his arms overtake me. The rest of the ride was quiet, the road jostling us against each other from time to time. When the car finally slowed to a stop, I looked out of the window. The snow-capped mountains that surrounded us were breathtaking. I lifted my head, taking it all in while Elijah petted my shoulders and upper back.

I sighed, fully enjoying myself. Elijah cleared his throat and I turned back to face him. His expression was serious now and I cocked my head, waiting for him to clarify.

"We're almost there, Ashleigh. You will remain in the car while my pack and I deal with the vampire infestation here," he explained.

"I can help," I exclaimed, and he slowly shook his head.

"No, I will not have you put in danger needlessly. Theo will remain here with you. You will not fight him. You will stay put just like I told you, do you understand me?" he continued.

"Fine," I answered curtly, and his jawline tensed. He grasped the hair at the back of my head so roughly that a flash of agony radiated outward across my scalp. I whimpered and his snarl of warning made my blood run cold.

"If you disobey me in this, mate, you will be punished. I promise you that you will be a very sorry and very sore girl by the time I'm through with you. Do not push me. You will not enjoy it," he growled.

I didn't want to find out what he meant. My backside tensed as if it was anticipating the spanking I hadn't yet earned.

"I understand," I replied meekly. "I'll stay put."

"Good girl," he replied. The seriousness in him disappeared, only to be replaced with a warm joy that was fully focused on me. "You're very important to me. Seeing you hurt would tear me apart."

His tender feelings for me shone with every syllable that left his mouth. His grip loosened on my hair and his lips closed in with a heart-stopping kiss. When he pulled away, his eyes searched mine.

"Don't make me punish you tonight, little wolf. I would much rather take you to bed without having to make you sob over my knee first," he said softly.

My pussy clenched tight.

"I won't, alpha. I will stay with Theo," I whispered.

He growled in appreciation before he hit a button on the ceiling. The divider between the driver and us opened, revealing Theo at the wheel.

"Keep her safe. If you need to restrain her, you have my permission. If she resists, I will deal with her when I return," he ordered his second. Theo nodded in understanding.

"I will see to it that your mate does not come to harm, alpha," Theo replied. Elijah lifted me off his lap and sat me down on the seat. He quickly climbed out of the car and closed the door behind him.

His absence hit me harder than I expected it to.

I sat back against the seat and watched him walk toward the rest of his waiting soldiers. All of them were lined up, looking to him with absolute respect. The kind of loyalty they offered him was something that had never happened back home. This was what my father had always dreamed of.

He'd never earned it though. It was clear that, to these men, Elijah had.

They gathered closely around him, listening intently as he laid out the plan. Since the sun was still up, it was in their interest to act soon while the vampires were still sleeping.

I moved to the door and opened it, much to Theo's chagrin.

"I just want to stretch my legs. I'm not going anywhere," I said quickly, and he got out of the driver's seat along with me. He walked around to me and leaned against the car. I glanced back at him, amused by his brooding silence.

Fighting against boredom, but maybe more at the fact that Elijah was running straight into a den of dangerous vampires, I decided to poke at him.

"Must suck to have to play guard duty to a she-wolf instead of running into the fight with your boss," I smirked.

He glanced toward me and shook his head. "Nah, he gave me the most important job," he grinned.

I wanted to come back with some smart retort, but the words died on my tongue before I said anything at all. I looked back at Elijah as he headed off down the road. They had shifted into their wolf forms, sprinting off to take on the rogue vampire clan with a contagious sense of excitement.

"Is there a place where it would be safe for me to watch?" I asked quickly.

"You're worried about him, aren't you?" he replied, smirking.

I glared back at him. I didn't dignify him with an answer.

"You don't have to tell me. There's an overlook just up that trail. We can head up there and watch the devastation from above," he said. "It would probably be an easier trek in our wolf forms, however," he added.

I looked at the overgrown trail and had to agree with him.

"I'm going to go just behind the car," I replied, and he nodded.

"Don't do anything you'll regret, Ashleigh. I have my orders and I mean to stay true to them," he warned.

"I know. I just don't want to ruin my dress," I replied. I turned away, using the car as cover as I stripped. I folded my clothes into a small pile and shifted quickly, not wanting anyone nearby to see me naked.

My body folded toward the ground, my front paws reaching forward as my claws dug into the dirt. Gray fur sprouted all over my skin. My coat was thick, shielding me from the cold breeze that was cutting through the mountains right now. After shifting fully, I padded back to the other side of the car to the open door. Using my mouth, I placed my clothes inside safely. I used my body to close the door.

Theo had already shifted and was sitting there patiently waiting for me. His ears were up. He'd likely been listening for any sign that I was going to run.

I didn't plan on running. Home was a long distance away. Even at my fastest, it would take me several days on foot. Even considering that, if I ran off by myself there was a chance I could run into vampires, or my father's long list of enemies that would use me against him.

My identity was no secret in a world ruled by monsters.

Theo's yellow eyes appraised me. He was surprised, but he covered it up well.

"Follow me," he murmured, and he turned to climb up the trail.

"Lead the way," I offered, and I padded off behind him.

CHAPTER 9

lijah

Leaving Ashleigh with Theo was one of the hardest things I'd ever done. I kept telling myself that she would be safe, that he was the strongest man in my pack and he would jump in front of a bullet just to keep her safe, but it was still difficult.

I focused on the bond for several moments. I could feel that she was safe. She was worried slightly and that warmed my heart. It brought me relief that I could not sense her fear.

I took a deep breath and turned my attention to the problem at hand. My pack and I were working our way up into the mountains. I knew from the satellite imagery that there was a den of them stationed up on the cliffs, hidden away in the pine trees so that it was barely visible from below. I led the way for my wolves through the woods at the side of the road, using it as cover. I took precautions as we drew closer, scenting the air and taking several moments to observe my surroundings in case the vampires had laid any traps.

Surprisingly, I didn't find a single one. They were either supremely overconfident or just incredibly stupid. By the time the cabin came into my sights, I'd decided it was probably the latter.

I'd decided in my initial plans that this outpost would be the first to go. It overlooked the main road into the biggest town in the surrounding area, which also doubled as their main hub. They'd taken over a mansion in the center of town, using it as their base to rule over its people.

I crept closer to the outpost, taking note of the heavy curtains and boards that closed off the windows. My men circled it with me, and I noticed that there was a rear exit that seemed to have fallen into disuse. From the looks of things, it had been nailed shut long ago.

The only way in was through the solid front door.

I crept along the perimeter, using the surrounding brush for cover. I doubted the vampires were looking out the windows themselves for fear of the sunlight burning them into a crisp, but from the looks of things, there were at least a few cameras mounted along the roofline.

I lowered myself to the ground, listening closely for signs of life. The rank scent of vampire was fresh on the air. One of the floorboards inside the cabin creaked loudly as someone walked around inside. The sound of hushed voices flittered on the breeze and the raucous roar of laughter soon followed.

I crept forward, noting that the conversation continued. There was one camera focused on me and either they were ignoring the feed, or it was only there for show. I expected some retaliation by the time my men and I climbed up onto the porch, but still none came.

I'd waited long enough though. I threw my entire body weight into the door, causing it to smash inward with a massive crash. My wolf form took up much of the entryway and a ring of male and female vampires looked up at me with abject surprise.

There were about a dozen of them in the cabin.

None of them looked particularly strong. It was as if they had all just entered their senior year of high school and all the guys had yet to actually hit puberty. They sort of looked at us like we were mythical creatures of some kind. To be honest, it was really quite amusing.

I burst forward and ended the one closest to me with my teeth. My men poured in behind me, swiftly tearing through the grisly group of vampires as if they were nothing more than paper dolls. It was bloody and extraordinarily violent, but in the end, it needed to be done so that I could create a safe place for my pack, my mate, and my future sons and daughters.

By the time we were finished, the floorboards were soaked through with blood, all of it from the unfortunate vampires that happened to be guarding this outpost.

I did a quick survey of the cabin, noting that it was outfitted with nothing more than basic necessities. There were two additional rooms and when I walked into one of them, I was horrified at what I found.

A woman hung from shackles on the wall. She was naked, her skin covered with fresh bites. She'd been here for a long time from the looks of it. There were a terrifying number of white scars that had long past healed over, as well as several that were still mending. There were no bandages or ointment and it appeared that she was barely hanging onto life. Her heartbeat was almost inaudible.

They must have freshly fed on her and it was clear that they'd taken it too far.

I took a step into the room, only to find out that she wasn't the only one. There were more inside. Both human men and women alike hung from the walls and all of them seemed to have been used like an endless buffet by the vampires we'd just torn through.

I tore the shackles from the walls. They crumpled under my strength into piles of rust. I caught the woman in my arms before she fell, hating how her skin was cool to the touch.

This was cruel even by vampire standards.

I laid her down carefully on the floor. Beside me, my fellow pack members destroyed the metal cuffs and freed all the humans that were still left alive.

"I want someone to stay behind and make sure everyone here gets the medical help they need. Kaden, Riley, since you two have the most experience, run back to the caravan and bring everything we've got. Keep them stable and once you're able, get them to the nearest hospital," I instructed once they were all free. The two wolves I'd called out nodded hurriedly. I watched them sprint off with urgency.

"I need one of you to stay behind until Kaden and Riley come back. The rest of you follow me. If this clan is allowing these kinds of atrocities out here, I can only imagine what's going on inside their stronghold," I added.

My wolves growled with restrained fury.

"What are your orders for the vampires?" Atreyu asked boldly. He'd always been a loyal soldier but had found it increasingly difficult to put his hatred for vampires aside while under Amir's rule. I, on the other hand, had no intention of limiting that hatred.

I would remember vampires for what they truly were. Monsters.

"I want them dead. Every last one," I growled, unable to tear my eyes off of the suffering humans they'd left behind.

"You got it, boss," Atreyu grinned.

"Let's go," I snarled.

We made quick work of the mountain. The men that followed me were battle-hardened soldiers. All of us were strong and fast, used to maneuvering our way through a fight and doing whatever it took to ensure that we came out as the victor.

When we reached the town, the roads were quiet. It was as if the town had been abandoned and the silence that reigned over the beautiful homes and shops was more suspicious with every passing moment. There wasn't a single face in the windows. No children laughing. The shops weren't open. Some of them were even boarded shut.

I didn't like it one bit.

I stopped several blocks away from the town center where the vamps had set up their home base. My ears flicked from side to side, listening for signs of life.

Then I heard something. It sounded like someone crying.

Now that my hackles were fully raised, I crept forward until the mansion in question came into view.

An army of humans was guarding its front gates. I stopped, still well out of the limits of the range of their vision.

"Circle around. We attack from the rear. Break into the mansion first and eliminate the vampires. Avoid killing the humans as much as you can. They are simply prisoners, and I will not punish them for that," I commanded.

Quickly, my pack broke apart. We used the cover of the abandoned buildings all around it and when we approached the back of the mansion, there were only a few humans guarding the back. With great care, we dealt with them as quickly and as quietly as possible, either sneaking around them or knocking them out when we had no other choice. They would eventually wake up with a headache, but they were alive when we left them.

We broke into the mansion all at once. Some of the windows were open, some had to be broken. A number of back entrances were locked, but that didn't stop us from barreling through the door and knocking it straight off its hinges. There were a few vampires we ran into as we rushed inside, but they were too caught off guard to do anything against the likes of us. I didn't give them the chance.

I tore through each one, ignoring the bitter taste of vampire blood on my tongue. We ran into more as we hurried through the halls, but we ended those too.

Word seemingly traveled fast. Soon enough, we started encountering larger groups of vampires. They didn't give us too much trouble, but they were prepared enough to start slowing us down. There were a few that rushed us with silver weapons, but we handled those quickly and efficiently so that none of my men got hurt.

By the time we finally managed to get to the central room of the compound, the vampires were fully armed and much stronger than the ones we'd encountered so far.

A large group of them were waiting for us. I paused, studying what appeared to be a hastily organized last stand. An alarming number of vampires were aiming guns in our direction. I assumed that it was more than likely that each one was loaded with silver bullets. Several were holding silver knives in their grasp too.

These ones at least knew who we were.

I hesitantly sniffed the air. The scent of wolfsbane burned at my nostrils. Some of them had sprigs of it tied around their necks.

Wolf shifters were weak to wolfsbane. Ingesting it would render us paralyzed. Aerosolized wolfsbane burned through our skin like actual fire. Touching it would be painful, but it would also weaken our strength. We would have to avoid it as much as possible.

My wolves were waiting at the perimeter, warily waiting for my command on how to move forward.

Atreyu and Noctis moved to either side of the front door, cutting off the exit in the process. I strode to the middle and sat down on my haunches, looking over the enemy. There were several weak points in their formation if they were meaning to protect the tall and skinny man at the center. They all seemed to be looking to him for direction. He was their leader.

I put my focus on him.

He did his best to not cower before me, but I could see the signs anyway. His Adam's apple bobbed up and down as he gritted his teeth. He tried to lift his chin bravely as he rolled his shoulders back, trying to make himself appear bigger than he actually was. His eyes were still glinted bright red, a mark of a young vampire, which meant that he had little experience in actually utilizing his abilities especially against a wolf like me. His fingers were shaking, and he hid them behind his back, but it was too late. I'd already seen his fear.

We hadn't even attacked yet and we already had the upper hand.

"I am Elijah, the alpha of the Rising Sun pack," I began, and he rushed to clear his throat.

"I am Timothy, the kingpin of the New Ravnos clan," he sputtered. All around him, the faces of his followers twisted with angry pride. The existence of their clan had never been officially recognized by the Council and after I was through with them, they likely never would. They'd been hiding out here in secret, likely hiding from the boss of the Ravnos clan, a feisty woman who went by the name Josephina. From what I knew of her, she wasn't the type of leader that would let their cruelty stand.

I wouldn't allow it to continue either.

From the moment I'd entered this unholy place, I could smell the suffering. There hadn't been time, but I knew that human men and women alike were barely hanging onto life behind most of the closed doors we'd passed. I'd hated having to leave them, but I hadn't had much of a choice.

We had to deal with the enemy before we could help them.

"You are breaking Council law here, Timothy. My pack intends to make you answer for it," I growled. His shoulders cowed at the sound. Good.

"We are living by our own decree. We do not bow before the Council," he vowed, and I had to chuckle.

The Council wasn't something you could just choose whether or not to exist under. They ruled over every single vampire clan and wolf shifter pack in the world, and they had done so for centuries. It was their role to govern and keep our identities secret from humankind. They would do whatever they thought necessary to protect that, including wiping out an entire clan or pack if need be.

I was quite certain the dissolution of this particular group of vampires would be their utmost priority if they knew what was happening here. I didn't particularly care for diplomacy though. I was a man of action. I'd deal with the problem before it got any worse.

"I don't care. You will bow before me," I snarled, and he took a step back nervously.

"My people will not cower before you, mutt," he exclaimed.

In the time I'd been speaking with the clan leader, my pack had situated themselves strategically throughout the room so that they could take out the vampires with weapons against our kind first. Through our pack link, I'd already delivered my instructions for how I wanted them to process. I would take care of the leader myself.

It was time for him to die.

I didn't tell him death was coming. I didn't give him any warning at all before I leapt forward. In a rush, he tried to un-holster his gun from his belt. I don't know if he was inexperienced or just dumb, but his gun got stuck in the process and he didn't even get it out of the holster before I was on top of him. When my claws dug into his chest, he squealed like a pig, and I had to stop myself from openly snorting with amusement.

My teeth captured his wrist, rendering it immobile before I splintered the bones inside it with a vicious bite. His screams echoed the loudest, but I ended him quickly and without remorse. I separated his head from his body in a practiced maneuver and I welcomed the silence that came with it.

My pack deftly avoided the silver knives, along with the bundles of wolfsbane. Several vampires got off a gunshot here and there, but the majority of them went wild and were so poorly aimed that they ended up blowing holes in the plaster walls instead of in the flesh of my wolves.

The battle was swift and bloody. We outnumbered them by a wide margin, so it was simply a matter of time before we came out the victor. Several vampires tried to escape out a window or off into the rest of the house, but they were quickly dealt with.

By the time it was over, there wasn't a single vampire left standing. When I was certain all of them were good and dead, I barked another order.

"Find every human in this place and free them. Those who are stable, see to it that they are cared for. Clear out this room and set it up as a makeshift hospital. Whatever we can do to mitigate the damage they wrought, I want done," I commanded.

My wolves howled in agreement.

"Atreyu, come with me. You and I are going to search the town to see if there are any vampires we missed," I added, and the black wolf leapt to follow. His yellow eyes swept the room. He loved the fight, and it would mean a lot to him that I would afford him the opportunity to come with me. I knew he'd hate to miss even a single one.

I bounded through the front door, and he sprinted along with me. Because of our innate ability to scent a vampire from afar, especially out here in the expanse of the mountains, we only had to sniff the perimeter of several of the surrounding buildings. We'd have to deal with the remaining outposts in short order, but that would come after we made sure that the humans that they'd hurt were safe.

The sun was beginning to set, so if there were any more vampires to contend with, this would be the time were they would start to become active. They would be stronger and freer to move around outside when it wasn't daylight.

Before the sun rose again, I would make sure there wasn't a single one left.

CHAPTER 10

 shleigh

I didn't see Elijah for hours. From above, I watched as the human wall meant to defend the central mansion started to break apart. The wolf shifters had taken to their human forms, keeping their identity a secret as much as possible from the victims of the vampire clan. Those people returned to their homes in a daze.

I could see several people carried out on makeshift stretchers. The breeze carried the bitterly strong scent of blood, both vampire and human and I slowly came to realize that the situation was quite dire for the people here.

I'd never seen anything like it before. I wanted to do something, anything really.

"Theo, I feel useless up here. I want to go down and help. The threat has passed. As long as you're with me, it should be safe," I said bluntly.

He looked at me with uncertainty and then back down to the scene below.

"I won't run off. You can trust me," I pressed, and he nodded with understanding.

"You don't need to worry about that, mate," a familiar voice grumbled, and I turned my head. "You will come with me, and we will get you settled in our new home."

Elijah had come to us.

His wolf form still took me aback and if I didn't know that I was safe with him, it would have even scared me. His wolf was much bigger than any of his brethren. He was almost double the size of some of the other wolf shifters. His golden eyes shone like stars, glittering with a multitude of oranges, yellows, and reds. His undercoat was a dark gray flecked with white and black.

He was a beast of a wolf and my heart thumped, reminding me that he was mine.

I'd been doing my best to hide it, but I'd been worried for him. I knew he'd fought his way through a multitude of situations far more dangerous than this but seeing him now right in front of me safe and sound made me sigh with an overwhelming sense of relief.

He didn't appear hurt, but there were several places on him that were matted with blood. I could tell by the scent of it that it wasn't his though.

"But they could use me down there," I argued.

"Are you a doctor, little wolf?" he asked.

"Well, no," I admitted.

"Many of the humans are in critical condition. We were able to locate several human doctors and nurses among the humans that inhabit this town, so they are doing their best to stabilize and heal those that need it. It is better for them if we keep out of their way. Tomorrow though, if you still want to offer a hand, we will do that together," he explained.

At first, I wanted to resist him, but what he'd said made sense. I looked away for a moment, searching the streets of the small town below. The humans looked much less dazed and far more focused on the well-being of their fellow people. It was possible that the entire town had been under the rogue vampire clan's compulsion and their deaths had broken the spell. Either way, the over-whelming threat had seemingly been handled and now it was everyone's job to pick up the pieces.

Tomorrow, I would do whatever I could do to help put their town back together the way it was before the vampires destroyed it.

I glanced overhead, noting that there were not many hours of daylight left.

"Has the chalet been searched?" I asked.

"Not yet," Elijah answered. "Between the three of us, we can handle it. Come. Let's go."

Theo followed him without question. I wasn't used to taking orders from him and I hesitated for several more seconds. When Elijah gazed back at me, I finally took a step and began to trail after him. He paused and cleared his throat.

"As my mate, you will walk beside me, Ashleigh. All others in the pack follow not only me, but you as well," he dictated.

Theo took several steps back, allowing me to come forward. I walked to Elijah's side, and I felt a sense of pride immediately wash over me.

"You are the alpha's mate, little wolf. From this point onward, your word is as good as mine," he said.

We traveled the rest of the trail up the mountain. Along the way, Elijah explained that the area had been cleared of vampires. Down below, they had searched every building and structure that could be used as a hideout and had uniformly exterminated any one they found. All of their surrounding outposts had also been dealt with. Above us, several helicopters were flying in to medivac anyone out that needed more extensive care than the small town could provide.

The swiftness of Elijah's takeover was both inspiring and terrifying at the same time. He was a powerful man, a dangerous one and anyone who stood against him in the future would do well to remember that.

By the time we made it up to the chalet, there were a few cars parked out front. Several of my bags had been placed on the porch and about a half a dozen men were standing guard outside. There was a thick lock on the door.

"We thought you might look poorly on us kicking in the door, so we waited for you, boss," Atreyu smirked.

"Good choice," Elijah rumbled, his amusement obvious. He walked over to the car and shifted quickly. He didn't hide his nakedness and I couldn't help but admire his pride. He pulled on a pair of pants and shrugged on a shirt. He indicated for me to come over to him. When I arrived, he used his body to shield me.

"Shift into your human form, little wolf. If there are any humans inside, I'd like to not give them a heart attack from seeing a pack of wolves barge inside," he commanded.

"But someone might see," I whispered, sitting back on my haunches.

"They will not, but they will certainly hear what happens to a naughty wolf who ignores her alpha's command," he continued. I blanched at the insinuation.

"You don't have to do that," I replied bashfully.

"Then be a good girl for me, little wolf," he pushed.

With a sigh, I allowed myself to shift back into my human form. My nipples pebbled in the chilly breeze and true to his word, he used his big body to block any wandering eyes. No one was looking though. They appeared to actively be studying everything other than us.

Elijah reached for me and pinched my nipple firmly enough to make me cry out. I bit my lip in an effort to keep quiet. He grasped at the other and twisted both hard. I knew better than to try to knock his hands away. Agony radiated across my breasts and when he finally released them, it intensified to a sharp and painful sting. For several more minutes, my nipples ached from his cruel touch.

"In time, you will learn to trust me, but I will never hesitate to remind you that you're mine, my pretty wolf," he declared.

My heart swelled. I turned away, not wanting to accept it and understanding on a fundamental level that fate wasn't going to give me a choice. He opened the car door and handed me my bra and dress. He deftly tossed my shoes in front of me so that I could slip my feet inside them without losing the coverage of his massive frame. Quickly, I dressed myself. When I was done, Elijah grasped my chin roughly and pulled me into a kiss that left my lips sore and swollen.

I kissed him back just as greedily. By the time we finally pulled apart, we were both breathless with need.

"When I put you to bed tonight, I plan on wearing out that pretty little pussy," he murmured, and I couldn't help but quiver at the suggestion. "First, though, we need to make sure that our new home is safe for you."

He took my hand and led me to the door. I watched as he reached into his pocket and pulled out a key. Without hesitation, he unlocked the deadbolt and swung open the door. Immediately, my nose was hit with the thick aroma of dust and disuse. The porch creaked behind us, and I looked back to see both Atreyu and Theo at my back.

As a group, we walked into the chalet. The first room was a large living area, but most of the furniture was covered in sheets as a protective measure.

I didn't sense anything unusual. It just seemed like the place hadn't been occupied for a few years, but nothing was worse for the wear. We searched the ground floor and found it abandoned. There was nothing on the upper floors either and I was overjoyed to see how many of the rooms had massive windows that let in an incredible amount of light even though the sun was nearly set by now.

When it came time to search the basement, we traipsed down the stairs one by one. Elijah went first and once the four of us all reached the bottom, it soon became obvious that we weren't alone down here. There was at least one vampire below ground with us.

Elijah lifted his nose to the air, scenting the place and trying to determine exactly where and how many of them were there. He didn't move into action right away. Instead, he knelt down, closing his eyes and concentrating on the myriad sounds and smells all around us.

When he was ready, he crept forward.

The basement was far more massive than I had anticipated. There were several unused rooms and quite a few that were full of boxes and sealed crates. As we moved further inward, I started to hear signs of life not too far ahead.

Somewhere, a deep rattling breath echoed in one of the rooms. For a moment that seemed entirely too long, silence reigned and then another breath sounded. Elijah moved ahead slowly, lifting his arms while fully preparing to use his fists. He rounded the corner first and sucked in a horrified gasp. He lifted his arm to stop me just as one more rattling sigh reverberated and stopped. I waited to hear another, but it never came.

"It is too late for the both of them," he murmured. Quickly, he shut the door and I looked past him in concern.

"Both?"

"A man and a woman. Trust me, little wolf. He was already dead, and she has now followed along with him," he explained. I swallowed hard and turned away. His face had paled, and I knew enough to not ask any more questions. I had no desire to see the horrors behind that door.

He took my hand in his and squeezed tight. Cautiously, he continued forward until we reached the rear of the basement where there was one last door. It was a thick wooden frame and he paused, pressing his ear against the wood.

His eyes flared with anger.

"Step back," he instructed me. He'd tried to keep the fury inside him at bay, but I could still sense the precarious restraint in his tone. I gave him the room he needed, and he threw his weight into the door so hard that it nearly splintered as it crashed open.

My gaze tore into the room beyond and I understood what had made his rage escalate so quickly.

There was a young girl. She couldn't have been any older than five or six. She looked lost and frightened, backed into a corner by a man dressed in rags. He stilled and whipped his head back and I crinkled my nose at the rancid aroma of vampire. His red deranged eyes met mine and he leapt toward us like a wild animal.

From somewhere inside the mangy cloth that just barely covered his skinny frame a silver knife appeared. He moved quickly and with far more expertise than I expected from something that looked like him.

Elijah burst toward him. He roared like a beast, using his arm to knock the man aside to the floor with a crash. The vampire crawled toward the little girl, sharp canines extended with the full intent on feeding on her. Elijah went after him.

He didn't hold back. His fist crashed into the side of the vampire's head. There was a sickening crunch, but the feral creature didn't slow down. He slashed at Elijah, and I was horrified to see that he'd struck him several times. The sides of his abdomen were bleeding, as well as several cuts on his arm.

The vampire moved impossibly fast. Maybe he was young or just strong from feeding on the man and woman that we'd been too late to save. The little girl screamed, and the vampire tensed. Elijah roared and the man slammed the knife deep into Elijah's side.

He roared with pain, but he didn't slow down either. He tangled with the vampire once more before he pinned him to the ground and grasped its head with both of his hands. With a hard twist, he beheaded the vampire.

I turned away as he rose to his feet, not wanting to see the body. With haste, I rushed over to the little girl and knelt before her.

I grasped her hands, and she went to pull away. She needed comfort.

"It's alright. You're safe now, sweetie," I whispered and her pretty hazel eyes found mine. They were glassy with her tears.

"Where's Mommy and Daddy? They went with him, and they never came back. I don't know where they went," she sobbed.

My heart broke for her.

Elijah knelt beside me, and she trembled at his over-whelmingly massive size. She moved a bit closer to me and I wrapped my arms around her.

"Don't mind him. He looks big, but he's a big ole teddy bear," I told her reassuringly and she looked at him with a quizzical expression that said she didn't quite believe me.

"She's right, you know," Elijah added.

The little girl narrowed her eyes. If the situation wasn't so dire, I would have found the stare down between the two of them humorous. I squeezed my arms around this tiny little thing as she bravely judged the big hulk of a man before her.

"You don't seem like a teddy bear," she replied bluntly.

"Can I tell you a secret?" Elijah whispered. He looked from side to side adorably and the little girl cocked her head as she was considering his request. I could see her decision playing out on her face and finally she gave into curiosity and nodded.

"Yes. You can do that," she replied. This little one was smart. It was really quite cute.

"I like chocolate chips in my pancakes," he whispered, looking a bit guilty at his confession.

"That doesn't seem very healthy for you," she chided him, and I had to bite my lip in order to keep quiet.

"But it tastes so good!" he whined.

"I've never had chocolate chip pancakes," she replied warily.

"I have the best recipe. Promise," he tried, and she softened in my arms. He was getting to her. I couldn't help but smile despite the sadness surrounding the whole situation. We hadn't been able to save her parents. At least we'd been able to rescue her.

"Tell you what, why don't you come upstairs with Ashleigh and me. Then the three of us can find the kitchen and see if there's stuff for pancakes," he offered.

"There won't be. There's only boring stuff like green beans and canned peas in the cabinets," she scoffed. I waited to see what Elijah's next tactic would be.

"Don't you worry then. I'll send someone to the store to get everything we need," he offered gently.

"I'm not sure I'll like chocolate chips. I like blueberries though," she murmured.

"I'll make sure they get blueberries too," he said.

"Okay," she smiled, and she relaxed in my arms. He offered his and she looked at me nervously.

"Don't worry, he gives pretty good bear hugs. I bet he might even let you up on his shoulders when we get back upstairs," I told her, and a wave of excitement crossed over her features.

"Really?" she asked gleefully.

"Definitely," Elijah grinned.

"My name is Becca," she replied.

"I'm Ashleigh. That's Elijah," I said.

"Nice to meet you," Elijah laughed, and she jumped into his arms. He was careful to angle her so she couldn't see the bloody mess of the vampire on the floor. Behind us, Atreyu and Theo took a few minutes to search the remainder of the basement while the two of us made our way back up to the first floor.

CHAPTER 11

 shleigh

It was late by the time the chalet was fully cleared. As the night wore on, Becca started looking more and more tired and it soon became apparent that we were going to have to find her a safe place to sleep. I cleared out two bedrooms on the upper floors and Elijah carried her up the stairs, finding a bedroom and tucking her into bed.

"We'll be right next door if you need anything," he whispered. "I'll make those pancakes for you in the morning."

"You promise?" she asked, her small voice carrying in the tiny room.

"I promise," he replied gently. "Now get some sleep, Becca."

Her eyes were already closing. By the time I closed the door behind us, she was already fast asleep. I turned toward Elijah and wrapped myself around him. He winced and I pulled back, searching his face for the reason why. I gasped when I glanced down. It was difficult to see against the dark color of his shirt, but when I reached out and touched the side of his torso gently, I could feel that it was wet. I pulled my fingers away and the tips were stained red.

"Get inside. Let me tend to you," I demanded.

He didn't fight me when I ushered him inside the bedroom that had been prepared for us. The moonlight illuminated his features, revealing the paleness of his face and the tiredness in his eyes. Slowly, I led him over to the bed and started to unbutton his shirt.

"If you wanted to get me naked, little wolf, all you had to do was ask," he chuckled.

"You're hopeless," I chided him, but I didn't really mean it. Carefully, I peeled the fabric away from his skin. His left side was covered with blood. The silver blade had cut him deep, practically skewering him in the process.

"I didn't want Becca to see. She's already been through enough," he murmured. I used his shirt to gently pat away the blood.

"Stay here," I ordered. I rose to my feet and rushed off into the attached bathroom. I dampened several towels and found a first aid kit under the sink. There was a bowl that

I filled with water too. Elijah would heal, but his wound would need to be cleaned before it would get any better. I carried everything into the room with me.

"This part isn't going to be pleasant," I warned, and he nodded. I hesitated for a moment, and he grunted.

"It's alright. This isn't my first run-in with a silver knife," he added. I'd give him points for bravery, but he was losing a lot of blood. I dabbed at his side, trying to mop some of it up with the towels. He didn't flinch, so I slowly increased the pressure. I glanced up to see him gritting his teeth. I knew it was hurting him. I could see it written all over his face.

By the time I had his side cleaned of blood, he'd gone several shades paler. I laid him down and laid a cold compress over his eyes.

"I need to clean inside the wound now. You will heal much faster if I can get that done quickly," I ventured warily.

"Go ahead, little wolf. I can take it," he replied bravely. His voice was a little strained and I hated seeing him in pain more than anything. With a steadying breath, I started to dab at his wound. I squeezed water over it, rinsing it first before I wiped it clean.

Lesser men would be screaming and begging for mercy from an injury like this, but he hardly made a sound. I dried his wound and he sat up so that I could wrap his waist with bandages I tore from a clean sheet I'd found in a nearby closet.

"Thank you, my sweet," he murmured.

"Let me get you something to drink, maybe a bite to eat too," I offered, and he shook his head.

"Come lie with me. Let us rest," he whispered.

"But you should—" I began, but he cut me off.

"I'll be much better in the morning, little wolf. Trust me," he insisted.

I sighed, not wanting to argue with him when he was in a state like this. He reached for me, and I carefully crawled into bed beside him. I tried hard not to jostle him, but he wrapped his arm around my waist and pulled me against him anyway.

His body warmth surrounded me, and I closed my eyes. I didn't know what tomorrow would bring in this new place, what was supposed to be our new home.

His breathing evened out, and I listened to it for a long time. It was soothing. There was no wheezing or rattling thankfully and I closed my own eyes.

I didn't understand the need to care for him like I did. A part of me felt like I'd done it out of kindness, that I just didn't like to see anyone get hurt, but another part of me knew I hadn't taken care of him for that reason alone. There was more to it than that.

I'd been afraid for him. The possibility of losing him had cut through my heart. I didn't understand it. Maybe it was the bond. Maybe it was just fate playing with my heart.

It couldn't be that I was actually falling in love with him.

* * *

When the sun rose the next morning, I opened my eyes and yawned. An arm squeezed around my waist, and I turned my head to see a familiar set of sparkling gray eyes. He wasn't nearly as pale as last night.

"How are you feeling?" I asked quickly and he smiled in return.

"Much better," he whispered. He leaned forward and kissed the back of my shoulder gently.

"I should change your bandage before Becca wakes up," I said.

"I suppose you're right," he murmured. With a groan, he pushed himself up to a seated position as I climbed out of the warm cocoon of our bed. I tore through another sheet, quickly making a few additional bandages. When I was ready, I unwrapped his waist and gasped at how much the wound had healed since last night.

Our species could heal quickly, but I'd never seen it in action quite like this. Most of his flesh had knitted back together, leaving a pink cut that was only about half an inch deep. I used the bowl of water from last night to wet another towel before I cleaned it again. He didn't make any sound at all. When I was finished, I wrapped him back up.

"By tomorrow, I don't know if you'll have anything more than a scar," I mused.

"I'll add it to the collection, I suppose," he answered.

My gaze played along the other scars that marred his chest. I reached for one and traced my finger along it.

"That one was from a human. Had a switchblade on him," he explained. "He didn't survive the encounter."

"Good," I replied, and he smirked.

He stood up and opened his own bag. He pulled out another shirt and shrugged it on, covering the bandages. He strode into the bathroom, and I heard the sound of running water while he got ready.

I gathered all the bloody towels and stuffed them in a basket. I had only just put it in the bathroom when an excited knock rapped at the door.

"Can we make pancakes now?" Becca exclaimed and I had to suppress a chuckle.

"Coming!" Elijah bellowed as he exited the bathroom and stuffed his feet into his boots, hurrying so that he could finish getting ready. "You," he said, pointing at me. "We will go into town together today. Take all the time you need to freshen up. Breakfast will be ready for you when you come downstairs."

"Blueberry, please," I smiled, and he nodded. He winked in my direction before he headed out the door to a very excited little girl. I couldn't tear my eyes away from the way he grasped her around the waist and hoisted her over his shoulder. She giggled animatedly. I didn't turn away until they descended the stairs and were well out of sight.

I walked into the bathroom and brushed my teeth. After I was done, I stripped. I turned on the water and waited a minute until it grew nice and hot. I grabbed my toiletries from my bag and washed up, enjoying the warm spray of the rain shower above my head. When I was done, I dressed in a pair of jeans and a long-sleeve blouse. I slipped on a pair of boots and brushed my hair free of tangles. I found a hair dryer and dried it enough to where it wasn't dripping wet before I headed downstairs too.

The scent of fresh baked goods was overwhelmed by the delicious aroma of bacon. When I walked into the kitchen, there was a smorgasbord of food all across the kitchen island.

"How many of us are you trying to feed?" I chuckled.

"Theo bought some of it, but most of it was given as a welcome gift from the town," he answered with a grin.

"What for?" I asked. I took a seat on one of the stools by the island. I couldn't resist grabbing one of the ripe strawberries in front of me. When I popped it in between my lips, Elijah stared at me suggestively. I blushed, squirming just a little as an explosion of flavor burst across my tongue.

Strawberries were my second favorite fruit. The only thing better was raspberries. There was a bowl of them just outside of my reach. Elijah noticed me staring at them.

"Do you still want blueberry pancakes, or shall I make them raspberry just for you?" he asked, and I started. He was perceptive.

"I would love some raspberry pancakes," I answered. He grinned and grabbed the container of berries. He emptied some of them into his mixing bowl before he walked over and handed the rest of them to me. I popped one in my mouth and hummed happily. They were incredibly fresh and delicious.

Becca already had a full plate of both chocolate and blueberry pancakes. She smiled up at me, her mouth full. She waved and I grinned in return.

"How's the chef?" I asked her and Elijah glanced back at me with an expression that told me I was precariously close to earning a very red bottom. I snickered and turned back to Becca.

"He's pretty good. Not my mom, but overall, I could recommend him," she answered, and I had to bite my cheek to keep myself from laughing out loud. Elijah didn't though. His raucous laughter echoed through the room.

"I'm glad I could be of service," he added joyfully.

"Yeah," Becca replied, and I couldn't stop myself from giggling this time.

I turned my head when someone knocked on the door-frame. It was Theo.

"I've put together files for you, boss. There used to be an agency in town for this sort of thing, and there were a ton of applications already. I picked my favorites for you," he explained. I raised an eyebrow, but Elijah shook his head and looked pointedly at Becca before returning his gaze to mine.

Theo put down the files next to me and I opened the first one. There was a couple pictured together and at once I understood.

He was looking to place Becca with a human couple to give her a chance at a family. I understood the reasoning. She was human, after all. If she could have a chance at a human family, now was the time to give her that.

"Elijah," I began. "I still want to be involved in some capacity. Please."

"Do not worry, Ashleigh. You and I will choose together," he vowed, and I sighed in relief. I flipped through several more of the files while he finished cooking. By the time he slid the full plate of pancakes in front of me, I'd already settled on a few of my favorite couples.

He sat next to me, and I smiled back at him wistfully.

He picked up the maple syrup and covered my breakfast with the delicious treat. Then he took my fork and knife, using them to prepare the perfect bite for me.

I opened my mouth when he brought it to my lips. The decadent breakfast treat exploded with flavor across my tongue, and I moaned quietly with pleasure. I was definitely going to have him make this for me again.

"That is fantastic," I murmured, chewing slowly so that I could savor every moment of that first bite. When I swallowed that initial one, he was already prepared with the second.

"She probably knows how to use a fork," Becca declared disapprovingly, and my cheeks flushed in embarrassment.

"She needs help sometimes too, you know," Elijah scoffed. He fed me several more bites until he finally passed the fork and knife back to me.

"Okay. We'll see," Becca replied while looking pointedly at me, and I had to hide my face to cover up my amusement. I stuffed a big bite into my mouth, almost as if I wanted to prove that I could indeed use utensils all by myself.

He was so natural with her.

He turned when he saw me studying him and cocked his head.

"I grew up in an orphanage. To many of the kids there, I was something of their big brother. I was the one they went to when an adoption didn't work out or when they were looked over because people wanted younger kids. No matter what they needed, I was there for them. I got in trouble with the law when I was sixteen. That's when

Amir found me and took me under his wing," he explained.

"You weren't born into the Crimson Shadows?" I asked and he shook his head.

"No. I wasn't," he replied.

Most wolves felt the power of their alpha intensely. Elijah had only followed Amir out of loyalty. His actions had nothing to do with deferring to an alpha.

His background was a mystery. For all I knew, he could have been born of another pack and was an alpha of his own right.

I flipped the folders shut and focused on finishing my own breakfast. I thoroughly enjoyed every last bite. When I was full, I sat back and pushed it away. Elijah swiftly came to my side and took my plate, washing all the dishes shortly after that.

He made himself a quick plate of eggs, bacon, and chocolate chip pancakes. Becca hopped up away from the table and went off to explore the chalet. Theo went along with her and kept an eye on her.

"It will be best for her to grow up with humans," Elijah murmured when she was out of earshot.

"I know. It wouldn't be safe for her to stay with us, especially with my father still in the picture," I muttered.

"That doesn't make it any easier though, does it, little wolf?" he asked pointedly.

"No. It doesn't," I answered a little mournfully. "It's hard not to fall in love with that little girl. She's awfully sweet."

"She is," he said thoughtfully.

I pouted a little and he noticed.

"Come here, little wolf," he commanded gently. His arm wound around my waist, and he kissed my forehead.

"I'll make you a promise, my sweet mate. Whoever we choose will not only have Becca to contend with, but they'll also have us. They'll have to smile when we show up to her birthday parties and they will thank us gracefully when we help them with the costs to send her to college. Do you understand me?" he explained.

"Yes, alpha," I murmured.

"Good," he answered, and his hand dropped to lightly smack my bottom.

"You're getting a spanking tonight," he growled.

"What? Why?"

"Because the two of us are going to start training tomorrow and I want that pretty little bottom sore so that you remember who's in charge," he whispered, and my pussy convulsed. I shivered and his arm pulled me up against him.

"Will you use your hand?" I asked nervously.

"If you're a good girl while we're in town today. If you're a naughty one however, I'm going to use the wooden paddle I found on top of the fridge," he threatened.

"A paddle?" I squeaked anxiously.

"That's right, little wolf," he replied. He opened a drawer and I glanced down, seeing the light wooden implement inside. I reached for it, sliding my finger along it. He grasped it in his hand and lifted it out.

"Bend over the counter," he instructed. I swallowed hard but obeyed him. He swatted one cheek and then the other, swiftly popping me with it over my jeans. I gasped, the sting quick and instantaneous. I sucked in a breath, trying to keep myself from crying out.

"That hurts," I sighed audibly. I had little doubt that those two swats alone had made my bottom pink already. I didn't want to find out what a full spanking with that terrible thing would feel like, especially if he decided to take my pants down too.

"It does," he answered.

He put the paddle back in the drawer and closed it. His fingers grasped my bottom, rubbing the sting away a bit roughly. Wrapping me in his arms, he squeezed my body tight and then grasped my chin with both hands.

He pulled me into a fierce kiss. My ass still smarted from the paddle, but the throbbing of my pussy soon outweighed the residual sting. When his lips finally drew away from mine, I was overwhelmed with breathless neediness. His smoldering gaze left me with no doubt that he'd throw me up on that counter and fuck me if there wasn't a child in the house.

"I want you to remember how much that paddle stings, little wolf. I want that fresh on your mind while we're in town today. If you are a bad girl for me today, you will find out what it feels like on your bare bottom. Don't make me have to punish you with it tonight," he warned, and I nodded.

"I'll be your good girl, alpha," I promised.

He kissed me again, much more tenderly this time.

"Eww!" Becca exclaimed as she raced into the kitchen with Theo hot on her tail.

The three of us rode into town a short while later. The local school was reopening, and we dropped Becca off so that she could play with other kids her own age. All the humans we ran into were very appreciative, thanking Elijah and me profusely for freeing them from the vampires that had held their town prisoner.

The more the two of us explored the town, the more evidence I saw that the vampires had been even crueler than I had imagined. People cowered before us, expecting us to lash out at them each time we paused to talk with them. They almost seemed surprised when we didn't hurt them.

Everywhere I looked, people bore scars on their necks. The rogue vampires had ignored every rule the Council had about feeding on humans.

Many of the boutique shops along the streets were opening for the first time since the vampires arrived. Restaurants were at full capacity as people went out to eat together, enjoying each other's company out in the open.

It was a beautiful sight.

Elijah and I went to the makeshift hospital after visiting with the local townsfolk. There were so many that were still in critical condition. Already this morning, there were at least a dozen that had been transported via helicopter to local hospitals for more intensive care. Here, many of the humans were wrapped in bandages.

Because of my father's obsession with the Malkovian clan, I knew the rules of vampire feeding firsthand. Those rules were upheld by the Council.

Vampires were not allowed to leave overwhelming evidence of their feedings like this. If their activity alerted even just the local news, the Council would act and destroy those that endangered the vampire species as a whole. It was better for humans not to know of the existence of wolf shifters and vampires. The mass panic that would spread at the discovery of either species would turn the world upside down.

SARA FIELDS

Most vampire clans fed in secret. The Malkovians kept a small group of human slaves for feeding, but they were under compulsion and didn't fight their fate.

This was far more brutal and much more vicious than that.

I sat down beside one woman who was bandaged up on a cot. Her eyes brightened at my presence, lucid and clear.

"It's not as bad as it looks. The nurses have me all hopped up on the good painkillers," she explained when she saw me looking at the sheer number of bandages.

"Do you remember much of what happened?" I asked carefully.

"Most of it. I survived though. One day, maybe the story of the demonic cult of devil worshippers might make it into a movie," she joked.

I chuckled, but I knew the Council would never allow such a thing. In time, they would probably suppress all evidence that anything had ever occurred here. Elijah would have to report what happened here at some point, and then they'd get started right away.

"Will you tell me what it was like?" I asked her and her eyes darkened with memory, but she broke into her story anyway.

The rogue vampires had arrived nearly three years ago. They'd demanded monetary tribute from everyone. They'd bankrupted her and many of the people she knew.

When she couldn't offer anything else, they beat her and fed on her as punishment. They ruled over the town with an iron fist. A few people tried to escape, and the vampires killed them in front of everyone as an example of their vicious power.

It was horrifying and saddening to hear all about it. When she finished, I took her hand in mine and squeezed it tight.

"I will make sure no one gets hurt like that ever again," I vowed, and she smiled. A nurse came over to check her IV.

"You should be getting some rest, Eliza," the nurse scolded, and the woman smirked knowingly.

"But I've got a visitor, Jane," she teased. The nurse laughed lightly and released the flow of the intravenous drugs a bit more.

"Visiting hours are over soon, at least until this evening," Jane explained while looking pointedly at me. I nodded quickly, getting the hint.

"I'll come back later, Eliza. I promise," I added, but Eliza's eyes were already slipping closed. In seconds, she was fast asleep.

"How are your medical supplies? I can send out a request for more," Elijah asked. He had been away checking on a few things and had just joined us.

SARA FIELDS

"I can get you a list in just a little while. The injuries are far more extensive than I anticipated. We've almost gone through our blood banks. We'll definitely need more to replace what my patients have lost. There's plenty more we're going to need as well," Jane answered.

"I'll make sure everything you need is here tomorrow once you get that list to me," Elijah vowed.

"I need to make my rounds, but I'll have it to you in an hour or two," the nurse replied. Elijah nodded and Jane rushed off to another patient who seemed to be having a rough time.

We left the makeshift hospital after that. Neither of us wanted to get in the way of the doctors or the nurses there.

In a show of their appreciation, the town threw us a welcome dinner with an incredible amount of food and drink. They thanked us profusely for their freedom. When dinner was over, they all lined up and started offering tribute in exchange for the protection of the Rising Sun pack.

Elijah graciously accepted their tributes with the exception that they were to focus on getting on their feet first. One of the town leaders who'd survived the vampire ordeal led us into the basement of the central mansion. There was a massive safe inside, and he opened it to reveal the riches the vampires had gathered during their time in this small town.

"They demanded tribute from us all, but they didn't stop at our small town. In order for them not to attack the surrounding villages, this was the price," the man explained.

The room was full of gold bars, crates full of euros, and chests full of gemstones and jewelry. I walked over to one, running my fingers along a diamond tennis bracelet in awe.

"I will take this blood money and use it to protect your people and mine," Elijah vowed.

"Thank you. Already I know that you will be different," he answered.

"I promise you that I will be," Elijah said firmly.

CHAPTER 12

shleigh

By the time we returned to the chalet, the sun had already set. We'd taken a few hours after dinner to meet some of the prospective couples that were interested in becoming Becca's family. Elijah and I liked several of them, but in the end, we decided on a couple that had long been unsuccessful with having a baby of their own. They were married, both with stable jobs. The wife, Melissa, was a science teacher, and the husband, Sean, held a position at a local bank. They'd also agreed to allow us to be a part of her life if we decided to place Becca with them, which made me very happy.

We'd introduced them to Becca and the sheer joy on their faces had won both me and Elijah over. She'd gone with them for the night, and we planned to check in on them in the morning. In the end, we wanted to hear Becca's opinion, but she'd taken to them really well from the start. She even made them promise to make her chocolate chip pancakes in the morning and both Sean and Melissa seemed overjoyed to grant her request.

My hopes were high that she would be happy with the two of them. If it didn't work out, we'd find another, but this one felt like the right fit.

Elijah and I walked into the kitchen. I grinned when I saw a bottle of champagne chilling on ice on the counter. He grasped the note lying in front of it.

"Compliments of the Swiss Historical Society," he read with a grin. Without delay, he popped the cork and poured me a liberal glass while he dug into the pantry and found a bottle of whiskey for himself.

I remembered his threat from this morning and nervously glanced at the drawer where the wooden paddle was hidden. He saw the direction of my gaze and lifted me up to sit on the kitchen island.

"I'm proud of you, little wolf," he said first. "You can relax. You're not getting a paddling tonight."

I squeezed my thighs around his waist as he moved between them.

"But you're still going to spank me," I sulked. I made a show of it and his eyes sparkled. I could play at being mad that he planned to put me over his knee tonight, but right now the thought was simply turning me on. Already, I could feel myself growing wet just imagining it happening so soon.

"You're right, little wolf. You are going to go over my knee tonight. Do you know why?" he asked pointedly. His hand splayed against my lower belly and his thumb grazed over my pussy. I was still wearing my jeans, but his fiery touch was so intense that it felt like they weren't even there.

"No," I whispered hoarsely. He teased my clit with that thumb, and I gasped.

"Because your pussy gets soaking wet when I turn that perfect little ass bright red," he murmured, and I sighed with pleasure.

"Is it going to hurt?" I asked.

"Most definitely, little wolf," he answered. He lightly spanked my pussy over my jeans, and I squirmed with desire at the slight stinging sensation before it was replaced with fervent heated desire. I took a quick sip of champagne, and he grasped my chin. I looked deep into his eyes, and I was lost in the incredible emotion I saw there. He took my glass of champagne from me and put it aside.

"Since you were such a good girl today, I'm going to reward you with my tongue before I take you over my knee. When your bottom is as red as I want it to be, you're going to ride me and come all over my knot," he declared brazenly, and my entire body vibrated with anticipation.

He grasped my shirt and lifted it up over my head. With a quick pinch, he unclasped my bra and tossed it aside along with it. He pulled off my boots and socks, dropping them down to the floor beside us. He wasted no time in unbuttoning my jeans. He lowered the zipper and lifted me off the counter just enough so that he could slip them down my hips.

I still hadn't been provided with any panties, so I hadn't been wearing anything underneath my jeans.

Once I was fully naked, I was awash in sudden feelings of bashfulness. I covered my chest with my arms. I couldn't close my legs because his body was between them. He grasped my wrists and pushed my arms aside.

Swiftly, he used the flats of his fingers to spank my left breast. He punished my nipple especially hard and when he was through with that one, he moved to the right. I squirmed and cried as he spanked my breasts, the stinging pain far more intense than I could have ever expected.

"Do not cover yourself again. When I bare this beautiful body, I want to see it," he warned. My breasts burned and when I glanced down, I saw several pink fingerprints covering them. I bit my lip when I saw how hard my nipples had become.

"Yes, alpha," I said quietly.

He took a step back and looked at my pussy deliberately.

"Have you been thinking of your spanking all day, little wolf?" he asked, and I blushed. I nodded and he smirked.

"Yes, alpha," I replied shyly.

"I thought you might. You should know that I've been looking forward to it too."

He was leaning over me now and the closeness of his presence was driving me crazy. My core was tightening with need, and I nudged his cheek with my face. He grasped my chin a bit roughly and pulled me into a kiss. I wound my arms around his neck, boldly pressing my still-stinging breasts against his chest. His fingers slid up along my stomach until he grasped one nipple and pinched it hard. I cried out, but he swallowed my sounds with his kiss. By the time he pulled away, my lips were swollen, and my clit was throbbing along with my heartbeat.

"Alpha," I murmured.

"What is it, little wolf?" he answered. His fingers were sliding along my inner thighs, teasingly close to my pussy. I squirmed, wanting to make him touch me there, but he made certain that he didn't.

I closed my mouth, biting the inside of my cheek in order to keep quiet. I didn't want to admit to wanting him to touch me, that I wanted to come on his tongue. I hid my face in his shoulder and he spanked my pussy three times in quick succession. The burn spread like wildfire, and I keened, squeezing my arms around him as I contended with the stinging brand of his hand in between my legs.

"When I ask you a question, 1 expect an answer," he warned.

"But alpha," I whined. With a growl, he smacked my pussy again. It was much harder this time and I struggled to take it.

"Do I need to paddle you after all, little wolf?" he asked, and I shook my head against his neck.

"No, please, alpha," I exclaimed.

My pussy burned fiercely, and he grasped my chin, forcing me to look at him.

"Tell me what you need, little wolf, or we'll start this night very differently from what I had imagined," he demanded. His hand still cupped my pussy, possessing it threateningly. If I wavered any longer, I was putting both my pussy and my bare ass in danger. I glanced to the side at the drawer, and he saw. Slowly, he reached over and opened it. My mouth went dry as he grasped the paddle and laid it on the counter beside me.

"Elijah, don't," I began, and his jaw tensed in warning.

His movements were so fast that one moment I was sitting on the counter and the next I was face down over it with my bare bottom on full display. There was a big hand splayed across my lower back, holding me down. My hearing was on overdrive all of a sudden and I heard the sound of wood clinking against stone, which could only mean he'd picked up the paddle.

"Wait! Please!" I cried.

The coolness of the paddle pressed against my exposed skin, causing me to tense. I flushed, panicking a little that someone would walk in and see me about to get a paddling like a naughty little girl.

"Do you feel like answering my question now, little wolf?" he asked pointedly, and I pressed my thighs together nervously. My entire focus was forced on the paddle as he circled it over my backside.

"Please, alpha. Not the paddle," I whispered fearfully.

"Do you get to decide how your alpha deals with you, my naughty mate?" he asked.

"No, alpha," I murmured with a pout.

I don't know why I was pushing him. Maybe I wanted him to punish me. Maybe I didn't. Maybe I just wanted his roughness and the pain that came with it so that I could enjoy riding his cock soon after with my bottom still burning.

Something had to be wrong with me.

"Let me tell you what is going to happen then, little wolf. I'm going to paddle your pretty little bottom until you tell me what you need. I may give you what you want, or I might take you over my knee and finish paddling you hard enough to make sure you're very sore and very sorry for delaying in the first place," he warned, and I tried to push myself up from the kitchen island. I was high enough that my legs didn't reach the floor no matter how much I kicked. I felt so small, and he forced me back down with ease.

The paddle cracked against my bottom far harder than I expected. It was so loud, I almost thought it was a gunshot, but then the instantaneous sting that came with it was anything but that. I squeaked in surprise as the lick of fire scalded my left cheek.

He spanked my right side with it next. The burn was far more intense than I could have ever imagined.

"The paddle hurts on your bare little bottom, doesn't it?" he asked.

"Yes, alpha," I wailed, knowing that avoiding his questions right now would be to my own detriment.

He paddled me far more quickly after that. I would have tried to stay quiet, but that horrible piece of wood made it impossible from the start. I couldn't keep my legs still. I kicked and squirmed, but that terrible paddle painted a sizzling stinging burn across my backside so swiftly that it left me reeling.

He didn't leave a single inch of my bottom unpunished. I couldn't think or speak or do anything but take it. When I reached back to try to block it, he caught my wrist and pinned it behind my back. His body pressed against my hip, the iron-hard spike of his erection quickly apparent.

"Please! It hurts," I begged.

He paddled my thighs next, taking extra care to punish the area where my bottom cheeks met the tops of my legs.

"What do you need, little wolf?" he demanded. The paddle never stopped. It was quick, and I was soon overwhelmed by the stinging pain. I opened my mouth, fully intending to answer his question, but all I could manage were desperate cries for mercy. Finally, he paused long enough for me to squeeze my eyes shut and catch my breath.

"Please, alpha. I need to come on your tongue," I begged.

He paddled me much more firmly several times and I wailed. If this went on much longer, he was going to make me cry. My paddling went on for several more moments and just when my breath hitched in the back of my throat, he stopped and placed the paddle back down on the counter.

My backside was on absolute fire. He'd scalded me with that paddle all the way down to mid-thigh. Cruelly, he lifted me by my waist and deposited me back in a seated position on the counter. I yelped the moment my back-side connected with the hard stone. I sniffled, pouting as the stinging pain burned that much hotter.

"Do you need my mouth, little wolf?" he whispered darkly. My pussy was soaking wet now and he forced my legs open. His thumb glided along my inner thigh and my clit practically leapt at his touch.

"Please, alpha," I begged.

"I will give you my mouth, my sweet mate, but I want you thinking about something as you come for me. You will remember that you're still going over my knee after I lick that needy little pussy. Will it be your choice whether or not it's my hand or the paddle?" he pressed, and my thighs trembled a bit against him.

"No, alpha," I whimpered.

"Open your legs and lean back on your elbows. Put yourself on display for me. Show me where you need my tongue," he instructed, and I moaned softly as I followed his instructions. With my bottom still very sore from the paddle, I didn't need to be told twice. I knew now that he would not hesitate to use it again.

I spread my thighs as wide as I could, quivering as he studied me. I blushed heavily, but I didn't move. I let him look because that's what he wanted. There was a part of me that also wanted him to look, that wanted to know just the sight of me made his cock hard as a rock.

He kissed my hipbone, and I couldn't help but arch into him. He chuckled lightly. I expected him to reprimand me, but he simply continued the kisses across my thighs until he kissed directly on top of my mound.

He studied me for several moments, making me squirm with shame.

"This pussy is so very pretty, especially when it's been naughty and has had to be spanked bright pink," he observed, and my legs twitched. His shoulders prevented me from closing them, which made me feel increasingly out of control.

His arm pressed against my lower belly as he gently coaxed me to lie down on my back.

I practically shook off the counter when his lips lightly kissed my clit for the first time.

"You are not allowed to push me away with your hands. I will bind them if I have to, but that will most certainly mean you need another very hard paddling when I'm through with this pussy, little wolf," he said darkly.

"I understand, alpha," I whispered nervously.

I arched my back a little and slipped my hands beneath it, pinning myself for him. He watched, his eyes sparkling with approval.

"That's my good girl," he murmured, and my heart swelled.

"Please, alpha. Please let me come for you. Please let me show you I can be your good girl," I pleaded.

Suddenly, it was incredibly important to me that I prove myself. I wanted to be his good girl. I didn't want to earn any more of that terrible paddle. It had been brutal, but now my entire body was vibrating with need. I wanted to come. I wanted to please him and ride him till he came inside me, to show him that I was everything that he had ever wanted and needed in a mate.

I opened my thighs as wide as I could manage, and he growled low in appreciation.

"I want five orgasms from you tonight, little wolf. Two of them are going to be on my tongue. The rest will be on my cock," he snarled and just the sound of his words made something inside me snap. Visceral desire radiated through me, and I started begging once again.

"Please. Please," I mumbled, no longer able to focus on forming complete sentences when my pussy was pounding this hard with insatiable need.

His mouth slipped along my inner thigh, kissing me tenderly. I loved how it felt, but it wasn't where I wanted him the most. When I whined openly, he chuckled.

"Do you need something, little wolf?"

He was teasing me. Maybe this was a part of the punishment I'd earned from refusing to answer his questions. He was making me wait and there wasn't anything I could do to make it stop. He was in a position of ultimate control.

"Please let me come on your tongue, alpha," I finally managed. His mouth didn't surround my clit though. He kissed the top of my mound and not where I needed him the most.

He was going to make me come when he wished it and not a moment sooner. He held power over me, and I felt it even more deeply than when he'd whipped me with his belt or paddled my bottom.

I was desperate for him. I didn't dare move my hands, but I did everything else I could to show him just how much I needed him. My hips were rocking back and forth, seeking his mouth as he denied me. The whimpers that escaped my lips were pitifully needy, but I no longer cared.

My pussy was burning with fire. The paddling had hurt, but it had stoked something inside me to render me a writhing mess of needy woman. My clit was pulsing constantly, a ferocious drumbeat that refused to quell.

"Please. I'm begging you. Please let me come. I'll be your good girl and come hard for you," I wailed.

My eyes nearly rolled back in my head when his tongue flicked forward to slide over my clit. I gasped loudly and his mouth surrounded me there. His fingers teased my entrance as his mouth closed over my clit and I knew it wouldn't take very long for me to fall apart all over his tongue.

My scorched backside burned, but my pussy flared hotter. My clit throbbed underneath his tongue and when he sucked it inside his mouth, I knew that holding back my impending orgasm would be nearly impossible.

His warm wet tongue flicked my clit back and forth, circling and teasing it with varying pressure until I was a veritable mess of insatiable need. I whimpered and moaned endlessly, feeling my core tighten further until I felt myself begin to fray apart at the seams.

Boiling heat surged through my veins. My skin felt so hot that beads of sweat were forming at my brow. I closed my eyes, and all of my senses were immediately focused on the man who'd taken my life and turned it upside down.

His mouth tortured me, taunting me with orgasm many times until I could do nothing more other than desperately plead for release. I arched up against his tongue, scraping my clit against it and the fingers that had been teasing my entrance thrust up into me with vivid force.

I cried out and his lips locked onto my clit. It was time for me to come for him.

My back arched clean off the island as that first orgasm took me captive. I wailed from the very start, suffering through the delicious pleasure he'd stoked inside me. My core collapsed in on itself, spiraling and shattering with endless quakes of pleasure. I screamed as it intensified, my hips rolling against him as he wrenched every bit of pleasure out of me that he could.

His fingers danced inside of me, switching between petting a place deep inside me and thrusting into me with wild abandon. My inner walls clutched at them, both wanting to take them and force them out. I knew that he'd pressed more than one finger inside of me and as wet as I was, it still hurt a little bit.

That was probably making my orgasm that much harder, to be honest.

By the time that first one finally crested, a sizzling satisfied sensation settled over me. The fight in me had boiled away along with it. I no longer wanted to push him to punish me or anything else. I simply wanted to take what he gave me because he wanted to give it.

My body relaxed against the counter. My clit felt especially sensitive, and when his tongue settled on top of it once again, I flinched. I knew better than to pull away though.

"Please. Let me come for you again, alpha," I whispered hoarsely.

He stoked my pleasure more slowly this time, taking advantage of the languid state of my body. I rode his tongue shamefully, seeking out its flat wet surface time and time again. Just when I was ready to come, he pulled back and cleared his throat.

"I want to see you get yourself off on my tongue. Make it a good one, little wolf. I expect to be impressed," he chided, and my hips obediently rose toward his mouth. He suckled on my clit and pressed his tongue against me. I pushed back against him. My clit throbbed greedily, and I gasped as a frisson of fierce pleasure raced through me.

I quivered hard, knowing this next orgasm was going to be even stronger than the last.

His tongue rolled against my clit, and I rocked against him. I blushed at first, unable to look at him knowing he was watching the way my body desperately sought him out, the way my desire was playing out across my face, everything. He could probably see my nipples hardening, giving away how much I desperately wanted to come for him again.

I rolled my hips a bit faster, rode him a bit more shamefully. Soon enough, the raw need pulsing through my clit became too much for me. I no longer thought about what I might look like, how much I would blush when I thought about this later. I lost myself on his tongue.

When my orgasm finally began, he took back control. He tortured my clit more firmly. His fingers thrust into me more cruelly. When my second orgasm broke, I could feel my entire core trembling with it. My inner walls grasped desperately at his fingers, milking them for every last bit of pleasure they offered. I wailed and shook against that countertop, breaking hard as he took my pleasure and made it his.

By the time that second orgasm finally ebbed, I closed my eyes, reveling in the continuous aftershocks that rattled my body long after it was over. His mouth pulled away and I whined as his fingers pulled out of me. Those same two fingers were suddenly forcing their way in between my lips, and I opened my mouth for them.

The taste of my orgasm was much stronger than just my arousal. It was sweet and heady and milky, which only made my pulse surge with greater need. I suckled at his fingers, doing my best to clean off all the evidence of me the best I could.

He pulled them free of my lips with a pop when I was done.

"Good girl," he murmured. His arms wrapped around me, and he lifted me clear off the counter. Roughly, he tossed me over his shoulder and slapped my bottom. It wasn't a particularly hard smack, but it was enough to reignite the leftover burn from my paddling. He paused just long enough to grab the horrible piece of wood before he carried me into the living room. He sat down on the massive plush couch and quickly deposited me face down over his lap.

"This pretty bottom is still very red from the paddle," he mused, and he laid the paddle in front of my face.

"Yes, alpha." I squirmed. I couldn't look away from the deceptive wooden implement. It looked so innocent but was far more sobering that it appeared. His fingers slid over my bottom, exploring me slowly and tracing the red that he had painted there himself.

"You wanted me to remind you who was in control, didn't you, little wolf?" he asked, and his hands squeezed one side of my ass and then the other.

"Yes, alpha," I admitted, feeling my cheeks flush almost immediately at having to confess such a thing.

"I thought so," he replied thoughtfully. Something about his tone made me a bit anxious and I chewed my bottom lip. He reached into his pocket and then he was holding something else in front of my face.

I swallowed hard. It was a very large butt plug with a purple jewel at the base. It was made out of steel, bulbous and round and just looking at it made my asshole tense nervously.

"It makes my cock very hard to remind you that I am your alpha, and you are my mate, little wolf," he said darkly. "Now, if you don't want another paddling, you will reach back and spread your cheeks for me. You will then ask me to plug your pretty little asshole," he demanded.

I froze, remembering how his finger had felt inside my bottom and how shameful it had felt. I couldn't forget how hard it had made me come either.

"Hold the paddle in your hands, little wolf," he directed. Hesitantly, I took it in my fingers and gulped hard. "Now put it back down and obey my instructions before I decide to take it and paddle this bottom until you're sobbing over my knee before I spread your cheeks and plug you myself. Either way, you're going to be wearing this plug for me," he continued.

I put the wooden paddle down like it had scorched my skin. I swallowed hard, staring at it as I reached back and took my bottom cheeks in my fingers. I spread myself a little and waited, only to have him demand that I open myself wider. With a whimper, I spread my cheeks as wide as I dared. I couldn't stop thinking about how my asshole was on complete display.

He slipped the plug inside my pussy, twirling it back and forth as he coated it with my wetness. As if to tease me, he pumped it in and out of my entrance several times before he pulled it out and dragged it up the cleft of my ass before settling it on top of my very reluctant hole.

He waited. I knew what he wanted, and I knew what was at stake if I delayed any longer. I stared at the paddle and opened my mouth, begging for the far more shameful thing instead.

"Please plug my bottom, alpha," I whispered, the words barely audible because that was all I could manage.

"Louder," he commanded.

"Please plug my asshole, alpha," I wailed, clutching at my bottom cheeks as I held them apart.

"Good girl," he replied, and he pushed the plug against my bottom hole. I didn't dare let go of my backside, but my cheeks tensed under my grip. My asshole fought its entrance, but the metal surface was slick with my arousal. The tip was small, stretching me just a little at first. I tried to relax, but as more of the plug forced its way inside me, it soon became impossible.

The plug was far bigger than his fingers, but I knew his cock would be that much larger. I struggled, crying out as the burning pain radiated around my asshole. It surged up and down my spine. I wailed and he roughly pushed the rest of it inside me.

A cruel spiral of deep agony rendered me helpless for several long seconds. I whimpered and the pain eventually lessened, leaving my bottom hole aching. I squirmed a little over his lap, trying to take in the feeling of heavy fullness inside my ass.

As much as I wanted to hate it, my pussy was throbbing once again.

"This asshole is so very pretty when it's properly jeweled," he observed, and I blushed heavily at his words. He gripped the top of the plug and pumped it in and out of me, making me moan out loud at the very shameful reminder of his power over me.

"You may let go. I'm going to spank you now and then you're going to lower this perfect little body down on my cock with your bottom sore inside and out," he said, and my pussy tightened, which only reignited the soreness around my asshole. I released my bottom. I whined when I realized that the plug was holding my cheeks open just enough to reveal the purple jewel at the top, that he'd be able to see it even when he spanked me.

His arm wound around my waist and then he slapped my bottom cheeks hard several times. Unlike the paddle, his palm felt that much more personal and with each stinging spank, my pussy practically sizzled with want. When he slapped the bottom curves of my cheeks, it jostled my pussy just enough to make my clit throb irrationally. My hips rose to meet his touch and occasionally, he would pause long enough to tease my clit with his fingers.

Every spank reminded me of the fullness of the plug in my bottom. When he spanked directly over it, I was so needy that I could hardly stand it.

I needed him to fuck me.

His cock was impossibly hard beneath me. With a little bit of sassy feistiness, I reached beneath my belly and stroked his cock. I wanted it inside me more than anything.

"Do you think you've earned my cock, little wolf?" he asked darkly, and my fingers grasped it greedily.

"Yes, alpha?" I answered tentatively. He didn't reply with words, but with a series of hard spanks that lift me whimpering and gasping by the time he was through.

"Is your ass sore?" he questioned.

"It is very sore, alpha," I answered, and I meant every word. I had a feeling I'd probably even have trouble sitting down in the morning.

"What about that pretty little asshole?" he asked as he gripped the end of the plug and roughly pumped it in and out of my bottom. I whined, fresh waves of pain and pleasure surging through me at the deliciously cruel treatment.

"It hurts, alpha," I cried out and he pushed it back in brutally. My asshole radiated with soreness, and I waited over his knee, unsure of what he might do next, which only made my pussy react with visceral need.

"Stand in front of me," he demanded. I rushed to obey him, even though my legs felt like jelly. He stripped off his shirt and tossed it aside. He kicked off his shoes and socks next before his hands finally reached for the button at his waist. Slowly, he undid it, sliding down the zipper without a hurry. My thighs rubbed against one another in anticipation. I clenched around the plug several times, imagining what it would feel like to have both of my holes filled at the same time.

Would it hurt? Would I come really hard? Would I like it?

He pushed his pants down to the floor. Then he slid each foot free. When he was finally naked, he sat back against the couch with the handsome arrogance of a god. His cock was impossibly hard, and I worried the inside of my cheek.

Would his massive cock even fit inside me with my ass full of his plug?

"Climb on top of me. Situate yourself so that you take just the head of my cock inside you and no more," he instructed.

Anxiously, I climbed up and wrapped my arms around his neck for support. I rose just high enough and tentatively wrapped my fingers around his shaft. It was difficult for me, but I lined him up and lowered myself just enough so that only the tip of his cock was inside me.

Fuck. He was so big.

I didn't think I could ever get used to his massive size. With the plug inside me, I felt that much tighter, and his entry hurt. I whimpered and cried out, struggling to take him and he watched every moment of my struggle as it passed over my face.

When he was ready, he grasped my hips roughly and lowered me a bit further himself, making me take his cock deeper. My inner walls clutched at him, both wanting to take all of him and force him out at the same time. I whimpered and he thrust upward, slamming the rest of his cock inside me with brutal force.

I cried out, not knowing if it was from pain, surprise, or relief that he was giving me his cock.

Fully seated on top of him now, I leaned against him. My nipples brushed against the thickness of his chest hair, and I couldn't stop the way my body instinctually rocked on top of him. One of his hands dipped down and his thumb lightly caressed my clit.

I couldn't stop from moaning out loud. It was shamefully desperate in nature.

"I think you've earned my cock, little wolf. Ride me now. You're going to come three times for me before I fill that pretty pussy full of my seed," he growled, and I gasped as my body immediately began to obey his demand.

With every roll of my hips, he teased my clit, showering me with delicious sensation. The fullness of both my ass and my pussy was almost too much all by themselves, but with his teasing fingers on my clit I knew that I was going to break for him, and hard.

I rocked back and forth, slowly at first before I was brave enough to pick up the pace. My pussy grasped at his cock. His other hand gripped at my hip, helping me along whenever I faltered. Occasionally, he would smack my bottom to spur me to move faster, but it didn't take long for that next orgasm to tear me open on top of his cock.

My arms clutched at him. I couldn't help but dig my nails into his flesh, simply trying to hold on as that next release destroyed me. His cock constantly pounded against my cervix, deeper and deeper until it felt like the two of us had become one. There was no holding back anymore.

The world fell down. Nothing else mattered but the two of us.

I came a third time. Then a fourth. Soon enough, I could only fathom pain or pleasure. Raw vicious sensation pounded through me, taking me captive and holding me prisoner to its will. I screamed and moaned, suffering through those blissful releases at the same time that they left me soaring. My body moved of its own accord, riding him harder with every passing second just so that I could come that much harder.

"I love the way your body squeezes my cock when you come, little wolf," he groaned. His thumb worried my clit a bit harder. He paid no mind to the fact that it was sensitive. He pushed past that, made me experience the pain because he knew that the release that would come after would render me undone.

The base of his cock flared, and I cried out. He grabbed the back of my neck and forced me all the way down. His knot inflated, larger and larger until it hooked us together as one. My eyes watered, staring into his shadowy depths and searching for something to hold onto.

The mate bond between us flared hot. It was an invisible tether, a golden thread that connected the two of us for the rest of our lives. In those moments, I lost myself in it and finally fully accepted that I was his and he was mine.

His seed spurted up deep inside me, splashing against my cervix like a firebrand. I keened, trying to pull away but his knot was locked inside my pelvis like a hook. There would be no escape for me. He increased the pressure on top of my clit and my over-sensitized body quickly responded to his command.

That final orgasm ripped through me. I screamed until my voice went hoarse. My legs started to convulse as his arm wrapped around me.

I broke so hard that I saw stars.

My cheeks were wet with tears, not from sadness or pain, but from the sheer power of the pleasure that my one true mate could give me. I panted, struggling to draw in air. When that fifth release finally crested, I finally remembered to relax my hands. I had been clutching at him like my life depended on it.

"That's my good girl," he murmured.

His knot didn't deflate right away. Instead, it stayed locked inside me. He stood up and carried me upstairs to our bedroom with his massive cock still inside me. I shivered in his arms, my pussy tensing around his thick shaft time and time again with an endless number of aftershocks.

He tucked me beside him in bed, petting my ass absent-mindedly. I was so numb with pleasure that it wasn't even sore from the paddle anymore.

I hadn't expected a man like him to come into my life, but fate had a funny way of doing things. I needed a mate like him. I needed a man to shower me with love and to be as rough with me as he pleased. I needed that because it was an intrinsic part of me that I'd never known existed before.

I pressed my forehead against his chest. "I love you, alpha," I murmured.

"I've loved you for a long time, little wolf," he replied.

My heart swelled with hope.

CHAPTER 13

lijah

The next day, I began training Ashleigh in defense. She was a good student, but she tended to get ahead of herself, which meant she spent a good deal of time over my knee getting her pretty little ass spanked. She was feisty and she impressed me constantly with her ability to adapt. Her strength was impressive, even for a female wolf.

Sometimes I just liked to watch her practice, fully enjoying the way her toned body moved when I switched things up and made her train with Theo or Atreyu. They were both much bigger than her, but I'd kept that in mind when I taught her to fight. Both of them were strong fighters and they bested her many times, but the occasions where she was able to defeat them were particularly extraordinary.

As a reward, I'd taken her into my office, tore her pants down, and pleasured that sweet little pussy with my tongue.

She especially liked being rewarded with my mouth and I gave it to her whenever I could because it brought me pleasure to do so.

Over the next several weeks, her muscles got harder, leaner, and more pronounced. She was strong and I knew it would be time to enter the next phase of training. I taught her how to use daggers made of wood to both attack and defend herself. She excelled quickly, her body more than ready to take on such a challenge.

I taught her how to use a gun next.

With the introduction of new and far more dangerous weaponry, I also increased the stakes of her reward and punishment system. If she did well, I'd not only pleasure her with my mouth, but she'd also get to choose the manner in which she received my cock. Sometimes she would have me bend her over the desk. Other times, she would ride me or if she hesitated long enough, I would fuck her impossibly hard right on top of the mats in the middle of the training room floor.

Her punishments for mistakes were more severe too. For every few mistakes she made, she would get a stroke of the cane. I would make her bare herself and ask for my correction each time.

She would bend over a pile of mats with her bare vulnerable bottom in the air and I would give her six hard strokes. I didn't rush either, taking my time and enjoying the way the welts rose on her pretty flesh. After I was done, I would run my fingers over each one, thoroughly enjoying her pretty stripes as they continued to pinken and eventually redden into raised welts. Sometimes I would surprise her with her plug right after, punishing her little bottom hole as much as I saw fit. There were times that I just used my fingers. Then I would make her come for me. Hard and rough enough to make her scream.

Some days, I was convinced that she made mistakes on purpose to earn a punishment. She would get her little pussy spanked bright red on those days until she begged me for forgiveness and for the mercy of my cock in between her thighs.

She was absolute perfection.

In those weeks, my pack established our place as the reigning heads of the surrounding territory. I started with the small towns around us and eventually moved to take meetings with the diplomatic leaders of the nearby city of Zurich.

Our accounts were overflowing from the sheer amount of tribute the humans offered us in exchange for our protection. They were exceedingly thankful for us and that afforded me and my pack a great deal of power.

I used it to my advantage to gain even more.

I had an unshakable number of allies at my back. Many had followed me from my days in the Crimson Shadows, but I'd earned a great deal more for my actions in freeing the humans from the terrible rule of the rogue vampires. I found out that their reach had spread like a virus. They'd lorded over Zurich with constant threats, attacking at will if they were not paid the tribute they deserved. They kidnapped and tortured members of the mayor's family, blackmailing his cooperation by coercion and cruelty.

They'd kept their actions secret in order to hide from the Council and I'd been the one to undercover their treachery. As a result, the Council sent members to thank me personally, while also providing a pretty incredible stock of anti-vampire weapons in order to show their appreciation. I began to store them, knowing that my quick ascent into power would not only grant me allies, but a fair number of enemies too.

I kept an eye on Amir and what remained of his pack. There were still plenty of wolf shifters that stayed loyal to him, but many of those had never served under me. I didn't blame them for staying, but I was wary of them all the same.

His alliance with the Malkovian clan was still as strong as ever. He'd never wavered from that even in the slightest, going so far as to share the compound with the vampires for good. I rolled my lip in disgust, imagining the rancid smell of vampire around me all of the time and immediately gagging at the thought.

For a while, Amir was quiet. He stayed in his corner, and I

stayed in mine, but soon enough rumors started to circulate about his intentions long term. I knew my decision to leave had never sat well with him. He'd never had anyone turn their backs on him before, especially someone who'd been as loyal to him as I had been for a long time.

Whispers of a planned attack began to surface.

Every day, Theo would come to my door and update me on the Crimson Shadows' movements. On the surface, it appeared that they were simply existing in their own territory, but I knew better. Atreyu hacked into Amir's accounts and small things began to come to light. Amir was paying an awful lot of money into an offshore account and when I dug a bit deeper, I found out that the owner of the account was a man who lived in Belarus. He was an arms dealer.

I'd contacted a man on the inside of Amir's pack who I'd placed there on the day I'd left. He was a long-time loyal supporter of mine who had always exceled at undercover work.

He'd told me to be careful, that there was an incoming attack and to be ready. He warned me that something else was in play, but he wasn't sure what it was yet. He needed more time, but when he found out, he would inform me as soon as he could.

I trusted his word. I'd known something like this was coming, to be honest. It had been weeks since I left the compound, more than enough time for Amir to make plans and begin preparations to remove me from power.

Amir wasn't the kind of alpha that would let things lie. He would take his time and prepare as best he could. He wouldn't rush something like this because the only option for him was to come out the victor.

Even before I'd been in contact with my informant, I'd taken measures to protect my own. My wolves were on a constant watch. I'd fixed up the surrounding outposts and always had my people on guard. I'd been stockpiling weaponry too, expanding on the original gift from the Council so that we could fight a war if it came to our door.

I had an overwhelming stock of sun fire bullets. I had stakes and powerful crossbows to fight them. I'd taken over the human water system and laced it with black-thorn, a specialized herb that would protect them against vampire compulsion. There were spray bombs that exploded and emitted droplets of blackthorn, which would burn a vampire's flesh on contact.

I had a full armory of anti-vampire weaponry, but I didn't stop there.

I made sure our stocks were complete with anti-wolf shifters weapons too. I had silver bullets, silver swords, daggers, and knives. I had silver-tipped arrows that could be loaded into crossbows just like the wooden stakes. I had aerosolized preparations of wolfsbane that could be used to fight against Amir's pack.

It was only a matter of time before they showed up at my door.

I would be ready when they came. Not only that, but I would make sure that Amir would regret the day that he thought he could stand up against a man like me.

CHAPTER 14

shleigh

"I can't wait to try all the flavors!" Becca exclaimed and the musical sound of her giggling flittered around me. Her joyful mood was contagious, and I couldn't help but laugh along with her.

"Which one is your favorite so far?" I asked and she skipped along, squeezing my hand tight as she pulled me forward on the sidewalk.

"The cotton candy one. No. Maybe cherry. Or blue raspberry," she answered thoughtfully, and I giggled. I'd taken her out for ice cream today and the shop owner had been amazingly sweet, even when Becca had wanted to try out seven different flavors before settling on a single scoop of three other ones she hadn't even tasted. I'd made sure to tip her well by the time we got to the register.

"Mom would have liked the strawberry one," she said softly and I squeezed her hand tighter.

"I bet she would have," I replied gently.

Becca was doing exceedingly well with Melissa and Sean. They doted on her, spoiling her rotten at every turn as if she was their own. She was exceling in school and was at the top of her class. She was showing great promise and had already begun to grasp the concept of reading even though it was still pretty new for her. Sometimes, she even insisted on reading them stories at night. Earlier this afternoon, she'd even read one to me.

She had both good days and bad ones. Sometimes, she would struggle and miss her parents or wake up with nightmares, but those became less and less with the passage of time. Melissa and Sean were great with her during those episodes, either playing hooky and spending the whole day with her or distracting her with something else. She cried a few times, but she was consoled with a big hug until her tears dried. It was a process and I knew it would get better eventually, but it was hard for her adoptive parents and for me and Elijah.

The two of them had been true to their word in allowing Elijah and me a place in the young girl's life. Occasionally, we'd take her overnight for sleepovers and other times I'd take her out to eat or to a movie. The more time I spent with her, the more I realized that I would really love to have my own family someday.

I wanted that family to be with Elijah. One day, I hoped to carry his son or daughter in my belly.

I strode along the sidewalk with Becca's hand in mine, thinking over the events of the past few weeks. I felt settled, like I'd finally accepted my new life here as the mate of the kingpin of the Rising Sun pack. Every day, I felt his love for me and mine grew for him.

He showered me with gifts, constantly surprising me with a piece of jewelry, a designer dress, a pair of one of a kind Jimmy Choos, and surprise bouquets of flowers to brighten up the chalet. He took me out to fancy dinners constantly and made sure that I was never left wanting, whether it be for pleasure or pain or something else.

He'd spent an inordinate amount of time teaching me to defend myself. I took to his lessons readily. I adored those sessions because he never went easy on me, and I understood why. Someday, his training might save my life and if neither of us were serious about it, my overconfidence could cost me my life. For the most part, I treated every session like it was the real thing.

That didn't mean it was all serious. There were definite moments that were special between the two of us during those sessions.

I smiled wistfully. I liked his reward and punishment system very much. I'd become fond of his desk simply because I'd been fucked over it endlessly. I'm not sure how, but he'd gotten even better with his tongue in these past few weeks. He had gotten to a point where he could

SARA FIELDS

suckle my clit for a scarcely a few seconds, and I'd be ready to fall apart. Occasionally, he'd make me ask for permission to come and when I didn't sometimes, he'd spank my pussy as hard as he pleased, which just made me increasingly needy for his cock. He'd make me beg for it and I always did.

The punishment cane was an interesting addition. It made me feel naughty and needy and the whole routine of baring myself and asking him to punish me with it ran through my mind often. I'd never admit it to him, but I sometimes made mistakes on purpose just so that he would use it. The orgasms he gave me afterward always made it worth it.

Even now, the backs of my thighs were achy and welted. Yesterday, I'd intentionally missed a cue. I'm not sure if he knew, but he had been even more vicious than usual, doubling his usual six strokes to a full dozen with the cane before he spanked my pussy hard, plugged my bottom, and fucked me hard enough to make me cry while I came for him.

My heart swelled.

I sighed, trying to rein in my thoughts and focus on the little girl at my side. She bounced as we rounded the corner and closed in on what was her new home. It was a beautiful townhome that wasn't far from the town center, which meant she was close to pretty much everything. The door opened and Melissa waved to us from inside. I let go of Becca's hand and she skipped toward her adoptive mother, going on about how I'd bought her the best bowl of ice cream she'd ever had.

I loved hearing things like that.

"See you for dinner this weekend, Becca!" I called out and she blew me a kiss. My heart melted into a puddle of goo.

When she disappeared behind the door, I finally turned away and began walking back to the chalet. The sun was setting, and the streets were beginning to grow dark. It was in that weird place where the lampposts hadn't turned on yet to illuminate the shadows. I looked up at the sky and smiled, enjoying the way the stars were just starting to glimmer.

There was a scuffle behind me, and I stopped, turning around quickly. There was nothing there. I searched the area carefully, sniffing the air and sensing nothing. When I looked up, I saw a number of pigeons flying up into the sky. I shrugged and shook my head at my edginess. I'd startled them somehow, that's all that had been.

I shook my head and continued on, anxious to get back to Elijah. He'd told me all about the suspected threat from my father and how they were planning an attack. Knowing that made me pretty uneasy. I wanted to return to the safe place that was his arms.

Maybe I'd even ask him to plug me tonight. I'd never told him, but I loved the orgasms he gave me when I was full of his cock and the toy at the same time. Those were quickly becoming some of my favorites.

With a heavy sigh, I rounded the corner. Immediately, a cloud of steam enveloped me, and I coughed almost just as quickly. My throat was suddenly on fire, flames licking down my throat until it settled deep in my lungs. I struggled to breathe. At once, I knew that it wasn't just water. It was aerosolized wolfsbane. I screamed, trying to wipe the burning solution off my face and having no luck. My skin sizzled and I screamed in agony.

A black bag was shoved over my head. Someone grabbed my arms and I tried to do my best to use the defense training Elijah had taught me to get myself out of it. I didn't know how many there were. He'd mainly taught me to fight one on one. Right now, there were at least three large creatures making a grab at me. One of them seized my left wrist. Another clutched at my right one. I struggled hard enough that my muscles began to protest, but it wasn't enough for me to break free.

One of them growled and I quickly scented the air. They were wolf shifters, which was why I didn't sense them right away.

I snarled in return, renewing my struggles, but there were too many of them. I kicked and tried to twist away from them, but they pinned my arms behind my back and tied them with rope. I cried out when it touched my skin, realizing it was rope woven with silver thread. My flesh sizzled. I screamed for help.

Everything inside me was roaring with agony.

I don't know whether it was just to keep me quiet or save me from the pain they'd brought on me, but someone forced a soaked cloth over my nose and mouth. I tried not to breathe, but someone punched me in the stomach, and I gasped as air flowed into my lungs anyway.

This was really bad.

The last thing I remembered was the sweet aroma of flowers before I passed out.

* * *

Fucking hell, my head hurt. I blinked, trying to make the terrible ache go away with sheer force of will. I sighed and stretched, stiffening immediately when the events of the night finally came back to me. I'd been taken and I didn't yet know by who.

There were thick curtains on the window, but I could tell that it was well into the afternoon. I sat up quickly, pushing my hands against the soft mattress beneath me. I stared at my wrists, pink evidence of the rope that they'd tied me with still very apparent on my skin. I rubbed at them absently, wincing a little at the stinging ache that came with even a gentle touch. I looked around, chewing the inside of my cheek.

Where the fuck was I?

This wasn't the chalet. Elijah's scent was nowhere to be found.

My heart hurt worse than both my wrists and head combined. I could feel that he was pretty far away and that was painful. The tether that held us together was strained over that kind of distance and my whole body ached from it. I pressed my palm over my heart, closing my eyes and taking several deep sobering breaths, trying to compose myself before I began to panic.

I had to stay calm. I needed to figure out where I was before I did anything drastic.

There was a glass of water on the nightstand table, along with a bottle of over-the-counter pain relievers. I grabbed both of them and climbed off the bed, padding into the attached bathroom of the bedroom I'd found myself in. I dumped the glass of water, rinsing it several times before I filled it with water straight from the tap. For all I knew, it could be poisoned.

I investigated the bottle of Tylenol, taking note that the seal inside it was untampered. I ripped it open and popped two of them, swallowing the pills with a gulp of fresh water. I took another steadying breath. The wolfsbane had burned my skin, but there wasn't any more evidence of it on my face or anywhere else. They'd already healed. My lungs no longer felt like I was breathing fire, so that was good too.

Other than the pink marks on my wrists, nothing else hurt enough to alarm me. I left the glass and the medicine on the counter and made my way back in the bedroom and to the window. The inside of the bedroom wasn't familiar, so I quickly opened the curtains in order to take in my surroundings.

I was in the center of the Malkovian clan compound. I'd been here several times as a girl, but I'd never stayed for long. Today though, there was only one reason I could be here and that was my own flesh and blood.

I growled fiercely when someone knocked at my door. I'd always hated this place.

"I'm glad to see you're finally awake," a very prim woman said as she walked in. She hadn't even paused to wait for my permission to enter. She'd just come in. Immediately, the scent of vampire assaulted my nostrils, but I had been groomed not to react to it all my life. I smiled politely, all while imagining the various ways I could tear her heart straight out of her chest with nothing but my bare hands.

"Who are you? Where am I?" I demanded.

She smiled tensely, running her eyes up and down me in the most judgmental way possible.

"You wolf shifters are always so impatient," she drawled, and I stood a bit taller. My gaze bored into hers and she eventually sighed. "You're here so that the alliance between the Crimson Shadows, the Malkovians, and the Venuti can finally be secured. It took time to gather the resources so that we could retrieve you and put you in your rightful position beside your future husband's side."

"Future husband?" I asked, furrowing my brow in confusion.

"Vincenzo Venuti," she answered, peering back at me like I was stupid for even asking the question.

I took a deep breath, quelling the desire to gauge her eyes out with nothing more than my fingers. Of course. My father was going through with the alliance he had planned. What I wanted didn't matter to him. He'd decided I was going to marry a vampire and he'd do everything in his power to ensure that marriage took place. To him, I was nothing more than a pawn that he could use to further his own position in the world.

"Where is my father?" I asked.

"He is in a meeting with Augustus and Vincenzo. They are finalizing the alliance agreement as we speak. You will dress in something more fitting of your station and meet them for dinner shortly," she explained, looking down at my jeans in disgust. With a flourish, she opened the closet doors. "I am here to prepare you."

The concept of an attendant wasn't foreign to me. I'd had them all my life. I lifted my chin and slipped back into my old persona, becoming the person I'd abandoned the night Elijah carried me off.

"Which one is the most expensive?" I asked and the aristocratic vampire grinned enthusiastically.

She pulled out a deep purple gown that would leave no doubt in anyone's mind that I was my father's daughter. It was a dress that was also befitting of an alpha's mate.

The bond between Elijah and me pulsed. There was no way in hell he'd allow this wedding to take place. He'd burn the whole place to the ground first.

* * *

Several hours later, I found myself seated at a table with my father, the leader of the Venuti clan and my future husband to be, Vincenzo, as well as the Malkovian kingpin Augustus. They talked like I wasn't even there. They were supremely overconfident in the way they spoke to one another, letting several important details slip out right in front of me about the upcoming attack on the Rising Sun pack and my Elijah. I knew what kind of weapons they had, how many of their followers they planned to show up with, the exact time and date. I took mental notes of everything.

I stared at Vincenzo when he wasn't looking. All my life, I had been groomed to marry a powerful man like him. I'd just never imagined him being a vampire. I had woken up every day knowing that as the daughter of an alpha, I would one day marry someone that would strengthen the power of my pack, but now that he was right here sitting in front of me, it felt like a hollow pipedream. The whole thing left a bitterness on my tongue that I couldn't shake no matter how hard I tried.

With Vincenzo, I would never find happiness. As a vampire, he would live forever, and I would live a normal life. When I died, he would find another and never look back. I would be nothing more than a possession to him, a wife he'd let out of the cage only when he desired.

I would never be able to have a family. Vampires were by nature infertile. They could not sire children, so Vincenzo would never be able to give me one. I wouldn't be able to conceive on my own either. Wolf shifters could only have children with their own kind. IVF wasn't an option for me either. It never took for female wolves. We needed the additional component of a mate bond to start a family and there was only one man who could ever give me that now.

This was what I'd been promised, the life of a kept princess that I'd dreamed of ever since I was a little girl.

I would have all the riches I could ever want. Clothes. Gems. Jewelry. Travel. Shoes. Whatever I wanted, all I'd have to do was ask. I could have it all, but it would mean nothing without Elijah by my side.

"She is a beautiful female, Amir," Vincenzo murmured, and my gaze flicked to him. I lifted my chin haughtily. His compliment made my stomach churn.

"She is quite a prize," my father replied without emotion. I glared back at him. He didn't know anything about me.

"How is this going to work?" I asked, sitting back and taking a bite of the dinner that had been put in front of me. I was vaguely aware of the fact that it was steak, but I could hardly even enjoy the taste of a prime cut of filet under current circumstances.

"Tomorrow, you will be taken to a fitting for your wedding dress. When that is complete, we will be taking a trip to Switzerland together to deal with the problem that is Elijah," my father explained.

"What are you going to do to him?" I pressed protectively.

"You will convince him to surrender and offer his territory to us in exchange for the continuation of his people's life. If he listens to you and goes willingly, he will survive the day. If he doesn't, well then, he will suffer," Augustus explained. His red eyes flared with excitement. It was clear he was looking forward to the prospect of battle.

"You would use me to force him out," I replied. My disgust was very clear this time.

"Yes," my father said arrogantly. I licked my lips and stood back up.

"I'm sorry. I've lost my appetite," I declared.

"Fine. Be sure you're ready in the morning," my father said, his exasperation and annoyance painted all over his face.

I pushed in my chair, following the basic expectations of decorum in my father's court. I bowed my head and walked out of the room, knowing with absolute certainty that Vincenzo was feasting on the vision of me walking away from him. I gagged with overwhelming disgust.

I had only just turned the corner before someone rushed up behind me. They grabbed me and covered my mouth with their hand before I could make a sound. Quickly, they thrust me up against the wall and I cried out into their palm.

"It's me, Ashleigh. Please don't scream," the male voice pleaded gently. I recognized him and relaxed slightly. It was one of my favorite teachers growing up, a man who went by the name Ronaldo. He'd always been especially kind to me and there were several times that I knew he'd shielded me from my father's anger and expectations. In many ways, he'd been one of the important figures in my life that had actually meant something to me.

When he pulled his hand away from my mouth, I stayed quiet. Slowly, he uncurled his arms from me, and I turned to face him. He said nothing but cocked his head in the direction of the room where the heads of the families were still discoursing noisily. Their voices carried, even outside the room.

"Cheers, men! To long time alliances. We will conquer the world together!" my father roared, and I turned my head, listening more closely. "Tomorrow we will end the Rising Sun pack and punish Elijah for daring to stand against us."

"Ashleigh will be the means to an end. Elijah will burn before the day is done. His death will secure our growing power here in Europe," Augustus chimed in.

"What if she dies tomorrow and I never get to enjoy her in my marriage bed?" Vincenzo whined a bit grumpily. I tensed at his sordid suggestion. The need to vomit slammed into me and I swallowed hard.

My father laughed out loud. "No matter, Vincenzo. We will find you another," he replied.

"I have many more women at my disposal for you to choose from," Augustus confirmed, and I stilled.

"My life or death has never mattered to him," I whispered, unable to hide the sorrow I felt. I'd always known my father hadn't wanted a daughter, that he'd done every-thing in his power to ensure that he wasn't actually a part of my life. I told myself time and time again that I didn't care but hearing his disdain for me put so bluntly was painful.

"Either way, Elijah and his pack will be destroyed tomor-row. Anyone that turns their back on my allies will die," Augustus added.

"Hear, hear," Vincenzo cheered.

I turned my head to the side. I'd heard more than enough.

"I needed you to know the truth," Ronaldo whispered.

I wanted to cry, but I wouldn't allow myself to lose control like that, not for the likes of them. I took several moments to gather myself before I looked back at him.

"What do you need?" I asked carefully. I gazed up into his eyes, trying to find it in me to trust him. I wanted to, but I needed to be cautious right now.

"Elijah knows you're here," he said, his voice so low that even I could hardly hear it. I stared at him, trying to make a quick assessment of his end goal. Was it his job to trick me into saying something? He was still a part of my father's pack. He hadn't left with Elijah on that day several weeks ago. He'd made his choice and stayed, which meant that he'd chosen my father instead of Elijah and me.

But... the way he was looking at me at that moment made me question that assumption, so I decided to ask him point blank. I didn't have time for pomp or circumstance.

"Whose side are you on?" I asked pointedly.

"The same side as you. We both answer to the same alpha," he whispered hoarsely.

"I only answer to one man, and he is not sitting in that room," I replied carefully, looking back in the direction of the room I'd just left behind.

"Elijah wants me to tell you that he loves you. He also wants me to tell you to trust him. He will not allow you to marry a monster, not when you already belong to him," Ronaldo added. I stared into his soft brown eyes. I could trust him after all.

"That sounds like him," I murmured tearfully. My heart ached.

"I want to help you," he added. He slipped something metal into my hands. I glanced down to see that it was a small handheld gun. The metal was cold against my fingers, but its grip was familiar enough to the one I'd trained with. It fit my hand well.

"This is full of silver bullets. Keep it hidden and use it at the opportune moment," he whispered. "I have hidden a number of other small weapons that might be useful to you in a small shoebox at the very back of your closet. There is an extra magazine full of sun fire bullets inside it too."

"Why would you take such a massive risk for me?" I asked him.

"It is a matter of loyalty, Ashleigh," he replied.

"Did you hear the rest of what they were saying?" I asked.

"I did. I know everything that they are planning. I wasn't able to find out their plan for you until it was already in motion, but I was able to prepare for your arrival. Return to your room now and familiarize yourself with the weapons. Elijah said he's been teaching you, so none of them should throw you off."

"I will," I replied.

"Now, keep yourself safe. Elijah will be waiting for you," he murmured.

"Tell him that I love him," I pressed, and he nodded.

"I will. If anything goes wrong tonight, scream as loud as you can. I won't be far. Your safety is my most important directive," he added before he released me and disappeared around the corner.

I took several deep breaths and hiked the decorative garter I was wearing higher up on my thigh. I slipped the

gun inside it, checking that it wasn't revealed by the salacious slit in my skirt. When I was certain that it was fully
hidden, I walked off down the hall and returned to my
room.

I used a chair to bar the door and opened the closet door.
The box that Ronaldo had left for me was there. It was full
of everything he'd said and more. There were a few
designer purses on the top shelf. I grabbed one of the
bigger Kate Spade bags and packed the weapons he'd left
me inside it. I hunted around the room and packed a few
additional outfits on top of it, a pair of pajamas, the
works. I twisted around and stripped myself out of the
dress, tucking the gun away in a hidden pocket inside the
bag too.

I wasn't going to let it out of my sight tomorrow.

The morning flew by faster than I thought it would. The
wedding dress fitting was mercifully quick. The dress had
already been chosen for me. It was gaudy and ostenta-
tious, seemingly something out of the mid-1800s. The
skirt was massive and covered in embroidery. The upper
half was demure, covering me completely in a thin veil of
white lace. The sleeves went all the way to my wrists and
the neck towered up my throat. I assumed that it was
probably a dress that was special in some way to the
Venuti clan.

To be honest, I didn't much care.

No one took a second glance at my bag. They didn't search inside it or even question the fact that I had taken it along with me. They underestimated me and I let them.

After the fitting, I was ushered to a small airport and hustled inside the Malkovians' own personal private jet. It spoke of old money. Many of the fixtures were lined with pure gold. The leather seats were the softest I'd ever felt, and the wood grain accents were deep stained mahogany.

I kept my head in a magazine I'd taken from my room, making a show of admiring several images of models in fancy clothing. Soon enough, no one was really watching me at all. Augustus and Vincenzo were chatting together while my father snoozed in a seat toward the front of the plane.

The flight itself was fast and I had hardly enough time to stuff my magazine into my bag before I was shuffled off and into a waiting Range Rover. The car shot off down the road and I studied the surrounding scenery. Some of it started to seem familiar.

The vampires had loaded into their own car. The windows were tinted pitch black, which must have made it safe for them to travel. On the plane ride, all of the windows had been shut and the only light inside the cabin had been artificial. We reached a ritzy old mansion, and I was ushered inside to a room of my own and left there.

I dressed in a pair of jeans and a loose-fitting long-sleeve t-shirt. I buckled a holster that Ronaldo had left for me around my waist beneath it, slipping the gun inside it. I'd decided to load it with sun fire bullets, not knowing if I'd have the heart to shoot my fellow wolf shifters with silver bullets, even if some of them may deserve it. I hid a few stakes in a holster at my ankle, using the wide flared cut of my jeans to conceal them. Lastly, I slipped a silver switchblade into the back of my waistband.

By the time they finally came to retrieve me, I was fully armed and prepared. Even after being left to my own devices, they didn't bother patting me down or even remotely checking me for signs of betrayal. They just assumed that I would come with them willingly and I did nothing to shatter that false veil of compliance.

The sun was almost fully set by the time we set out again. They stopped a short distance away from the chalet before I was forced out. My father gripped my arm roughly, forcing me to stay at his side as one carload after the next was unloaded beside us.

I looked out in the direction of the chalet I'd come to know and love. It was only a short walk down the road. All was silent in that direction, but I knew Elijah and his pack would be waiting. My hands pressed against my belly nervously.

I just wanted this all to be over with so that I could return to the safety of my alpha's arms.

lijah

Waiting for them to show up at my front door was the hardest thing I'd ever had to do in my life. Every instinct in my body was screaming for me to rush to my mate's side, to rip through everyone that threatened her and end them. I wanted to rain down blood until she was returned to my side.

Doing so would be foolish. I knew that, but the wolf in me was saying otherwise.

I had called in every favor in the book. I had allies fly in from all over the world. Every local hotel and bed and breakfast was fully booked. The overflow split into the surrounding towns and even into the outer edges of Zurich. The weapons I had stored and collected were distributed and by the time I got word that an unscheduled flight had landed at a private airport only a short distance away, I was ready.

At the front of my army were myself and my pack. Behind us were several other packs that had come from New Orleans, Las Vegas, Chicago, Belarus, and other places around the world. My numbers had swelled to over a thousand, and that didn't even include the townsfolk who had insisted on joining the battle as well.

They wanted to defend not only me, but Ashleigh too.

They loved Ashleigh like one of their own. In her free time, she'd helped out at the hospital and spent time with them and in those moments, they had fallen in love with her too. She had become their queen just like she was mine.

In preparation for the arrival of the Crimson Shadows and their vampire allies, I directed much of my numbers to hide in side streets. They were under strict orders not to reveal themselves unless I signaled for them to come.

To the unobservant eye, I would look ill prepared and easily subdued. Below the surface, however, I had everything at my disposal to destroy those that threatened my little slice of heaven here in Switzerland.

They would rue the day they'd challenged me.

My enemies crested over the hill only a few minutes after the sun had fully set. Their numbers were vast, and they kept coming. They bled in from the road, from the surrounding mountains through the less traveled passes and from the sides. They didn't attack outright at first.

I was used to action, but this appeared to be like the conflicts of old. They wandered in and lined up like a battle straight out of the revolutionary war. I squinted my eyes. Most of them had handguns and a few of them had much larger rifles, but many of the vampires seemed almost disgusted by the weapons in their own hands.

I recognized many as Malkovian and others as Venuti. Amir and my former pack members crested the hill last, and it tore at my heart to see them by his side.

I would do everything in my power to make sure that I was able to keep as many of them alive as possible. It wasn't their fault that their alpha was both a madman and a monster. I wondered if many of them even knew that he planned to sell off his daughter's hand in marriage to a vampire.

I stepped to the front of my forces with Theo close by my side. I had two guns tucked into the back of my jeans, one loaded with silver bullets and the other of the sun fire variety. I had several more magazines full in my pockets.

I spotted Ashleigh almost immediately. When she saw me, she lifted her chin a bit higher. I'd received word from my inside man that she'd been outfitted with the weapons I'd sent and that she was safe, but seeing her alive with my own eyes was something else entirely.

I wanted her back in my arms right now. I wanted to take her back to the chalet and remind her in every way possible that she was mine and that I'd never allow another man to touch her. Not now. Not ever.

She belonged to me.

I pulled my shoulders back and readied myself for battle. I took several steps forward and my enemy soon followed suit. I recognized Vincenzo Venuti when he grabbed Ashleigh's arm roughly and forced her on ahead with him. I had to stop myself from grabbing the crossbow out of Theo's hands and shooting the monster in the heart with the biggest wooden stake that I could find.

I didn't though. Not yet. It wasn't the right time.

Amir followed several steps behind, alongside Augustus Malkovian.

When we reached a place that was directly in the middle of the two forces, we paused and stared back at one another. Vincenzo forced Ashleigh forward, and I couldn't keep myself quiet this time.

"Take your hands off of her," I growled.

True to her nature, Ashleigh's jaw tensed. She stood with a strong sense of pride and yanked her arm from Vincenzo's grasp first.

"I will do what I want with *my* bride, wolf," Vincenzo sneered. I decided then that he would be the very first one I killed.

"Let me do what I came here to do," Ashleigh exclaimed. The two vampires and her father stood haughtily behind her. They didn't know that I was already fully aware of their plans to take over my newly established territory. I knew that they planned to kill anyone that stood in their way, and I also knew that they planned to use Ashleigh to force my hand at surrender.

I was far more prepared than they gave me credit for.

Amir looked out at my pack behind me. To him, it would look like I only had several hundred at my back at best. He'd underestimated me and I was looking forward to the moment when I saw the realization that he'd lost painted all over his face.

"Elijah, I'm here to beg you to surrender. If you do, your people will live," Ashleigh pleaded. Her voice was begging for me to heed her words, but her eyes sparkled with rebellion. She curled her hands around her waist, pulling the fabric just taut enough so that I could see the faint outline of a gun. She didn't have to say it, but I knew she had some kind of a plan forming in her head.

I'd play along for a little while. I wanted to see how it would play out.

"What will happen if I refuse?" I asked pointedly.

"They will kill your entire pack. My father will spare no mercy in your destruction if you refuse to bow to him," she continued. Behind her, Amir preened with arrogance, and I glared at him over her shoulder.

SARA FIELDS

"Perhaps before we come to blows, I should invite the rest of my allies to join me," I replied cockily.

Amir started a bit in surprise but covered it up quickly. Atreyu bounded to my side, fully in wolf form, and lifted his snout up into the air. I snapped my fingers and he howled so loudly that the sound would carry for miles. Behind me, a series of howls followed. Wolves and humans poured onto the streets, bulking up my forces and joining alongside my pack.

Amir's face paled a little bit. He had a great deal of his own, but my numbers were far more than his and now he could see it. I enjoyed the way his brow furrowed with worry, the way his eyes narrowed with fear. I lapped up every second of it.

"You cannot think to defeat the Malkovians, the Venuti, and the Crimson Shadows," Augustus murmured, and I turned my glare to him. I didn't answer. I just smiled and said that was exactly what I planned on doing without words.

"You will die, wolf dog, and I'm going to enjoy taking what was promised to me on my wedding night," Vincenzo countered, and Ashleigh lifted her chin in fury.

What happened next was the most beautiful thing I'd ever seen in my life.

Ashleigh side-stepped out of Vincenzo's reach and quickly slipped her fingers beneath her shirt. She didn't even hesitate as she whipped the gun out of the holster.

She pressed the barrel directly against his temple and squeezed the trigger. The piercing sound of a gunshot echoed deafeningly up here in the mountains. The bullet tore through his skull and a sudden brilliant flash of light ruined him from the inside out. His head exploded, splashing a shower of blood down onto the ground before his headless body followed.

Everyone around her gasped in shock. They probably hadn't even known she was armed. Her father was the most stunned of all. He stared at Ashleigh like she was a perfect stranger and I smiled. I couldn't be prouder of her.

In the confusion, I un-holstered my own gun and narrowed in on Augustus. I took aim with the experience of a thousand gunshots. My finger was already on the trigger by the time he realized what was happening. He made a move to get out of range, but I'd had my fair share of vampires that I shot dead in my time. I guessed his movements and pulled that trigger. He did exactly as I thought he would do, and my aim was true.

His fate was the same as Vincenzo, ending in a flash of light, blood, and gore. My wolves rushed at Amir, but he'd already turned tail and run. The vampires folded in around him, encompassing him with their protection. My pack surged forward, and the battlefield became chaos in a matter of moments.

I raced ahead, trusting in my pack to deal with the matter of Amir.

I had something more important to contend with. I had to get back to my mate. I reached out at the same time as her, taking her hand in my own and holding it tight. Her glittering eyes met mine, full of love and beauty and strength.

"Let me fight," she exclaimed.

"You may fight, but you will stay by my side as you do it," I declared, and she nodded once. She used me to gain momentum as she sprinted toward another vampire, grasping one of the stakes at her ankle and slamming it straight into its heart. The look of shock on his face was almost comical. She tossed him to the ground, grinning in my direction with triumph.

She and I fought side by side for hours. She emptied her magazine of sun fire bullets, and I was proud to see that she ended a vampire with every single shot. Eventually, the vampires began giving her a wider berth.

I saw one approaching her from behind. He lifted his weapon and shakily aimed in her direction, but I was much faster than him. He didn't even have a chance to get off a shot before I put a sun fire bullet directly in the center of his skull.

The darkness of night dragged on. The brilliant flashes of light all around me were a sight for sore eyes because I knew it was my men fighting to keep what was theirs.

The vampires fought on like they had no other choice. They were leaderless and they fell into chaos. I observed the battlefield while searching for signs of the rest of Amir's pack, but there didn't seem to be any. They'd most likely retreated at Amir's command.

Either way, it didn't matter to me. I'd never intended to kill my former brethren anyway.

When we ran out of bullets, we kept fighting with stakes. I had several stored on the belt around my waist and I gave Ashleigh a quick lesson on how to properly stake a vampire in a way that was quick, deep, and brutal, while also allowing her to reuse it on the next one that came her way.

I swatted her bottom hard and she squealed, but she leapt up and jumped on an unsuspecting vamp's back. She slammed the stake down and used her body to roll off of him before he fell, bringing the stake along with her as she went.

She stood up, smirking back at me with victory.

"How was that?" she sassed.

"That'll do," I replied with a grin.

She spun hard, gripping the stake tight in her fingers and taking out another. Her movements were like a dance, swift, graceful, and utterly breathtaking. I found myself getting distracted by her a fair number of times. One time, I almost ran straight into a vampire and a stake from Theo's crossbow was the only thing that stopped him dead in his tracks.

The battle lasted long into the night. My allies fought hard. When the vampires finally realized that they were quickly losing numbers and their defeat was inevitable, many of them started to flee. I knew several would escape. I made no move to hunt them down or stop them if they stopped putting their hands on my pack and the people under my protection.

They would return to their homes and tell everyone of my power. The stories would spread that my mate and I had killed Vincenzo Venuti and Augustus Malkovian, two of the most powerful vampire kingpins on Earth.

By the time the sun rose, the road was littered with dead vampires and the battle had ended. Immediately, my pack switched into recovery mode. The bodies were gathered and disposed of. Big bonfires popped up all over the place. Vampires disintegrated pretty quickly when directly exposed to an open flame, leaving the only evidence of their existence a smattering of dark ash on the wind.

There was no sign of Amir and his wolves. In the chaos, several of my own pack members had fallen. The vampires had been armed with guns, but many of them had forsaken them in the interest of fighting with their own hands instead. Some of them, however, had been good enough shots to take out my men.

Theo and Atreyu directed my allies in the gathering of the bodies. Over the next several days, we would bury them and give them the sending off that they deserved, but I wanted to make sure my still living people were taken care of first.

Ashleigh helped as much as she could, but soon enough her exhaustion outweighed her. I took her hand in mine and put a stop to it before she collapsed.

"Wait. Let me go, Elijah. They need my help," she replied, trying to jerk her fingers free from me.

"Unless you want me to tear off those pretty jeans and spank your bottom in front of everyone here, you will come with me and get some rest," I warned, and her lips slammed shut. Her eyes narrowed though, so I decided to continue.

"My belt is much thicker than the one I've used before, little wolf. It will sting far more when I mark your bottom, your thighs, and your bare little pussy with it," I said loudly.

Her face flamed beautifully as she glanced around to see if anyone had heard me. Theo smirked not far away from me, which only served to deepen her shame.

"I understand you wish to help, little wolf, and I commend you for it. You are exhausted though. You will get some rest and if there is more to do when you wake, I will be by your side doing whatever needs to be done. Do you understand me?" I pushed.

The fury almost seemed to bleed right out of her. After several tense moments where I very seriously contemplated the fate of her bare ass, she sighed and nodded, almost as if she was finally accepting the fact that she was, in fact, very tired. She nodded and licked her lips.

"Yes, alpha, I understand," she replied, and I sighed happily at her obedience.

"That's my good girl," I answered, and her face lit up. Her fingers squeezed mine and I held her close as I called Theo over. I quickly gave him orders, insisting that the wolves that were hurt be attended to as a priority.

"Don't worry, boss. I've got it handled," Theo shouted with a grin.

"I know you do. You will inform me if there are any problems," I continued.

"I will. Take your mate somewhere safe," he answered, winking heartily as he did so. I smirked in return as Ashleigh studied the exchange between us. I was delighted to see her blush redden even further.

"I plan on it," I replied, and I didn't listen to a single word out of my mate's mouth when I tossed her over my shoulder and carried her off to my chalet.

CHAPTER 16

 shleigh

Though this was not the first time Elijah had carried me off over his shoulder, I fought hard, earning myself several hard swats on my ass along the way. They stung, but the thick fabric of my jeans took the brunt of it.

"I'm warning you, Ashleigh," he snarled. He placed his hand directly over the cusp of my thighs, making me pause. My body reacted almost viscerally to his touch, and I bit my lip to keep myself from reacting in a way that would shame me.

Eventually, I gave into the fact that he was forcibly removing me from the battlefield. The sun was rising and very few skirmishes were left. Most of the vampires had already escaped, had been killed, or were about to die with the coming daylight.

He carried me off to the chalet with intent. He didn't put me down until he reached our bedroom. He was silent as he stripped me of my clothes. In a matter of moments, I went from feeling like a warrior on the battlefield to a blushing she-wolf about to be dealt with by her alpha.

He started with my shirt, tearing it off in one rapid motion. He made quick work of the rest of the clothes covering my body. He ripped them into tatters, but I didn't much care because they were torn and stained with the blood of a countless number of vampires anyway.

Soon enough, I was standing in front of him in nothing more than a pair of white lacey underwear. He stared down at them and I fidgeted nervously.

"Did I give you permission to wear these, little wolf?" he asked, and I whimpered openly. His eyes were dark with promise, and I chewed my lip.

"No, alpha," I whispered. My fingers intertwined together as I fidgeted. He approached me and slid his fingers around the back of my neck.

"Let me tell you what's going to happen then, little wolf. I'm going to bathe you and then we're going to go to bed. When we wake up, we will have breakfast and I will deal with your disobedience after that," he growled.

My body pulsed with desire.

"What are you going to do to me?" I asked shakily.

"All you need to know, my beautiful mate, is that your pretty little asshole is going to be very sore after I'm through with you. It won't be from your plug either. It will be from my cock," he continued firmly, and my entire body clenched down in anticipation.

I swallowed hard. Even though I'd worn the plug for him a good deal, it still hurt when he put it in. I knew that his cock was thicker than my toy and it would probably hurt a lot more.

I opened my mouth several times, but nothing came out.

"Take off your panties for me. I want to see you bare that pretty little pussy for me," he murmured seductively. My clit throbbed and I worried my bottom lip with my teeth.

Hesitantly, I slipped my fingers below the hem of my panties and slowly pushed them down my hips. Having to expose myself like this felt especially shameful. Would he allow me to wear clothes tonight? Would he make me stay naked?

He held out his palm expectantly. I stepped out of my underwear and placed it in his waiting hand. I shivered, watching him rearrange it so that the seat of my panties was visible. There was a wet spot there and I squirmed a little in shame.

"Oh, little wolf. I'm very much looking forward to taking your bottom tomorrow. It would appear that you are too," he said. He snarled with his desire and a single drop of arousal rolled down my thigh. With a knowing smirk, he placed my panties on top of his nightstand. I licked my lips, and he took my hand in his.

He led me into the bathroom and readied the shower. I didn't fight him as he pulled me inside. He shampooed my hair gently, taking care to massage my scalp. I couldn't keep myself from moaning in appreciation. He took extra care to wash my body with a loofah, scrubbing off any evidence that we'd spent all night fighting vampires. When he was done, he slicked conditioner through my hair. I stood under the rain shower and rinsed while he washed himself beside me. I peeked to see the soap running down his body. My body burned at the image of it.

I pressed up against him, very aware of the fact that his iron-hard cock was firmly between us.

"I don't want to wait until morning," I pouted. He grasped my upper arm and swiftly turned me around, landing several hard swats on my bottom. With my ass soaking wet, each one stung far more fiercely than I expected.

"You will rest tonight, little wolf. Keep resisting your alpha and you'll end up very well paddled before you're put to bed, very wet and very needy without coming for me at all," he warned. His threat gave me pause.

"Please, alpha?" I tried instead. I wiggled my bottom, trying to entice him to take me.

He didn't answer. He shut the water off and wrapped me in a towel before he grabbed one for himself. I followed him into the bedroom, grabbing my brush and taking it along with me. I brushed through my tangled wet hair, pouting a little in the process.

"Time for bed, little wolf," he replied.

"But please?" I whispered.

"Do I need to get the wooden paddle?" he asked. His tone was no longer playful.

I swallowed hard and grabbed his fingers with mine. "No, alpha," I murmured.

"That's my good girl. You need your rest. I will not take your bottom for the first time when you can hardly keep your eyes open," he answered, taking the towel and drying me off. I put down my brush and he willfully carried me into bed. He climbed in beside me and pulled up the covers. I cuddled against him, and his finger delved between my thighs. He brushed them against my clit, and I had to stifle a moan.

"But I thought you wouldn't," I gasped.

"Hush and let me spoil you," he demanded, and I arched into his touch. My body flared with fire and my orgasm slammed into me so fast that I saw stars.

"That's right, mate. Come hard for me," he purred, and I grasped onto him while I writhed beside him. I could hardly control the way my thighs were trembling. I moaned hoarsely, bright white light blinding me for what seemed like an endless display of incredible bliss.

When that orgasm finally ended, all of my remaining energy sapped away along with it. His fingers pulled away from my pussy and curled around my waist. He pressed a single kiss to my forehead. His lips made my skin tingle.

"Sleep now, sweet girl," he whispered, but my eyes were already closing. I snuggled up against him, thankful to be in his arms once again.

I'd missed him.

* * *

When I woke, the sun was already setting again. I yawned, snuggling in closer to the safety of Elijah's warmth. He groaned as I placed my cheek against his chest. I breathed in his scent and sighed happily, wanting to memorize the feeling of this moment forever.

I'd chosen him. I'd chosen my mate.

The pull of childhood dreams and the path that I thought I'd always take had paled under the power of my bonded mate. Fate had other ideas for me and now that I'd turned my back on my old life, I embraced it fully.

We belonged to each other, and no one would ever tear us apart.

"I know you're awake, beautiful," he said, and I snuggled in closer to him.

"No, I'm not," I whispered, unable to stop myself from giggling a little.

"Naughty girl," he chided, and his hand squeezed my bare bottom hard. He grunted as he massaged it and I pushed harder against him. Now that I was fully rested, my body was ready for him to take me, hard.

My stomach growled and I groaned out loud as he chuckled at the sound.

"Let's get some food in you before I remind you who you belong to," he said firmly, and I pouted. He saw my reaction and gently grasped my chin. My pussy pulsed as he looked down at me. His cock was rock hard against my belly.

"That pretty pout just earned you a dose of my belt. Keep it up, little wolf," he declared firmly. My thighs pressed hard against each other. I bit my lip, keeping myself quiet.

"I'm going to freshen up now. If you're not up and getting ready yourself by the time I'm out, then that little pussy is getting a spanking before we go down to breakfast," he warned.

"Yes, alpha," I whimpered.

"You are forbidden from wearing clothes. You will remain bare for me so that when I'm ready to fuck that pretty little bottom, all I have to do is bend you over and take it," he murmured against my ear. I shuddered hard. I didn't tell him that my nipples pebbled almost instantly, and my pussy was dripping with excitement.

I squirmed, imagining what his big cock would feel like as it slid into my last virgin hole.

He kissed my forehead again before slipping from underneath the covers. I whined at the sudden loss of his warmth. I curled up in a ball before I stretched with a yawn. I rubbed my eyes, listening to the sound of the water running in the bathroom. With a reluctant groan, I climbed out of bed with a shiver and the door to the bathroom opened not long after. He smirked, grasping me around the waist and clutching my pussy as if he owned it.

"Good girl. You will meet me downstairs in the kitchen when you're finished," he murmured. When he finally released me, I was already panting with desire. He smacked my ass lightly, causing it to jiggle. My pussy practically spasmed at his touch. Now fully blushing, I rushed into the bathroom and shut the door behind me.

I brushed my teeth, used the restroom, and splashed some water on my face. I dried myself off and went back into the bedroom to retrieve my hairbrush. I tamed my tangled case of bedhead, all while ignoring the constant throbbing of my clit.

The scent of cooking food spiraled up the stairs and I felt my cheeks heat with shame as I descended them still fully naked. I knew that there probably wasn't anyone else here, but the possibility of it made me a little worried and horrendously aroused all the same.

When I rounded the corner into the kitchen, I saw that Elijah was cooking over the stove. He was wearing a pair of gray sweatpants that hugged the firm globes of his ass deliciously. I sat down at the island, putting my elbows on the counter as I watched him flip several pieces of thick cut French toast. When they were done, he plated them, slathered them in butter, and topped them off with a generous helping of berries and maple syrup.

"Eat up, little wolf. You're going to need your energy for what's coming," he warned. His grin widened and his gaze darkened dangerously, glinting with promise as he stared back at me. I cut myself a large bite and popped it into my mouth, groaning when the flavors burst across my tongue.

He really was a fabulous cook. He prepared me a mug of coffee next, pouring in the perfect amount of creamer. I sipped it greedily, enjoying the sweet taste at leisure.

I had no problem finishing my plate of food. With my belly full, I sat back and watched him finish his own plate. He gathered the dishes and loaded them into the dishwasher. When he stood back up, he leveled me with a stern glare.

"You will go to the living room and kneel on the rug. You will wait for me while I go and fetch my belt," he directed.

"Yes, alpha," I whispered anxiously in anticipation. I climbed off the seat and slowly walked into the large living room. He'd already moved the coffee table out of the center of the room, and I knelt there. The carpet was plush against my knees as I sat on my heels. The stairs creaked as he climbed them, and I couldn't help but fidget nervously as I waited for the belting I had coming. My fingers clutched at my bottom. I remembered the feeling of his belt well, even though it had been some time since he'd chosen to use it. I'd fought him fiercely that night. Would he put it around my throat again?

His footsteps sounded on the stairs again and I anxiously pressed my palms against my thighs. When he walked into the room, my eyes dropped to the floor.

"The sight of you waiting for me like this is absolute perfection," he crooned, and I sighed with pleasure at his unexpected compliment. I raised my gaze, seeing that his cock was rigid, the outline of it fully visible despite the looseness of his sweatpants.

I licked my lips.

"I'm going to mark every one of your pretty holes tonight, little wolf. I want to make sure you fully understand how much you belong to me by the time I'm through with you," he groaned. He moved in front of me and started petting the top of my head. When I turned my head to the side, he used his palm to press my cheek against his cock.

"Do you feel how hard I am for you, my sweet mate? How much I'm looking forward to using every part of you?" he asked, and my cheeks flushed knowingly.

"Yes, alpha," I gasped. My core spiraled with heat as I pressed my palm against my belly.

"Open your lips. I'm going to start with that perfect little mouth," he demanded, and my thighs quivered. My lips parted and I watched greedily as he pushed down his pants and freed his cock. I leaned forward as he pushed his length into my mouth, taking him as readily as I dared.

The taste of him immediately burst across my tongue, causing my pussy to shiver with excitement as I moaned around him. I carefully pressed one palm against his left thigh, not to push him away, but to steady myself. With my other hand, I grasped the base of his cock. I stroked him up and down with my fingers as I took the whole of his cockhead in my mouth.

My tongue slid along the slit at the top, licking away the arousal that had formed a droplet there. I suckled gently at first, teasing him with my mouth as I took more and more of him down my throat. He groaned with desire, but before long he was growling in warning. His fingertips lightly petted the back of my head, and I knew it was time to show him how much I enjoyed taking him this way.

I drew my head back and bobbed it forward, taking him deep as I swirled my tongue around his thick length. With enthusiasm, I sucked his cock more vigorously, tasting him and suckling him like candy. The masculinity of his scent and taste surrounded me. He was sweet and salty and absolute perfection and I worshipped him.

He groaned as I worked the base of his cock with my hand. I squeezed him tighter, and he made that same sound again, which only caused my pussy to spasm as I imagined him filling me there too very soon.

I moaned around him.

"Your alpha is going to fuck your mouth now. Clasp your hands behind your back like a good girl," he directed, and a rubber band of desire snapped hard inside of me.

His fist tightened at the back of my scalp as I slowly released my hold on him and folded my hands together behind my back like he'd instructed. I gazed up at him with my mouth still full of him. His other hand cupped the side of my face as he lovingly dragged his thumb across my cheekbone. I leaned into his touch and suckled him gently.

"I love everything about you, my little wolf," he purred, and his fist tightened a bit harder. I whimpered, but it did nothing to stop the mouth fucking I had coming.

He thrust roughly and I choked from the beginning. He didn't give me any time to recover, just continued using my mouth as hard as he pleased. I struggled to open my throat. I whimpered, crying out around his cock and that only seemed to spur him on faster. He forced my head down further until I knew that my throat would be very sore by the time that he was done with me.

Eventually, I managed to get a hold of myself. I opened my throat and was able to keep my choking to a minimum. I gagged several times, but I pushed through it even as a few tears of exertion dripped down my cheeks.

I did everything I could to please him. I sucked him as much as I could, the wet slurping sounds as he fucked my mouth embarrassingly loud. My cheeks were already sore, as were my lips, but I didn't dare slow down. In time, I got through the pain and was rewarded with a mouthwatering groan from him that made me quiver.

His thighs trembled just slightly as he jerked into my mouth. His cock went even more rigid against my tongue, pulsing hard several times before his cum splashed against the back of my throat. It caught me off guard for the briefest of seconds, choking me before I was able to swallow it down. One eruption after another spurted inside my mouth and I swallowed every last drop. When he was done, I pulled back and suckled him lightly before I used my tongue to make sure I cleaned away all evidence of his seed.

He grasped the back of my neck and lifted me up to my feet. His lips crashed down onto mine, kissing me so fiercely that it left me feeling lightheaded. His arm wrapped around my waist, holding me steady as he pulled away from me. My lips were bruised and sore, ravaged by both his cock and his kiss. Without delay, he lifted me up off the floor, carrying me and tossing me over the back of the couch high enough so that my feet no longer touched the floor.

I saw him reach over me and take the belt in his hands. The jingle of the buckle was like music and before long, the sound of it cutting through the air met my ears. I should have tensed, but I was still reeling from the taste of him on my tongue.

The first line of fire that flared across my ass nearly stopped my heart. My legs straightened with shock at that initial sting, and I did everything I could to keep still, knowing that another one was coming. He whipped me hard and fast. I cried out with each lash, but that didn't slow him down.

"You are mine, mate," he roared.

"I'm yours, alpha," I whimpered. The belting didn't stop. It marked every inch of my bottom and down my thighs. Several hard thrashes caught in between my legs, licking against the sensitive folds of my very wet pussy. I snapped my thighs shut in an attempt at protection, but when another harsh lash whipped against the bottom curve of my cheeks, I had trouble keeping them together. His palm pressed down on my lower back, pinning me over the couch as he ruthlessly whipped me with that piece of leather.

By the time the entirety of my bottom was welted and burning, I was very close to tears. I begged him for mercy. I pleaded for his cock. Even though it was agony, my pussy was dripping for him. I needed him to take me, and I needed it hard.

"Please, alpha. I need you," I begged, and he tossed the belt aside. I gasped as the stinging welts rose on my flesh, looking back as he grasped at my cheeks roughly. His fingers dug into his marks, making them burn even more fiercely.

He tossed the belt beside me on the couch and suddenly his rock-hard cock was pressing firmly against my entrance. I moaned, lifting my hips so that he had easier access and he thrust inside so roughly that I wailed at his intrusion. My body had no time to get used to his size. My inner walls grasped at him, struggling to take him at the same time they tried to squeeze him out. None of that did anything to slow him down.

I was so wet that his entrance had been easy. The sound of his sliding in and out of me was shameful, but I didn't care. I wanted this. Badly.

His rigid length surged in and out, slamming against my cervix again and again as he took me as hard as he saw fit. The burning stretch of his thick girth continued to ache, and his rough fucking only made it hurt more.

At the same time though, my pleasure surged, quickly overwhelming the soreness coursing through me. His pelvis slammed against my ass, giving me a shameful spanking of a very different kind as the welts from the belt flared hot with every forceful thrust.

This wasn't just a fucking. This was a mounting, a claiming, and a rutting all in one.

I could feel my core fluttering as my desire catapulted into the clouds. There was nothing for me to do but lay there and take his cock, over and over again as my womb readied itself for him. Raw heat made the blood boil in my veins. My flesh shone with glistening sweat and several beads of it rolled down my back.

He fucked me harder, and I closed my eyes, enjoying the way every massive inch of him pistoned into me over and over. My core squeezed tight, and my inner walls clutched at his girth. Raw need spiraled faster until the pleasure far outweighed the pain. Soon enough, the two sensations married into one deliciously consuming one that left me needier than I'd ever felt in my life.

"Please. Alpha. Please let me come," I begged. I didn't know how much longer I could hold back. His cock was breathtaking in the best way and already my head was reeling, and my body was on the edge.

He didn't respond right away.

My clit throbbed and I wailed. I muttered the word please over and over, begging in desperation as I felt myself begin to teeter over that threshold.

"You want to come on my cock, little wolf?" he teased.

"Yes, alpha," I cried. My voice was shaky and desperate, my need pitifully apparent with every syllable that rolled off my lips.

"Come for me, little wolf. I want to feel that pussy squeeze my cock before I mark it with my seed," he growled and not a second later, I shattered for him. My orgasm slammed over me like a tsunami, powerful, consuming, and destructive. I screamed as it tore through me, intense sensation overwhelming me from the second it broke.

I writhed beneath him, my pussy grasping at his cock like my life depended on it. My core convulsed, spasming with one rattling wave of pleasure after the next. He thrust into me harder than ever, forcing my release even higher with every single one.

His hands grasped firmly around my hips as he groaned, jerking harder several times before he roared with his own release. His seed pelted inside me, crashing against my cervix with lashes of red-hot fire.

With his belt, he'd forced me to let go. Now he was taking everything with his cock.

I could feel my womb radiating with heat. His cum inside me was impossibly warm and when my orgasm finally ebbed away, I sighed with happiness at the feeling. He thrust into me more slowly now and some of his seed dripped down my thighs.

"Thank you, alpha," I whispered hoarsely, and he chuckled.

"I'm not done with you yet, little wolf," he answered, and I blushed hard. My muscles clenched nervously as if I could hide myself from him. His hand quickly spread my cheeks open, revealing my reluctant hole to his view.

He pulled free of my pussy, and I whined at its absence. He swirled the fingers of his hand in the cum dripping from me and used it to lube my asshole.

"I've been waiting to fuck this pretty little hole for a long time, mate," he said softly. I whimpered, feeling at a distinct disadvantage right now. I was exposed and vulnerable.

"You don't have to," I mumbled.

"I do, little wolf," he replied curtly, taking his time to admire me before he spread me open wider and pressed the tip of his cock against my last virgin place.

I cried out nervously before he even moved a muscle.

"Oh, I can't wait to hear the sounds you make when I fuck this tight little hole for the very first time," he whispered, and my body quivered hard in anticipation. I tensed, trying to tighten my muscles. I knew it would probably hurt more, but no matter what I did I couldn't get myself to relax.

I expected him to take me there hard and fast, but he didn't rush, not this time. He slowly pushed the tip inside me and I cried out, the burning pain of being stretched there by something as big as his cock instantly overwhelming. He didn't stop at the sound of my cries, he just pushed onward.

I squirmed, trying to pull myself off of him, but there was nowhere for me to go, and his cock only sank deeper into my bottom. My asshole tensed around him again and again, which only made blazing spirals of pain surge up and down my spine. The ache ran deep, so constant and overwhelming that I couldn't help but whimper through it in hopes of making it better.

"It hurts, alpha," I cried. "Please!"

"You can take it, mate. You were made for me," he encouraged, and my fingers clutched the sofa. My eyes squeezed shut as he pushed the rest of himself inside me. By the time his cock was fully seated, the pain had lessened and the shameful aching soreness that followed made my legs quiver. Slowly, he thrust into me again, reawakening that terrible pain, but it was lesser this time.

"That's my good girl. Your tight little ass is so very pretty when it's full of my cock," he whispered, and my clit throbbed to life. My muscles tensed and a flare of agony radiated around my bottom hole. I bit my lip as he started to pick up the pace.

The feeling of his cock sliding in and out of my asshole was so taboo that I forgot to breathe. It was so different from the metal of the butt plug, and it was so much bigger than his fingers. It was rigid and much thicker and as the shock of that first thrust began to wear off, I found that I was enjoying the feel of every veiny ridge sliding in and out of me in such a shameful way.

My hips arched up to meet each thrust. I moaned appallingly loud, and my pussy pulsed so greedily that I knew that an orgasm was inevitable. All of a sudden, something was in his hand, and he passed it to me. I looked down to see a small round toy. It was a bullet and it flared to life in my palm. I gulped, glimpsing a small remote in his hand.

"Hold this against your clit, little wolf. Do not remove it until I give you permission. Am I clear?" he instructed.

"Yes, alpha," I answered quickly, unable to help the way my asshole tensed around his cock. He groaned low in his throat, and I knew that he had felt it.

He wound an arm beneath my torso and lifted my hips, just enough for me to slip my hand underneath. I gasped openly the moment the toy touched my clit. He lowered my torso just enough to pin my wrist very lightly in place.

"You may come as many times as you like, little wolf. Your fucking will not end until my seed marks this last little hole," he said darkly, and he thrust into me hard.

He had been gentle with me before. I realized that now. His thrusts slammed into me, over and over as the little toy sent waves of vibrations through my whole body. He rutted my ass roughly, mounting me from behind.

"Who do you belong to?" he growled.

"You! I belong to you, alpha," I wailed.

"That's right you do. Now come for your alpha, I want to feel this little asshole squeeze my cock before I come inside it," he demanded.

With my asshole burning, I teetered over the edge and fell down into an endless chasm of dark consuming pleasure. My clit pulsed against the toy, the steady vibrations forcing my release to devastate me.

I screamed. I cried. I suffered on that toy as his cock fucked my ass ruthlessly hard. He was forceful and rough, and I came endlessly beneath him because of it.

I don't know how many orgasms I had. To be honest, it didn't matter. I broke for him again and again. My body fought each orgasm, but the sheer destruction of them did nothing to slow the inevitable. My clit was too sensitive, but I didn't dare take the bullet away from it. Every single nerve in my body was on overdrive, but it kept answering to him, over and over until I was a breathless writhing mess.

My throat was hoarse from the mouth fucking I'd taken and all the screaming orgasms he forced from me so far.

My pussy was so well used that I knew I'd feel my fucking with every step I took tomorrow.

My ass was marked red with stripes from his belt, but it was the shameful achiness in my asshole that would remain sore long after he finished fucking it.

His cock slammed into me, over and over again as I came for him one final time. I wailed as his seed spurted deep inside my bottom, claiming my last hole as his once and for all.

I belonged to him and there would never be any doubt in my mind after this.

His arms curled around me, and he lifted me so that his chest was at my back. His cock remained in my bottom, a shameful reminder of what had just taken place.

"I love you, alpha," I whispered, my voice cracking.

"I love you, little wolf. Your life is with me now and no one will ever hurt you again."

EPILOGUE

 *shleigh*

The scars from the battle against the Crimson Shadows, the Venuti, and the Malkovians took a few weeks to clear away. In that time, several rumors of my father's fate had surfaced. Elijah did his best to look into each one until it became clear that his demise was certain.

The Crimson Shadows pack dissolved. Much of them were disgusted at being forced to follow a man that would marry off his own flesh and blood to a vampire, a creature that was by very nature our enemy. Amir had kept the details of my marriage a secret from most of them, but it hadn't stayed that way. Many former pack members arrived on our doorstep, swearing fealty to Elijah in exchange for their lives.

Ronaldo had stayed behind after the battle, offering to serve as my own personal security guard. I accepted his service readily, happy to have someone I could trust at my side.

Upon the arrival of the new pack members, even more rumors began to circulate about my father's disappearance. I asked Ronaldo and Elijah to investigate and they were able to figure out the true story to his end.

Both vampire clans blamed him for the loss of their leaders. They had suffered great losses at our hands, and they were working tirelessly to refresh their numbers while also keeping out of the watchful eyes of the Council.

A small group of former Crimson Shadow members captured my father not long after the battle. They questioned him and when they were displeased with the betrayal that my father had brought on our species, they took him to the vampires he held in such high standing. They left my father bound and gagged in a room with freshly sired vampires that had not yet had a taste of blood to complete their transition.

My father never left that room. When they opened that door, there wasn't a single sign of him other than the stain of his blood on the floor.

With his removal, I knew that my place as Elijah's mate would never be questioned or interfered with again. I settled into my new life with a sense of peace. I put my own touches on the chalet, making it my home once and for all.

With a shake of my head, I tried to stop thinking about what happened in the past and focus on the future instead. Needing a breath of fresh air, I walked out onto the balcony and looked down at the mountain town beneath us. People were walking along happily, going about their day with a joy that had not been there before we arrived. I smiled and one of the floorboards behind me creaked.

My hand dropped to my swollen belly, protectively covering the growing child inside of me. I turned, breathing a sigh of relief to see that it was only Elijah.

"You frightened me," I scolded him lightly.

"Did I now?" he asked pointedly. His gaze darkened with desire. He never tired of looking at me and my pregnant belly only seemed to make him more insatiable.

"I love seeing you swollen with my child, little wolf. It makes me want to bend you over and fuck that perfect little pussy right here on this balcony," he growled, and I bit my lip. He grasped the waistband of my stretchy yoga pants, baring my bottom in one quick motion.

"Elijah!" I gasped.

He slapped my ass several times, hard enough to sting and make me cry out.

"You've got a fucking coming, little wolf. Either you make your way inside, or you're getting that little asshole fucked right here," he threatened.

I blushed furiously. I glanced around, hoping no one had heard his open threat.

I curled up against him, pressing my belly to his. "Will you still fuck me there if we go inside?" I asked pointedly, staring into his dark gaze with sordid desires of my own.

"Definitely. I'll give you everything you've ever wanted and more, little wolf. Now get inside, you're testing my patience," he warned, and I squealed with glee as I scampered in the door with my bottom still bare and exposed.

I bent over the bed and waited.

He growled behind me. My entire body tensed with anticipation.

I couldn't wait for what came next.

The End

AFTERWORD

Stormy Night Publications would like to thank you for your interest in our books.

If you liked this book (or even if you didn't), we would really appreciate you leaving a review on the site where you purchased it. Reviews provide useful feedback for us and our authors, and this feedback (both positive comments and constructive criticism) allows us to work even harder to make sure we provide the content our customers want to read.

If you would like to check out more books from Stormy Night Publications, if you want to learn more about our company, or if you would like to join our mailing list, please visit our website at:

http://www.stormynightpublications.com

BOOKS OF THE WOLF KINGS SERIES

Alpha King

I thought I could defy the most powerful mafia boss in the city, but as Lawson Clearwater rips off my nightgown and pins me to the bed I'm certain he can smell more than just my fear.

This beast isn't just here to punish me. He's here to mount me, rut me, and mark me as his.

Forever.

Alpha Boss

She came here to find her sister. Her mate found her instead.

When she blew off my offer to help rescue her sister, Natalia Kotova learned the hard way that defying an alpha shifter will get you spanked until you are sobbing, then mounted and rutted.

But she's not bound to my bed with her dress and panties in shreds and every hole sore just because she needed a shameful lesson in manners from the most powerful mob boss in the city.

She's here because she's my mate.

MAFIA AND BILLIONAIRE ROMANCES BY SARA FIELDS

Fear

She wasn't supposed to be there tonight. I took her because I had no other choice, but as I carried her from her home dripping wet and wearing nothing but a towel, I knew I would be keeping her.

I'm going to make her tell me everything I need to know. Then I'm going to make her mine.

She'll sob as my belt lashes her bottom and she'll scream as climax after savage climax is forced from her naked, quivering body, but there will be no mercy no matter how shamefully she begs.

She's not just going to learn to obey me. She's going to learn to fear me.

On Her Knees

Blaire Conrad isn't just the most popular girl at Stonewall Academy. She's a queen who reigns over her subjects with an iron fist. But she's made me an enemy, and I don't play by her rules.

I make the rules, and I punish my enemies.

She'll scream and beg as I strip her, spank her, and force one brutal climax after another from her beautiful little body, but before I'm done with her she'll beg me shamefully for so much more.

It's time for the king to teach his queen her place.

Boss

The moment Brooke Mikaels walked into my office, I knew she was mine. She needed my help and thought she could use her sweet little body to get it, but she learned a hard lesson instead.

I don't make deals with silly little girls. I spank them.

She'll get what she needs, but first she'll moan and beg and scream with each brutal climax as she takes everything I give her. She belongs to me now, and soon she'll know what that means.

His Majesty

Maximo Giovanni Santaro is a king. A real king, like in the old days. The kind I didn't know still existed. The kind who commands obedience and punishes any hint of defiance from his subjects.

His Majesty doesn't take no for an answer, and refusing his royal command has earned me not just a spanking that will leave me sobbing, but a lesson so utterly shameful that it will serve as an example for anyone else who might dare to disobey him. I will beg and plead as one brutal, screaming climax after another ravages my quivering body, but there will be no mercy for me.

He's not going to stop until he's taught me that my rightful place is at his feet, blushing and sore.

Pet

Even before Chloe Banks threw a drink in my face in front of a room full of powerful men who know better than to cross me, her fate was sealed. I had already decided to make her my pet.

I would have taught her to obey in the privacy of my penthouse, but her little stunt changed that.

My pet learned her place in public instead, blushing as she was bared, sobbing as she was spanked, and screaming as she was brought to one brutal, humiliating climax after another.

But she has so many more lessons to learn. Lessons more shameful than she can imagine.

She will plead for mercy as she is broken, but before long she will purr like a kitten.

Blush for Daddy

"Please spank me, Daddy. Please make it hurt."

Only a ruthless bastard would make an innocent virgin say those words when she came to him desperate for help, then savor every quiver of her voice as she begs for something so shameful.

I didn't even hesitate.

I made Keri Esposito's problems go away. Then I made her call me daddy.

The image of that little bottom bare over my lap was more than I could resist, and the thought of her kneeling naked at my feet to thank me properly afterwards left me as hard as I've ever been.

Maybe I'm a monster, but I saw the wet spot on her panties before I pulled them down.

She didn't come to my door just for the kind of help only a powerful billionaire could offer.

She came because she needed me to make her blush for daddy.

Reckoning

Dean Waterhouse was supposed to be a job. Get in. Get married. Take his money and get out.

But he came after me.

Now I'm bound to his bed, about to learn what happens to naughty girls who play games.

The man who put his ring on my finger was gentle. The man who tracked me down is not.

He's going to make me blush, beg, and scream for him.

Then he's going to make me call him daddy.

Bride

This morning I was a businesswoman with no plans to marry, but that didn't matter to him. He decided tonight was my wedding night, so it was. All he let me choose was the dress he would tear off me later.

When I told him I wanted him to be gentle, he laughed at me, then ripped off my panties.

I shouldn't have been wet. I shouldn't have moaned. But I was, and I did.

When he threw me on the bed, I told him I'd never be his no matter how he made me scream.

He just smiled. The kind of smile that said this was going to hurt and he was going to enjoy every moment of it. Then he bent down and whispered something in my ear that shook me to my core.

"You're already mine. You always have been."

SCI-FI AND PARANORMAL
ROMANCES BY SARA FIELDS

Feral

He told me to stay away from him, that if I got too close he would not be able to stop himself. He would pin me down and take me so fiercely my throat would be sore from screaming before he finished wringing one savage, desperate climax after another from my helpless, quivering body.

Part of me was terrified, but another part needed to know if he would truly throw me to the ground, mount me, and rut me like a wild animal, longer and harder than any human ever could.

Now, as the feral beast flips me over to claim me even more shamefully when I've already been used more thoroughly than I imagined possible, I wonder if I should have listened to him...

Inferno

I thought I knew how to handle a man like him, but there are no men like him. Though he is a billionaire, when he desired me he did not try to buy me, and when he wanted me bared and bound he didn't call his bodyguards. He did it himself, even as I fought him, because he could.

He told me soon I would beg him to ravage me... and I did. But it wasn't the pain of his belt searing my naked backside that drove me to plead with him to use me so shamefully I might never stop blushing. I begged because my body knew its master, and it didn't give me a choice.

But my body is not all he plans to claim. He wants my mind and my soul too, and he will have them. He's going to take so much of me there will be nothing left. He's going to consume me.

Manhandled

Two hours ago, my ship reached the docks at Dryac.

An hour ago, a slaver tried to drag me into an alley.

Fifty-nine minutes ago, a beast of a man knocked him out cold.

Fifty-eight minutes ago, I told my rescuer to screw off, I could take care of myself.

Fifty-five minutes ago, I felt a thick leather belt on my bare backside for the first time.

Forty-five minutes ago, I started begging.

Thirty minutes ago, he bent me over a crate and claimed me in the most shameful way possible.

Twenty-nine minutes ago, I started screaming.

Twenty-five minutes ago, I climaxed with a crowd watching and my bottom sore inside and out.

Twenty-four minutes ago, I realized he was nowhere near done with me.

One minute ago, he finally decided I'd learned my lesson, for the moment at least.

As he leads me away, naked, well-punished, and very thoroughly used, he tells me I work for him now, I'll have to earn the privilege of clothing, and I'm his to enjoy as often as he pleases.

Marked

I know how to handle men who won't take no for an answer, but Silas isn't a man. He's a beast who takes what he wants, as long and hard and savagely as he pleases, and tonight he wants me.

He's not even pretending he's going to be gentle. He's going to ravage me, and it's going to hurt.

I'll be spanked into quivering submission and used thoroughly and shamefully, but even when the endless series of helpless, screaming climaxes is finally over, I won't just be sore and spent.

I will be marked.

My body will no longer be mine. It will be his to use, his to enjoy, and his to breed, and no matter how desperate my need might grow in his absence, it will respond to his touch alone.

Forever.

Prize

Exiled from Earth by a tyrannical government, I was meant to be sold for use on a distant world. But Vane doesn't buy things. When he wants something, he takes it, and I was no different.

This alien brute didn't just strip me, punish me, and claim me with his whole crew watching. He broke me, making me beg for mercy and then for far more shameful things. Perhaps he would've been gentle if I hadn't defied him in front of his men, but I doubt it. He's not the gentle type.

When he carried me aboard his ship naked, blushing, and sore, I thought I would be no more than a trophy to be shown off or a plaything to amuse him until he tired of me, but I was wrong.

He took me as a prize, but he's keeping me as his mate.

Alpha

I used to believe beasts like him were nothing but legends and folklore. Then he came for me.

He is no mere alpha wolf. He is the fearsome expression of the virility of the Earth itself, come into the world for the first time in centuries to claim a human female fated to be his mate.

That human female is me.

When I ran, he caught me. When I fought him, he punished me.

I begged for mercy, but mercy isn't what he has in mind for me.

He's going to force one brutal climax after another from my naked, quivering body until my throat is sore from screaming and he's not going to stop until he is certain I know I am his.

Then he's going to breed me.

Thirst

Cain came for me today. Even before he spoke his name his power all but drove me to my knees.

Power that can pin me against a wall with just a thought and hold me there as he slowly cuts my clothes from my quivering body, making sure I know he is enjoying every blushing moment.

Power that will punish me until I plead for mercy, tease and torment me until I beg for release, and then ravage me brutally over and over again until I'm utterly spent and shamefully broken.

Power that will claim me as his forever.

Alien Conqueror

He's going to take me the same way they took our planet. Without gentleness or remorse.

I dared to defy him, but as this alien brute rips my clothes off and mounts me with my bottom still burning from his punishing hand it is clear what is in store for me isn't mere vengeance.

It is conquest.

Soon I will know what it means to be utterly and shamefully broken, my helpless body ravaged and plundered in every way imaginable, and when he is done I won't just be sore and spent.

I will be his.

Guardian

After watching over this world for millennia, a girl wandering in the woods should have been of no interest to me. But the moment I saw her bathing in a stream, I knew Emma was mine.

I kept myself from throwing her over a fallen tree and ravaging her… but only for a few hours.

If she had been obedient, I might have held instinct at bay a little longer. It was the scent of her helpless arousal as I reddened her bare bottom that tore away the last vestiges of my self-control.

But it would have made no difference in the end.

Sooner or later, she was always going to scream my name as I mounted and rutted her.

A beast must claim his mate.

BOOKS OF THE ALPHA BROTHERHOOD SERIES

Savage

I thought no alpha could tame me. I was wrong.

Many men have tried to master me, but never one like Aric. He is not just an alpha, he is a fearsome beast, and he means to take for himself what warriors and kings could not conquer.

I thought I could fight him, but his mere presence forced overwhelming, unimaginable need upon me and now it is too late. I'm about to go into heat, and what comes next will be truly shameful.

He's going to ravage me, ruthlessly laying claim to every single inch of me, and it's going to hurt. But no matter how desperately I plead as he wrenches one screaming climax after another from my helplessly willing body, he will not stop until I'm sore, spent, and marked as his.

It will be nothing short of savage.

Primal

I escaped the chains of a king. Now a far more fearsome brute has claimed me.

The Brotherhood gave him the right to breed me, but that is not why I am naked, wet, and sore.

My bottom bears the marks of his hard, punishing hand because I defied my alpha.

My body is slick with his seed and my own arousal because he took me anyway.

He didn't use me like a king enjoying a subject. He took me the way a beast claims his mate.

It was long, hard, and painfully intense, but it was much more than that.

It was primal.

Rough

I came here as a spy. I ended up as the king's property.

I was captured and locked in a dungeon, but it was only when I saw Magnar that I felt real fear.

He is a warrior and a king, but that is not why my virgin body quivers as I stand bare before him.

He is not merely an alpha. He is my alpha.

The one who will punish and master me.

The one who will claim and ravage me.

The one who will break me, but only after he's made me beg for it.

Wild

She's going to scream for me and I don't care who hears it.

I traveled to this city to disrupt the plans of the Brotherhood's enemies, not tame a defiant omega, but the moment Revna challenged me I knew punishing her would not be enough.

Despite her blushing protests, I'm going to bare her beautiful body and mark her quivering bottom with my belt, but she won't be truly put in her place until I put her flat on her back.

I'm her alpha and I will use her as I please.

Enigma

An alpha could not tame her. Now she will kneel before a god.

For endless ages I've kept this world in balance, and over the centuries countless women have writhed and screamed and climaxed beneath me. But I've never felt the need for a mate.

Until today. Until her.

When I touch her, she trembles.

When I mark her defiant little bottom with my belt, her bare thighs glisten with helpless arousal.

When she lies next to me blushing, sore, and spent, my lust for her only grows stronger.

The world be damned. I'm going to claim her for myself.

BOOKS OF THE OMEGABORN TRILOGY

Frenzy

Inside the walls I was a respected scientist. Out here I'm vulnerable, desperate, and soon to be at the mercy of the beasts and barbarians who rule these harsh lands. But that is not the worst of it.

When the suppressants that keep my shameful secret wear off, overwhelming, unimaginable need will take hold of me completely. I'm about to go into heat, and I know what comes next...

But I'm not the only one with instincts far beyond my control. Savage men roam this wilderness, driven by their very nature to claim a female like me more fiercely than I can imagine, paying no heed to my screams as one brutal climax after another is ripped from my helplessly willing body.

It won't be long now, and when the mating starts, it will be nothing short of a frenzy.

Frantic

Naked, bound, and helplessly on display, my arousal drips down my bare thighs and pools at my feet as the entire city watches, waiting for the inevitable. I'm going into heat, and they know it.

When the feral beasts who live outside the walls find me, they will show my virgin body no mercy. With my need growing more desperate by the second, I'm not sure I'll want them to...

By the time the brutes arrive to claim and ravage me, I'm going to be absolutely frantic.

Fever

I've led the Omegaborn for years, but the moment these brutes arrived from beyond the wall I knew everything was about to change. These beasts aren't here to take orders from me, they're here to take me the way I was meant to be taken, no matter how desperately I resist what I need.

Naked, punished, and sore, all I can do is scream out one savage, shameful climax after another as my body is claimed, used, and mastered. I'm about to learn what it means to be an omega...

BOOKS OF THE VAKARRAN CAPTIVES SERIES

Conquered

I've lived in hiding since the Vakarrans arrived, helping my band of human survivors evade the aliens who now rule our world with an iron fist. But my luck ran out.

Captured by four of their fiercest warriors, I know what comes next. They'll make an example of me, to show how even the most defiant human can be broken, trained, and mastered.

I promise myself that I'll prove them wrong, that I'll never yield, even when I'm stripped bare, publicly shamed, and used in the most humiliating way possible.

But my body betrays me.

My will to resist falters as these brutes share me between the four of them and I can't help but wonder if soon, they will conquer my heart...

Mastered

First the Vakarrans took my home. Then they took my sister. Now, they have taken me.

As a prisoner of four of their fiercest warriors, I know what fate awaits me. Humans who dare to fight back the way I did are not just punished, they are taught their place in ways so shameful I shudder to think about them.

The four huge, intimidating alien brutes who took me captive are going to claim me in every way possible, using me more thoroughly than I can imagine. I despise them, yet as they force one savage, shattering climax after another from my naked, quivering body, I cannot help but wonder if soon I will beg for them to master me completely.

Ravaged

Though the aliens were the ones I always feared, it was my own kind who hurt me. Men took me captive, and it was four Vakarran warriors who saved me. But they don't plan to set me free…

I belong to them now, and they intend to make me theirs more thoroughly than I can imagine.

They are the enemy, and first I try to fight, then I try to run. But as they punish me, claim me, and share me between them, it isn't long before I am begging them to ravage me completely.

Subdued

The resistance sent them, but that's not really why these four battle-hardened Vakarrans are here.

They came for me. To conquer me. To master me. To ravage me. To strip me bare, punish me for the slightest hint of defiance, and use my quivering virgin body in ways far beyond anything in even the very darkest of my dreams, until I've been utterly, completely, and shamefully subdued.

I vow never to beg for mercy, but I can't help wondering how long it will be until I beg for more.

Abducted

When I left Earth behind to become a Celestial Mate, I was promised a perfect match. But four Vakarrans decided they wanted me, and Vakarrans don't ask for what they want, they take it.

These fearsome, savagely sexy alien warriors don't care what some computer program thinks would be best for me. They've claimed me as their mate, and soon they will claim my body.

I planned to resist, but after I was stripped bare and shamefully punished, they teased me until at last I pleaded for the climax I'd been so cruelly denied. When I broke, I broke completely. Now they are going to do absolutely anything they please with me, and I'm going to beg for all of it.

After nineteen-year-old Jenny Monroe is caught stealing from the home of a powerful politician, she is sent to a special prison in deep space to be trained for her future role as an alien's bride.

Despite the public bare-bottom spanking she receives upon her arrival at the detention center, Jenny remains defiant, and before long she earns herself a trip to the notorious medical wing of the facility. Once there, Jenny quickly discovers that a sore bottom will now be the least of her worries, and soon enough she is naked, restrained, and shamefully on display as three stern, handsome alien doctors examine and correct her in the most humiliating ways imaginable.

The doctors are experts in the treatment of naughty young women, and as Jenny is brought ever closer to the edge of a shattering climax only to be denied again and again, she finds herself begging to be taken in any way they please. But will her captors be content to give Jenny up once her punishment is over, or will they decide to make her their own and master her completely?

Taming Their Pet

When the scheming of her father's political enemies makes it impossible to continue hiding the fact that she is an unauthorized third child, twenty-year-old Isabella Bedard is sent to a detainment facility in deep space where she will be prepared for her new life as an alien's bride.

Her situation is made far worse after some ill-advised mischief forces the strict warden to ensure that she is sold as quickly as possible, and before she knows it, Isabella is standing naked before two huge, roughly handsome alien men, helpless and utterly on display for their inspection. More disturbing still, the men make it clear that they are buying her not as a bride, but as a pet.

Zack and Noah have made a career of taming even the most headstrong of females, and they waste no time in teaching their new pet that her absolute obedience will be expected and even the slightest defiance will earn her a painful, embarrassing bare-bottom spanking, along with far more humiliating punishments if her behavior makes it necessary.

Over the coming weeks, Isabella is trained as a pony and as a kitten, and she learns what it means to fully surrender her body to the bold dominance of two men who will not hesitate to claim her in any way they please. But though she cannot deny her helpless arousal at being so thoroughly mastered, can she truly allow herself to fall in love with men who keep her as a pet?

Sold to the Beasts

As an unauthorized third child with parents who were more interested in their various criminal enterprises than they were in her, Michelle Carter is used to feeling unloved, but it still hurts when she is brought to another world as a bride for two men who turn out not to even want one.

After Roan and Dane lost the woman they loved, they swore there would never be anyone else, and when their closest friend purchases a beautiful human he hopes will become their wife, they reject the match. Though they are cursed to live as outcasts who shift into terrible beasts, they are not heartless, so they offer Michelle a place in their home alongside the other servants. She will have food, shelter, and all she needs, but discipline will be strict and their word will be law.

Michelle soon puts Roan and Dane to the test, and when she disobeys them her bottom is bared for a deeply humiliating public spanking. Despite her situation, the punishment leaves her shamefully aroused and longing for her new masters to make her theirs, and as the days pass they find that she has claimed a place in their hearts as well. But when the same enemy who took their first love threatens to tear Roan and Dane away from her, will Michele risk her life to intervene?

Mated to the Dragons

After she uncovers evidence of a treasonous conspiracy by the most powerful man on Earth, Jada Rivers ends up framed for a terrible crime, shipped off to a detention facility in deep space, and kept in solitary confinement until she can be sold as a bride. But the men who purchase her are no ordinary aliens. They are dragons, the kings of Draegira, and she will be their shared mate.

Bruddis and Draego are captivated by Jada, but before she can become their queen the beautiful, feisty little human will need to be publicly claimed, thoroughly trained, and put to the test in the most shameful manner imaginable. If she will not yield her body and her heart to them completely, the fire in their blood will burn out of control until it destroys the brotherly bond between them, putting their entire world at risk of a cataclysmic war.

Though Jada is shocked by the demands of her dragon kings, she is left helplessly aroused by their stern dominance. With her virgin body quivering with need, she cannot bring herself to resist as they take her hard and savagely in any way they please. But can she endure the trials before her and claim her place at their side, or will her stubborn defiance bring Draegira to ruin?

BOOKS OF THE TERRANOVUM BRIDES SERIES

A Gift for the King

For an ordinary twenty-two-year-old college student like Lana, the idea of being kidnapped from Earth by aliens would have sounded absurd... until the day it happened. As Lana quickly discovers, however, her abduction is not even the most alarming part of her situation. To her shock, she soon learns that she is to be stripped naked and sold as a slave to the highest bidder.

When she resists the intimate, deeply humiliating procedures necessary to prepare her for the auction, Lana merely earns herself a long, hard, bare-bottom spanking, but her passionate defiance catches the attention of her captor and results in a change in his plans. Instead of being sold, Lana will be given as a gift to Dante, the region's powerful king.

Dante makes it abundantly clear that he will expect absolute obedience and that any misbehavior will be dealt with sternly, yet in spite of everything Lana cannot help feeling safe and cared for in the handsome ruler's arms. Even when Dante's punishments leave her with flaming cheeks and a bottom sore from more than just a spanking, it only sets her desire for him burning hotter.

But though Dante's dominant lovemaking brings her pleasure beyond anything she ever imagined, Lana fears she may never be more than a plaything to him, and her fears soon lead to rebellion. When an escape attempt goes awry and she is captured by Dante's most dangerous enemy, she is left to wonder if her master cares for her enough to come to her rescue. Will the king risk everything to reclaim what is his, and if he does bring his human girl home safe and sound, can he find a way to teach Lana once and for all that she belongs to him completely?

A Gift for the Doctor

After allowing herself to be taken captive in order to save her friends, Morgana awakens to find herself naked, bound, and at the mercy of a handsome doctor named Kade. She cannot hide her helpless arousal as her captor takes his time thoroughly examining her bare body, but when she disobeys him she quickly discovers that defiance will earn her a sound spanking.

His stern chastisement and bold dominance awaken desires within her that she never knew existed, but Morgana is shocked when she learns the truth about Kade. As a powerful shifter and the alpha of his pack, he has been ordered by the evil lord who took Morgana prisoner to claim her and sire children with her in order to combine the strength of their two bloodlines.

Kade's true loyalties lie with the rebels seeking to overthrow the tyrant, however, and he has his own reasons for desiring Morgana as his mate. Though submitting to a dominant alpha does not come easily to a woman who was once her kingdom's most powerful sorceress, Kade's masterful lovemaking is unlike anything she has experienced before, and soon enough she is aching for his touch. But with civil war on the verge of engulfing the capital, will Morgana be torn from the arms of the man she loves or will she stand and fight at his side no matter the cost?

A Gift for the Commander

After she is rescued from a cruel tyrant and brought to the planet Terranovum, Olivia soon discovers that she is to be auctioned to the highest bidder. But before she can be sold, she must be trained, and the man who will train her is none other than the commander of the king's army.

Wes has tamed many human females, and when Olivia resists his efforts to bathe her in preparation for her initial inspection, he strips the beautiful, feisty girl bare and spanks her soundly. His stern chastisement leaves Olivia tearful and repentant yet undeniably aroused, and after the punishment she cannot resist begging for her new master's touch.

Once she has been examined Olivia's training begins in earnest, and Wes takes her to his bed to teach her what it means to belong to a dominant man. But try as he might, he cannot bring himself to see Olivia as just another slave. She touches his heart in a way he thought nothing could, and with each passing day he grows more certain that he must claim her as his own. But with war breaking out across Terranovum, can Wes protect both his world and his woman?

Claimed by the General

When Ayala intervenes to protect a fellow slave-girl from a cruel man's unwanted attentions, she catches the eye of the powerful general Lord Eiotan. Impressed with both her boldness and her beauty, the handsome warrior takes Ayala into his home and makes her his personal servant.

Though Eiotan promises that Ayala will be treated well, he makes it clear that he expects his orders to be followed and he warns her that any disobedience will be sternly punished. Lord Eiotan is a man of his word, and when Ayala misbehaves she quickly finds herself over his knee for a long, hard spanking on her bare bottom. Being punished in such a humiliating manner leaves her blushing, but it is her body's response to his chastisement which truly shames her.

Ayala does her best to ignore the intense desire his firm-handed dominance kindles within her, but when her new master takes her in his arms she cannot help longing for him to claim her, and when he makes her his own at last, his masterful lovemaking introduces her to heights of pleasure she never thought possible.

But as news of the arrival of an invader from across the sea reaches the city and a ruthless conqueror sets his eyes on Ayala, her entire world is thrown into turmoil. Will she be torn from Lord Eiotan's loving arms, or will the general do whatever it takes to keep her as his own?

Kept for Christmas

After Raina LeBlanc shows up for a meeting unprepared because she was watching naughty videos late at night instead of working, she finds herself in trouble with Dr. Eliot Knight, her stern, handsome boss. He makes it clear that she is in need of strict discipline, and soon she is lying over his knee for a painful, embarrassing bare-bottom spanking.

Though her helpless display of arousal during the punishment fills Raina with shame, she is both excited and comforted when Eliot takes her in his arms after it is over, and when he invites her to spend the upcoming Christmas holiday with him she happily agrees. But is she prepared to offer him the complete submission he demands?

The Warrior's Little Princess

Irena cannot remember who she is, where she came from, or how she ended up alone in a dark forest wearing only a nightgown, but none of that matters as much as the fact that the vile creatures holding her captive seem intent on having her for dinner. Fate intervenes, however, when a mysterious, handsome warrior arrives in the nick of time to save her.

Darrius has always known that one day he would be forced by the power within him to claim a woman, and after he rescues the beautiful, innocent Irena he decides to make her his own. But the feisty girl will require more than just the protection Darrius can offer. She will need both his gentle, loving care and his firm hand applied to her bare bottom whenever she is naughty.

Irena soon finds herself quivering with desire as Darrius masters her virgin body completely, and she delights in her new life as his little girl. But Darrius is much more than an ordinary sellsword, and being his wife will mean belonging to him utterly, to be taken hard and often in even the most shameful of ways.

When the truth of her own identity is revealed at last, will she still choose to remain by his side?

ABOUT THE AUTHOR

Do you want to read a FREE book?

Sign up for Sara Fields' newsletter and get a FREE copy of
Sold to the Enemy!

https://www.sarafieldsromance.com/newsletter

About Sara Fields

Sara Fields is a USA Today bestselling romance author
with a proclivity for dirty things, especially those
centered in DARK, FANTASY, and ROMANCE. If you
like science fiction, fantasy, reverse harem, menage, pet
play and other kinky filthy things, all complete with
happily-ever-afters, then you will enjoy her books.

Email: otkdesire@gmail.com